For the Bear's Eyes Only

ALSO BY KATHY LYONS

The Bear Who Loved Me
License to Shift

For the Bear's Eyes Only

Book Three of Grizzlies Gone Wild

KATHY LYONS

New York   Boston

Forever Yours
Hachette Book Group
1290 Avenue of the Americas
New York, NY 10104
forever-romance.com
twitter.com/foreverromance

First published as an ebook and as a print on demand: November 2016

Forever Yours is an imprint of Grand Central Publishing. The Forever Yours name and logo are trademarks of Hachette Book Group, Inc.

The publisher is not responsible for websites (or their content) that are not owned by the publisher.

The Hachette Speakers Bureau provides a wide range of authors for speaking events. To find out more, go to www.hachettespeakersbureau.com or call (866) 376-6591.

ISBNs: 978-1-4555-4099-0 (ebook), 978-1-4555-4097-6 (print on demand)

For the Bear's Eyes Only

Prologue

Three Years Ago

Alan Carman was so happy he was singing. Rarely in life was everything exactly perfect. The sun was shining. He'd just been paid, pitiful an amount though that might be. And now he was headed home, flying down the freeway on a beautiful late summer day to tell his brother the most amazing news.

Which made it typical for his life that sirens started blaring right behind him. Cop car. A quick look down showed that he hadn't been speeding, but the flashing lights were pretty clear, so he braked and pulled over.

Damn. Though—upside—even this wasn't dimming his mood because today was a great day. His life had just changed for the better. The amazing, the absolutely, wonderful, joyous yes- all-is-exactly-as-it-ought-to-be better! Then he looked back and saw the police officer step out of her car. He knew that walk. Knew that body even though it was encased in the intimidating uniform of a state police officer. And now that he saw her, he also knew that God had given him exactly the most perfect day.

He grinned and lowered his window. This was going to be fun.

"License and registration, please." Her voice was clipped, her eyes hidden behind mirrored sunglasses, and she in no way indicated that they'd grown up within a few miles of one another.

"Hi, Tonya. Guess what?"

Officer Tonya Kappes, gorgeous grizzly-shifter and all around badass, didn't react though he watched carefully for any hint of softening. No relaxation of her spine, no tilt to her lips. Nothing despite the fact that she'd been his one obsession since his fourteenth birthday. He knew from his brother Carl when she started working for the state police. And he'd watched the news just in case she hit the media spotlight. For years they'd had no direct contact while he went through law school and she flew through the police academy. But now, on this day of all days, she was here pulling him over.

Must be fate.

"Come on, Tonya. It's me on a beautiful day. Guess what?"

"Alan." Just his name spoken in a flat voice. "Hand me your license and registration, please."

Well, at least she recognized him. That was something, right? Still smiling—though the expression was getting more strained by the second—he pulled out his wallet and handed over his driver's license. A moment later, he passed her his insurance information.

"Do you have any idea how fast you were going?" she asked, her voice deadpan.

"Yeah. Seventy."

"You were in a fifty-five zone."

What? "No way. I know this route like the back of my hand. It's not—"

"Changed last week."

A speed trap. Of course.

"Damn it, doesn't Michigan have any other way to fund themselves?"

"There were notices in all the local papers."

"I've been working in Detroit." He huffed out a breath. "Hell, Tonya, I'll pay the ridiculous ticket. I'll even donate to the policeman's ball or whatever charity you want. Just do me one little favor and ask me what's up!"

Pause. A long one, damn it. And then she lowered her sunglasses. Her sweet baby blues appeared and he almost melted right there. Sure she was all Officer Ice Queen, but right there were the eyes that had lived in his fantasies for over a decade.

"What's. Up."

"I passed the bar. As of today, I'm a real, live, honest-to-goodness attorney."

He watched her face for her reaction. He waited for a whoop of joy or a slap of congratulations. Something that indicated she knew what this meant to him. Instead, her lips curved into a slow, shallow smile.

"Congratulations, Counselor."

He huffed out a breath. That was a bit anticlimactic. So he

abruptly twisted, crossed his arms, and leaned them against the car door such that he was as close as he could get to her without climbing out of his car. Then he smiled his most charming smile at her.

She arched her brows, but beyond that, didn't seem to react at all.

"Celebrate with me, Tonya."

"I'm in a relationship."

Ah. Well that put a damper on his hormones, but even so he still wanted to catch up with her. "That's great," he lied. "Tell me about him."

"Her."

His brows arched. "Really?"

She nodded slowly. "If you tell a soul—"

"Not a word. I swear. But only if you tell me all about it."

"Got a kink gene you want to indulge?" she drawled, her voice heavy with sarcasm.

He held up his hand. "No, Tonya. I got an interest in you. We grew up together. You gave me my first kiss—"

She flushed at that, and he took it with a measure of pride that she remembered it. Maybe even thought of it as pleasurably as he did.

"We've missed each other these last years. I've kept up through Carl but—"

"You still dating the Chinese girl?"

He shook his head.

"The brunette?"

So she had been paying attention. Good. "Jade and I are on

the outs right now. She's headed to New York and big city law. Couldn't understand why I was going back to Gladwin."

Tonya jolted. "You are?"

He nodded. "Carl really needs the help since Dad died. Has for a while, and I can't keep splitting my time between Detroit and home."

"So you quit Detroit?"

He grinned. "Yup. Turned in my notice today."

"But what are you going to do in Gladwin? The clan can't have that much legal work—"

"You'd be surprised. Plus, I'll be looking in the surrounding area for work. Bay City isn't that far. It won't be a lot of money, but my expenses are low." He shrugged. "Once Carl gets everything stabilized, I can look for a more permanent solution."

"He'll be grateful for the help."

"So what about it?" he pressed. "Tell me all about your girlfriend over dinner? My treat?"

"Of course it's your treat," she said as she handed him back his license and registration. "Since I just accidentally screwed up this ticket." She ripped up the moving violation, then gave him directions to a chain restaurant. "I'll meet you there in an hour."

"Bring your girl," he said. "I'd love to meet her."

She flashed him a sheepish look. "She's actually a guy named Brian. He's a dentist and the exact opposite of the meatheads I work with every damn day."

"So not a muscle guy?"

"More like a ninety-pound weakling, but he makes me smile."

"So why say you're with a girl?"

Her gaze canted away. "Because guys stop arguing when I say I'm on a different team. Plus it helps them understand a female cop. Apparently only lesbos can be butch."

He frowned and he tried to sort out what she'd just said. "You know that makes no sense, right?"

"And when did the human race ever make sense, Counselor?"

She had a point. And he had a desperate urge to learn more about what it took to be a female cop. What it had cost her and how it worked with the whole shifter thing. She started to walk away, but he reached out to touch her hand. Warm fingertips to hot skin. He brushed across the back of her hand and felt a jolt all the way through his body that lingered in his dick. And even more shocking, she seemed to have felt something, too. Her eyes widened and her breath caught. But that was the only reaction he could see.

"Alan?"

"Does he know? About the bear thing?"

Tonya's face paled and she shook her head. "He's so normal, you know? I liked that about him. Not macho, not paranormal, just a boring dentist raised by nice middle-class people. Hell, the weirdest thing about him is he's part Chippewa on his mom's side. He even has allergies and hates camping."

Alan listened carefully, keeping his expression neutral. She clearly had reservations about the relationship, but there was also a softness in her tone. A yearning that lay underneath her words that spoke of a deeper connection with the man.

"Do you love him?"

"I think so," she said. "Maybe. Or maybe I just want the whole white-picket-fence thing."

"Bring him to dinner. Let me meet him."

She arched a brow. "You looking to give dating advice, Counselor?"

He snorted. "Never. I just want you happy, is all." And wasn't that God's honest truth? "And I want to see if this dentist can do that." Apparently, he couldn't even say the man's name.

She swallowed. "He's going to propose soon. He bought a ring."

Oh shit. This was serious. "You're sure?"

"I saw the receipt. Didn't mean to snoop, but he was careless."

And Tonya noticed things. It was part of being a cop. "So that's a good thing, right?"

"So I'm going to have to tell him. About the bear thing."

Right. Always a dicey proposition. "Have you talked to Carl? Gotten his okay and all?" It was standard practice to ask permission from the alpha for revelations like this. It was rarely denied. Not in this day and age. But alphas liked to keep track of who was in on the secret and who wasn't. And since she was a woman who followed the letter of the law, Tonya would be particular about following clan rules.

"Everything's in place to tell Brian," she said. "I just can't seem to actually do it."

"Do you need help?"

Her eyes sharpened for a moment. She looked like she was about to bite his head off for suggesting such a thing, and so he held up his hands in surrender.

"It was just an offer. I don't know how I could help, but some-times—"

"I know," she said, cutting him off. Then she rubbed a hand over her face. "I haven't gone running in a while and it's making me antsy."

He didn't have to ask what kind of running she meant. Every shifter had to go animal wild for a time. Just let the bear out of the cage and go tromping through the woods in their natural form. "Have you tried Mark's new software program? It takes the edge off."

"Yeah. I love it, but it's not enough."

He nodded. He couldn't relate to the need to go native, but he did understand it. So he touched her hand again, and this time the electrical surge was more like a warm wash of energy—sweet and gentle. "Call Brian and tell him you're get-ting together with an old friend tonight. Celebrate my passing the bar and all," he added with a grin.

"Yeah, I will—"

"But then go get your bear on at the state park. I'll bring food to the campground for afterward and keep hold of your keys and stuff." Shifters always ended up ravenous after a run. And it was always reassuring to know that someone watched the home fires while the animal went native. This he knew from years of hold-ing car keys and warming the grill while bear play went on in the woods. They needed it, and he took comfort in keeping things safe while the clan went wild.

Tonya wasn't immune to the lure. She hesitated, clearly tempted. "It's been a *long* while, Alan. I might not be done until well after midnight."

He shrugged. "I got no plans."

Then she gave in. He saw it first in her eyes, which flashed gratitude even when her body was still trying to resist. But then every part of her sagged with relief.

"Thanks, Alan."

"No problem."

And it wasn't. Not even when she didn't return to the campsite until after three in the morning. Not when she ate two steaks and finished the last of his beer. It wasn't a problem until she kissed him on the cheek and hopped into her car, flushed and excited to return to her dentist.

Then he stood by his car and gave up hiding the boner that throbbed through every cell in his body. And he realized that while she was headed to her boyfriend, he was so very alone.

He thought the feeling would ease over time. He thought he would get past this childhood crush that was more about nostalgia than anything else. After all, she'd been his first kiss and it had blown his teenage mind.

But three months later, she showed up in Gladwin. She'd gotten a job as the sheriff's newest deputy. Carl told him that the bear revelation hadn't gone well with the dentist and she needed a change in scenery. And when Alan went to see Tonya, she was a totally different person.

All her defenses were up. Her shoulders were tight and her eyes were haunted. She declared in no uncertain terms that she wasn't gay, but she sure as hell was over men. Her exact words were, "I've decided I'm asexual."

Then she slammed the door in his face.

Chapter One

*N*_{ow}

Alan Carman dragged his eyes open to a room flooded with sunlight. He'd always liked the light, but this time he flinched away from it. And then suddenly, she was there.

Tonya.

Officer Tonya Kappes sat by his bed, her face drawn with worry, her hands gripping his arm tightly.

"What's wrong?" he rasped.

She blinked twice before speaking, her voice heavy with irony. "Nothing's wrong except you've been running a temperature higher than a volcano for nearly a week."

Huh.

Is that why he felt like an overbaked biscuit? God, even his skin seemed to crackle when he moved. Thankfully, she brought him water, and he drank from the cup greedily.

Flashes of memory returned to him.

He'd been abducted right in the courthouse parking lot. Then that damned cage and all the who-knew-what that had been shoved into his arm.

Evil Einstein and that cougar bitch. She had been the worst. Einstein had just looked at him like a science project, but that bitch had sat and stared at him. Hours upon hours just like a fucking cat, and she hadn't said a word. At least not English words. There'd been weird chants and strange potions shoved down his throat. And all the while, he'd felt the caress of her like slime on his skin.

And then…

Oh, hell. "Did I shift?"

Tonya's gaze slanted away. "Sort of."

He looked at her face, seeing the stark fear that she tried to hide. And then he remembered the rest. The prickly agony of fur spiking out of his skin. Not in a regular way, but in patches. The horror of a nose and mouth elongated. Teeth that were sharp and irregular inside his mouth. And the fever. He remembered the fever sapping his strength and the bitch hissing in his ear when he was too weak to move.

And he remembered how much he hated her.

"So I'm a freak now," he said as he looked at his arms before him. Same bones, but the skin was patchy with dark spots. Same hands except the knuckles were larger, the fingers blunter.

"No!" Tonya said, gratifyingly vehement.

"It's okay. I was one already, though in a different way."

She turned to look at him, her blue eyes laser bright. "What do you mean?"

He meant a lot of things, none of which he could process or explain right now. "How'd you find me?"

"Mark turned on your phone. Used the GPS."

Right. Good idea. But... "Why'd it take a week?"

Silence.

He looked at Tonya, and a familiar ache settled into his chest. *Good God.* He'd been gone for a week, trapped in that cage while Einstein experimented on him. He'd missed two court dates and at least one Gladwin pack meeting. And in all that time... "You guys didn't even realize I was missing."

She swallowed. "Carl got a text saying you had met someone. That you'd be gone for a while."

"Because I'm so irresponsible that I disappear for a week without finding a replacement, without emailing everyone at least twice. Without—"

He'd been covering the Gladwin clan's paperwork almost since he could read. His father had never been happier than when Alan announced the intention of becoming a lawyer. The Gladwins needed a lawyer in the family because good ones cost too damned much.

So he'd gone. He'd studied. And he'd become his brother's right-hand man for everything that the shifters were too twitchy to deal with. Paperwork. Court filings. Hell, he even did the taxes. Alan handled all the details of living in this modern age.

And no one had fucking realized he'd been missing.

"I'm sorry. We're all really sorry," she said.

Yeah. He got that. Except sorry wasn't cutting it. Fury itched right beneath his skin. A red haze of hatred rose up from his gut and choked off his words. Tonya was saying she was sorry. Tonya, the woman he'd loved since he was ten, was apologizing for not noticing him.

Like that was fucking unusual.

"Get out," he said. Except it didn't come out in cold, clipped tones. It wasn't his precise, businesslike way. No, the words were snarled, the meaning ripped from his heart and thrown at her face.

"Alan—"

"Get. The. Fuck. Out."

Carl would have blustered at him. Becca, Carl's fiancée, would probably pat his hand and offer to get him some pie. Tonya, however, was a straight line in his mind. No bullshit, no fudging. She'd screwed up. They'd all screwed up, but she took the brunt of his rage because she was here.

"If you ever want to talk, just call me," she said as she straightened up. "Day or night."

He glared at her. "Not going to happen."

She dipped her chin, and her short honey-blond hair brushed over her eyes. He didn't know if it was an apology, an acknowledgment, or if she just had that much trouble looking at the freak he'd become. Whatever it was didn't matter. After a moment, she stepped out of the room and was gone.

Six hours later, he was wide awake in his bed. It was night, the floor was quiet, and the nurses gossiped in low tones down the hall. Thanks to Becca he had a change of clothes. Thanks to Carl's visit an hour after Tonya's, he had a good idea of just how bad everyone felt for not realizing he'd been abducted.

Somehow that didn't mean jack shit to him.

Now it was night, and he was dressed.

He snuck out of his room and slipped down the stairs. Ten minutes later, he was hotwiring a motorcycle. He'd never stolen so much as a kiss from anyone, but he was stealing this Harley.

When he roared away, he relished the throb between his thighs and nursed the hatred in his soul. He couldn't deal with the Gladwin grizzlies. He refused to think about a single one of the ungrateful, self-absorbed bastards. Instead, he focused on the cat bitch.

He was going to kill her.

He was going to rip her heart from her chest, then laugh as the light died from her eyes.

And he was going to do it alone.

Chapter Two

*P*retty.

Alan looked up in shock at the colors of the stars. It was a dark night without moon or clouds, which left him a clear view of the heavens. Red. Blue. Yellow. Pinpricks of light with Christmas-like halos. As if the stars were a very far away holiday display.

He blinked, doing his best to focus his thoughts. It was getting harder, especially with his fever coming back. It had been a week since leaving the hospital and whatever focus he'd had was now slipping away. Colors distracted him. Scents overpowered him. And he enjoyed the brute force use of his muscles like a Neanderthal. He'd always been a man who valued thinking. He ferreted out the reasons behind the actions and quietly sneered at people who couldn't use logic.

Now he was one of the dumb ones. Distracted by trivialities. Happy in raw strength. And unable to remember anything beyond this moment in time.

Good thing he was dying. He didn't know how long he could hold on to his mission. Too much distracted him and his thoughts splintered into fragments. He remembered a command.

Look at your hands.

Something about his hands was important.

So he focused downward to the flex of tendon and bone. He remembered typing elegant phrases on a computer. Even before that, he'd played with calligraphy as a boy. Beautiful strokes of ink on parchment. But when he looked down now, he didn't see long fingers with neatly trimmed nails. He saw hairy fists, knobby knuckles, pinprick claws.

A monster.

He was a monster now, and he hated pretty.

He had to keep it together for his mission. One last thing to do before he died. Kill the bitch who'd done this to him. Kill her for making him despise pretty. Kill her for destroying a good man. And he'd been a good man, he was sure, but he wasn't anymore.

Refocused on his purpose, he looked out at the parking lot. He studied the rusted trucks and mentally dissected the stench of piss and vomit. His attention slid to minute sensations as he leaned against the brick wall of a topless bar. He was deafened by the music and nauseated by the slime on the brick where it slicked his skin. And yet, unwillingly, his gaze inevitably rose to the stars.

Pretty.

Then he winced as the already loud music exploded into the air. Someone was leaving the bar. Next came a man's voice, thick with liquor. A moment later, Alan saw his target draped around a tired-looking woman.

"Come on, honey," the bastard said. "It's a pretty night. We can see the stars."

"Nah, Johnny. I don't like the stars. I like what you got right here." She giggled, clearly drunk. But when Alan sniffed the air, working to isolate smells and their origin, he wasn't so sure. The man's scent was thick with alcohol, but hers wasn't so ugly. Then he watched her lift Johnny's wallet. Clever fingers, moving quickly as the two people wove their way to the back of the parking lot.

Good.

Alan kept himself in check while she pocketed all of Johnny's cash then went for his watch. Might as well let her get what she needed. He counted the seconds, forcing himself to get to twenty before he struck. Long enough for the couple to stumble into the shadows with him.

Now.

Easy-peasy to reach out and grab the bastard by the throat. Monsters had quick reflexes and could crush a man's larynx with a single squeeze.

He didn't do it, though it was disturbingly hard to control the impulse. Johnny was a drunk, a cheat, and a miserably bad father, but he didn't deserve death. So Alan held himself back. Besides, Alan needed the idiot alive. So he used his strength to pin the moron against a truck. And he didn't crush the larynx, though he did push it a little.

Fortunately, Johnny was sober enough to understand the threat. His eyes bugged out and his fists froze at his side.

"Whoa, mister," the woman began.

"Go back inside," Alan ordered. His voice was as rusty as the truck, but he forced the words out. "Johnny and I. Chat."

Once he'd been known for his delicate phrasing and precise word choice. But the monster was so close to the surface now, he had no complexity in his language.

"Call the—" Johnny tried, but Alan leaned in. No more oxygen for Johnny.

"Call the cops," Alan said. "I'll tell them about your hip pocket." It's where she'd stashed Johnny's watch.

The side of her mouth tilted up in a smirk. "Like anybody cares."

True. He knew cops, and they didn't much care about petty theft. Not when it was someone like Johnny getting picked. Time for a different tack. With his free hand, he pulled a few twenties out of his front pocket. He'd planned to use it for dinner, but after smelling Johnny up close, he'd lost his appetite. "Take this. We're gonna talk. About his wife. Kids."

She took the bills quickly but kept her tone hard. "If he ends up dead, I know what you look like."

No, she didn't. Not the real him. But he didn't argue. "Okay."

"Okay." She turned and sauntered back to the bar while Johnny sputtered in disgust.

Alan took a moment. It was a habit he'd developed as a man to organize his thoughts. But with the monster so strong, all he could do was think about Johnny's emotions as they marched across his face. Anger. Frustration. A slow relaxation of fear. That last one was a problem. He needed Johnny pissing-his-pants terrified. So he punched the man in his thick gut.

Johnny doubled over from the pain. Alan let him gag, but then straightened him back up. Except now he could see the bastard's eyes. Cougar slits, glowing a dull lime green. The man was trying to shift, but Alan knew it was too soon. The idiot had been a cougar just hours ago. No way was he capable of changing again this fast.

"Nice try," Alan said as he increased pressure on Johnny's throat. "How do you think I found you? I tracked cougar piss. Followed you here."

The bastard frowned, and Alan watched his nose twitch as he tried to sort out Alan's species by scent. Good luck with that. There was no species like him. But he did like seeing the terror of people's faces when they figured that out. So he let Johnny sniff. And just to make sure it was clear, he relaxed into the horror of his own body. It was as simple as breathing, and he could do it anytime he wanted, probably because he was a monster first, and a man a distant second. He let the patchy fur rise, bringing its own stench with it. His joints ached and his muscles thickened. His sharp nails became pronounced claws and, worst of all, his nose and mouth stretched around sharp teeth. Even if Johnny couldn't see clearly what was happening, the *wrongness* of Alan's cells became clear to anyone with a shifter's nose.

And that's when Johnny really began to sweat. "What are you?" he gagged. "Bear?"

"Monster. Looking for Elisabeth Oltheten."

"She ain't part of us no more. We kicked her outta the pride."

Lions had prides, not cougars. But maybe the cougar shifter knew best. Part of Alan wondered, but the rest of him didn't care.

"I need to find Elisabeth Oltheten," he said.

"I don't know where she is!"

"She's one of you—"

"She started the war with the wolves. The one that got all of us kilt!" Johnny was spitting now. The wet added its own reek to the encounter, and Alan wanted nothing more than to leave.

"*Killed*, you idiot. Not kilt."

"Wot?"

Not the brightest bulb and drunk as well. Alan focused on the basics: slowly choking Johnny until he had the man's full attention.

"Where's Elisabeth Oltheten?" he repeated.

"I don't know!"

"Find out."

"How? We got no one left!"

Not true. He knew that because he'd been carefully stalking the cougars for a week now.

"You didn't die, Johnny. Your brother didn't die. You got four people left in your clan, plus your kids. Someone has to know—"

"We don't know shit!"

Truer words were never spoken, but Alan didn't have the luxury of finding better sources. "Find out or I'm going to do to your kids what she did to me." He leaned in, making sure Johnny saw his sharp teeth in a bearlike jaw. "Take a good whiff."

The man choked on his fear, spitting out his terrified words. "Don't you touch my boy!"

The bastard had one son and two daughters, but clearly he didn't give a shit about the girls. Which was really stupid because among cat shifters, it was the females who had the brains.

"Find Elisabeth." He pulled a card out of his pocket. All it had was a single email address on it and a logo depicting an ogre. A little obvious, style wise, but it was meant for male cats with limited intelligence. He slid it into Johnny's shirt pocket. "You find something and email."

Johnny blinked, his eyes watering either from terror or the stench. "That's it? Anything? I just email you?"

"It better be true. Or I'll hurt your boy."

Alan waited a moment longer, letting the threat sink in. Then after a last shove against the bastard's neck, he spun around and loped off into the dark.

Chapter Three

Alan liked disappearing into the field of corn near the bar. It was the height of summer, so the scents were pleasantly ripe, and the deafening sounds from the bar quickly faded. The corn was face high, so he had to duck his head to avoid the whipping leaves. That allowed him to focus on his feet, the steady thud as his heels hit the ground. Children would be out here soon. The little ones would scramble through corn mazes. The teens would detassle the crop during the day and drink beer near the stream at night.

Memories crowded in. Happy moments better left untouched. He pushed them away in favor of the night breeze and not taking a header into an unexpected ditch. The gas station where he'd parked his motorcycle came up too fast, and his mind slammed back to his surroundings with an almost painful jolt.

Tonya.

He stumbled to a halt at the edge of the parking lot, barely twenty feet from her. How had he missed the scent of her vanilla shampoo and baby powder deodorant? The wind was blowing it straight at him, and even unconscious, he would know it was her.

She was leaning against his motorcycle. He drank in her long legs and short blond hair that was more practical than stylish. He also noted the mussed outline of her sheriff's deputy uniform. She looked tired, and the wrinkles in her clothing told him she'd driven up here straight from a shift. His first instinct was to ask her what he could do. Whatever was wrong, he would fix it.

He squashed that thought almost before it was born. He wouldn't help her or anyone in the Gladwin grizzly clan ever again. So he set his face into hard lines and walked straight up to the bike.

"I need that," he said.

She turned to look at him, the softness on her face so appealing. It was rare for her jaw to be relaxed, rarer still for her eyes to mist or her lips to curve into a smile. She did all three when she saw him. Then she exhaled a low breath as if she'd been holding it in for too long.

"Alan. Really glad you're alive."

"Tonya. Go home. Get some sleep. You look ragged."

Her brows arched. "You say the sweetest things."

He looked her straight in the eye. "Not anymore." And that was as clear as he could make the message. Whatever relationship they might have had, whatever torch he used to carry for her was gone. Terminated with prejudice.

He watched the message land. Her eyes widened and her jaw tightened. And then her shoulders slumped. It was a measure of how long they'd known each other that she allowed her spine to curve in front of him. Normally, her back and her life were as straight arrow as possible.

"Look, I know you have reason to be pissed," she said.

Ya think?

"But that's no reason to turn your back on the people who care most for you. Everyone's been searching for you nonstop since you disappeared from the hospital."

He felt his fingers spike into claws where they curled against his thighs. The run had helped clear his head. He could think right now, but that didn't mean he was safe. So he settled into his fury because it would end the conversation fast enough to keep her alive. He had no idea what he would do to her if the monster took hold.

"Who cares so much for me?" he snapped, hating that he sounded like a whiny child. "My family didn't notice I'd been captured. The clan I've served since I was three can't bother to pay for my services. Or did you mean Carl, my brother and alpha—"

"Carl offered you a generous salary. If this is about money, then—"

"Or is it about you? Finally ready to let me in when it's already too late."

She froze and her eyes widened. "I've been worried sick about you, Alan. Please come home."

He believed her. Everything about her screamed exhaustion. Nerves stretched too thin. But it was too late for them. "Our timing always sucked."

"So let's get it right—"

"I'm leaving, Tonya. You go home and get some sleep. Now get off my bike."

She huffed out a breath and he could see the resignation hit her. One thing about Tonya: she never lived in hope. It was all about the facts as presented to her at any given moment.

"About this bike," she said as she idly pulled out her handcuffs. She made it look like she was playing with them, but the threat that she'd use them hung like bad smoke in the air. "Turns out it's not yours. You're wanted for theft, Mr. Carman. And I'll be taking you in."

He snorted. "Nice try, but Carl bought this bike off the owner. He emailed that to me a couple of days back. So now it's mine."

"Wrong. Now it's Carl's—"

"And he's prosecuting?"

She grimaced. "If that's what it takes to get you home."

She was negotiating with him. Feeling out her options as to the best way to get him back to Gladwin. He'd known her their whole lives, so he knew she wouldn't let it go. If Carl had ordered her to bring him back, she wouldn't stop until she'd seen the truth. Might as well get it over with now.

So he let himself shift. The line was so slim between human and monster. In truth, he was all monster, but sometimes the worst of it didn't show. Sometimes he kept the *smell* of it hidden away. And sometimes he could pretend he was in control. He gave up that illusion now. He relaxed everything until he felt his nose lengthen and his jaw square off. Fur sprouted on his arms and legs, and the oil that allowed it to grow oozed out in a stench that always made him want to retch. His muscles thickened and his fingernails became claws.

Vile.

The smell hit her first. She was a grizzly bear-shifter, so her nose was the most sensitive. It wrinkled, and her gaze darted around. It took her two seconds before she realized the stench came from him. The *wrong* scent was him, the boy who'd adored her since he was fourteen years old.

"Alan…" she choked out.

He didn't answer, just let the smell thicken between them. He could do that, he realized. He could make the scent choke the air like a noxious fog. And then she straightened, facing him square on.

"I don't care, Alan. Make it stink to high heaven, but hear this: *I. Don't. Care.*"

He wanted to believe her. He wanted to feel accepted and loved, just as he was. But he knew it couldn't happen for him. He knew it was too late because he couldn't love himself. Not like this. Not as a monster. And besides, with his fever building again, he doubted he would live long enough to make peace with himself.

But rather than say that, he chose the cowardly way out. He ran, using his shifter speed.

He shoved her aside, careful to make sure she fell onto soft dirt and not the concrete rubble a few feet to the left. She rolled with the fall, adjusting easily, though he'd moved with lightning speed. But she was off balance and too far away. Plenty of time for him to leap onto the bike and kick it to life. Part of him wanted to wait, to see what she would do. Would she fight to keep him near? Or back away in horror? Maybe she'd shoot him because that's what cops did to monsters.

He didn't wait. He didn't want to know.

Chapter Four

Tonya listened closely, doing her best to track Alan's direction just from the sound of the bike. She didn't move until the roar was well out of range. And even then, she remained still, taking the time to remember every detail of their discussion.

Biggest in her brain was that five-alarm body odor. The kind that went well beyond personal hygiene and landed in skunk territory. Which is kind of funny, Tonya thought as she brushed the dirt off her uniform, because growing up, Alan had either smelled like chlorine from the local swimming pool or Axe body spray. And she'd spent years calling him a pretty boy.

Not something that fit now, though, but she'd never found him more appealing. There was a ruggedness to him now that hadn't been there when he'd dressed as a lawyer. He'd always been tall, and thanks to his swimming, his shoulders were almost bear-shifter broad. That inverted triangle on him? Hot. Which meant that the man looked fine in either a suit or jeans and a ripped tee.

But now he sported a five-o'clock shadow and an I-don't-give-a-shit attitude that appealed to her sense of danger. What could she say? She'd always had a secret longing for bad boys with an edge. It was the grizzly in her who respected physical power, while the woman in her wanted a father of the year. Which meant suddenly Alan was an incredibly appealing mix of Boy Scout gone bad and she was wet-her-panties attracted. Then he'd let fly with his skunk impression. The thing about skunks, though, was that they used their noxious spray to scare away predators. And that's exactly what he'd been doing: trying to scare her while he fled. And it had worked. She'd been horrified by the smell and too confident in their history to believe that Alan would ever hit her.

Wrong.

So wrong to think he was the same sweet boy from her childhood. So wrong to believe his captivity and torture hadn't fundamentally changed who he was. And a million times wrong to think that a simple come-hither smile from her would bring him home. But she had to find him. She had to get his head screwed on right. It went well beyond her responsibility as a cop or as beta to the Gladwin clan. She needed him in her world. He was the last remaining point of stability in her life, and she couldn't let him toss her away like moldy bread. It wasn't pride and it sure as hell wasn't simple attraction.

It was a need that burned so hot in her gut that it frightened her. Just what would she give up to keep him in her life? And what would she do if he said no? In fact, he *had* said no, and she was about to risk her job and her position as beta to keep looking for him.

Sometimes, a girl just had to embrace her inner stalker.

But first she needed a diet soda. Something with extra caffeine in it because she sure as hell wasn't going to sleep anytime soon. She headed for the convenience mart where she grabbed some dark chocolate peanut M&M's because there was nothing to dislike about that. She was just paying when her phone rang.

She toyed with the idea of ignoring it, but that would only delay the inevitable. Might as well deal with it now. She stepped outside, looked at the pretty stars, and tried not to bite the head off her alpha.

"Kappes," she answered, barking out her last name rather than hello.

"Tonya," Carl growled into the phone, the sound both anger and relief mixed together. "Where the fuck are you?"

She turned around, looking for the address on the side of the convenience mart. In the end, she pulled the information from her memory of driving through a zillion small towns in Michigan. "Bad Axe, I think." If Michigan was a hand, Bad Axe was near the tip of the thumb.

"What the hell? I made you my beta so you could help me here. In Gladwin."

"I *am* helping," she ground out. "I found him."

It took him less than a second to answer, and then his voice came out filled with excitement. "Alan? When are you two getting home?"

"We're not, Carl. He ran off. He's different."

She hated disappointing him. Not just because he was her alpha, but because Carl was Alan's brother and there was a wealth of love between them. Or there had been.

"Of course—"

"No, not of course!" How did she express what she'd just seen? What she was only now starting to process? "You're thinking of him as the same old Alan but traumatized. And he is. He's angry and defensive. But there's more."

"Look, I know he's been changed. I know he's had his shifter DNA activated."

"You think you know. I thought I knew. But he's not the same person, Carl. He's not even close."

"That doesn't make sense. He's still Alan, no matter what's been done to him."

She thought about the way he'd shifted and the smell. That was the surface result of what that cougar bitch had done to him. Then she rolled through all the things he'd done recently that the normal Alan couldn't conceive of doing, listing them off as they came to her. "He stole a motorcycle, he's been threatening were-cougars throughout Michigan, and he hit me."

There was a moment's silence. "So he's fast enough to surprise you." She could hear the smirk all the way through the phone.

Not the point. "He's strong, too. Physically, I mean."

"These are all good things, Tonya."

Jesus, when would men realize that the ability to do physical violence wasn't always good? Even Carl—as proactive and modern an alpha as she'd ever seen—wasn't immune to the idea that physical power was always a reason to cheer. The old Alan had taught her that wasn't true. If a man was capable of winning with violence, he tended to negotiate from that place first. Direct line to a win. It was only the physically weaker ones, the ones who got their butts kicked, who started with the brain first. Who talked and thought their way through before trying to punch their way out.

But Alan had stopped being a thinking man. He'd become an angry, violent puncher. In their short encounter, he hadn't tried to talk to her. What he'd said was simply a distraction until he could get into position to fight. That was a shift from the foundation. Which meant he wasn't the old Alan at all. Not even remotely.

And the ache of that hurt so deep in her soul that she could barely breathe. Even so, she had to make Carl understand, so she forced the words out though they cut at her on the way. "He's not Alan anymore."

"Bullshit."

Tonya closed her eyes, trying to find a way through. Carl was loyal to a fault. It was part of what made him a good alpha. He never abandoned anyone. But she was the beta, which meant it was her job to handle reality, no matter what ideals Carl still clung to.

Tonya exhaled. "Look, I'm wiped and it's a long drive home."

"Stay up there. I'll join you. We'll bring him home together."

"No." The word came out with a quick explosion of sound. No explanation. Just a gut feeling that Carl would only make it worse simply because he wouldn't see the truth. "He doesn't want help. He doesn't want to get better."

"He needs to know that we want him home. That we're sorry for everything."

Damn it, the man wasn't listening. "He knows that. He doesn't care."

"But—"

"Carl, do you trust me?"

Her alpha let out an aggravated sigh. "Of course I do."

"Then let me handle this. You've got plenty on your plate with the Detroit shifters going psycho. People need to see you in Gladwin looking out for our own."

"He's my brother," Carl ground out. "I need to—"

"Let me handle it. I can talk him around. Woman's touch and all."

Carl snorted. "No offense, but you're a little late to be playing that card."

True enough. In fact, she'd never made any claim to feminine intuition, wiles, or subtlety. Except for some exploration of her womanly side in college, she was entirely masculine in her approach to life and had made damn sure everyone knew it. Which made it doubly surprising to both of them that she was drawing on that now. And she couldn't even give a good explanation as to why. Just that perhaps it was time. Maybe it was past time for her to be both a cop and a woman.

"Just let me try, okay?"

"Two days, Tonya. That's it. And then I'm coming up there and dragging you both home."

She hung up the phone rather than answer. She didn't want to confess that she had no freaking idea how she was going to do what she promised. Or even how to find whatever shithole Alan was hiding in.

But that's why she was a good detective. She figured stuff like that out.

Fortunately, it didn't take her very long. The shithole in question turned out to be a resort in Bay City. He'd booked under the alias Harry D. S. Den. Alan probably thought he was being clever using the name and account Carl had created for his clandestine PI work. And truthfully, no one else would have thought to look for Alan under his brother's alias. But Tonya wasn't just anybody and so she'd found him within an hour of beginning the search.

Great. Except now she had to figure out some fast talking way to get Alan off the revenge bridge and back in Gladwin where he belonged. Problem was fast talking wasn't in her skill set. She was more in the do this or I'll arrest you camp and that had already failed. Which meant she had to lead with one of her other strengths.

The good news? Alan was in a resort that had an open gift shop.

Chapter Five

Booze and chlorine. They were the scents of Alan's adolescence, not to mention a few wonderful post-finals weekends in law school. The heat of the water sank into his bones, easing aches he hadn't even been aware of. Joints loosened, muscles relaxed, and he finished off the last gulp of his martini before closing his eyes and dropping his head back against the tile.

His pulse pounded in his throat, reminding him that he still had a fever and the Jacuzzi was going to make that worse. The booze probably wasn't good for him, either, but both the heat and the alcohol gave him easy excuses for his splintered thoughts.

Who needed to focus, anyway? Especially with the stars so pretty above and no one close enough to be in danger from him. He was alone out here except for the bartender on the opposite side of the roof. Down below, he could hear the chatter of other hotel guests, but he'd paid extra for a premium suite and the special rooftop view. Or rather Carl would pay it as Harry D.

S. Den since this was his brother's alias. Which meant that Alan could enjoy Bond martinis, shaken not stirred, and the color of the stars in gleeful peace. Especially since he absolutely refused to feel guilty about burning through Carl's money. His brother would inherit all of Alan's savings soon enough.

So Alan sank into the water and let his gaze wander through the stars. He was just about to signal for another drink when he saw her. At first he thought he was hallucinating. He was constantly discovering new "gifts" from his change like killer BO on command and itchy feet. Hallucinations couldn't be far behind, right? But this hallucination wasn't going away.

A blond who looked a lot like Tonya stepped onto the balcony, looking away from him. She was wearing a thong bikini and open skirt wrap. The whole outfit was midnight blue with tiny sparkles that made him think she was twinkling just for him. And then she turned around and headed his direction. Her luscious breasts were plump, her waist narrow, and her hips moved in a way that could only be called bewitching. Which meant it couldn't be Tonya. As far as he was aware, she'd never sauntered anywhere, much less in so frankly a sexual way.

And yet, as the woman drew nearer, his brain kept screaming, *Tonya*. Tonya as a Victoria's Secret model. Tonya as a Playboy bunny. Tonya looking even better than his adolescent fantasies of her. Tonya slowing as she approached to allow him to stare at every creamy inch of her exposed flesh. *Jesus*.

"Go away," he croaked out. It was all he could manage between the dry throat and the fact that all his blood had gone south.

"What? Why?"

Oh hell, it was Tonya's voice, too, only sounding strangely restricted and uncertain. As if she were as uncomfortable as he was horny. Then he watched her swallow. Oh God, how many of his adolescent dreams had involved that image?

Jesus, he was depraved.

He reached instinctively for his drink only to find he'd already finished it. Worse, his hands were shaking bad enough he fumbled with the empty glass.

Get it together!

Meanwhile, she stopped walking to twist sideways as she untied the filmy skirt. There was almost no breeze, and yet the fabric billowed about her legs, drawing attention to their muscled length. Tonya wasn't tall so much as strong, but her proportions made it look like her legs went on for miles. He couldn't stop himself from thinking about them wrapped around his ass. About the way she'd arch back, giving him a great view of her bobbing tits as he thrust home. And he thought about sucking on her berry tips until she orgasmed around his dick while both his heads exploded.

His thoughts were graphic, the images filthy, and he had to sink farther into the bubbling water to keep his boner from breaking the surface. Why, why, why was she here tempting him with a body he couldn't have? Suggesting things she'd never do with him?

And right there was the shot of ice water that he needed to regain his composure. Sure Tonya was here, and just like at his fourteenth birthday party, she had an ulterior motive. The difference here was that at fourteen, he hadn't cared why she'd kissed him silly. Now, nearing the ripe age of thirty, he more than cared. He despised her for it.

So he turned away from her to signal to the bartender. He didn't need more vodka screwing with his thinking, but it was better than looking at her as she slowly sank one sweet inch at a time into the Jacuzzi.

"Fair warning, Tonya. If you step all the way into the water, I'm going to fuck you right here, right now. Beneath the stars and in front of Marty the bartender." He turned his hard stare onto her. "And I won't wear a condom or give two shits what you want."

She paused, her eyes widening at his words. And then she shrugged, her lips curving into a taunting slash of a smile. "You could try."

"Planning to cry rape?"

She shook her head. "Wouldn't be rape with you."

His gut clenched at her words, but that was nothing compared to his dick's happy dance. He'd been waiting well over a decade for her to say something like that to him. He'd offered her respect in their teens, then courtly generosity in his early twenties. Over the last few years, they'd settled on suggestive banter, which she sometimes killed, but sometimes played along with. And whenever she'd teased him back, he'd jolt into a euphoric hope that one day they'd be more.

But then the bitch Elisabeth had kidnapped him and killed the man he was. The monster who currently inhabited his body was just hoping to strike back hard before he died. And maybe have a little cheap fun before the end.

And now Tonya wanted to play? Bullshit. She had an ulterior

motive. But apparently his dick didn't care because here she was, fully into the hot tub despite his warning. The bubbles played peekaboo with her belly button, and he felt the volcano inside him begin to churn. Was it lust or violence burning through his veins? Even he didn't know.

Marty brought him another martini, and Alan slammed it back like a shot. Not the way to treat fine vodka, but he was pissed and the burn at the back of his throat fired his blood. He put a fifty-dollar tip on the tab and told the man to stay at the far end of the roof. And then he stared at Tonya with hooded eyes.

She lifted her chin—and her breasts—then arched a brow at him. "Why are you angry at me?"

He stared at her, shocked to realize the depth of her ignorance. "Are you kidding?"

She folded her arms, plumping her cleavage even more. "I get why you're angry. You've got every right. But why be pissed at me?"

"Do you know when I fell in love with you?"

She flinched at the question. How could she not know how completely she'd owned him as a teenager?

"I was fourteen and you came to my birthday party. You wore a leather miniskirt, nearly spilled out of your bikini top, and batted your eyes beneath that goth eye shadow. And right there in front of all my friends playing Halo, you kissed me. For like ten minutes."

"It was a dare."

"*I know.*" He let that hang in the steam between them. She'd upended his world with one very public, very hot kiss. She'd smelled like vanilla and rocked her pelvis against his erection. She'd tugged on his lower lip and rubbed her breasts against his chest. And when she'd pulled back, her nipples had been tight pearls and her cheeks were flushed. He'd nearly come just looking at her wet ruby lips. All because some senior dickhead had dared her to go give Carl's little brother a big happy.

"We've talked about this, Alan," she said. "I apologized the next day. I was wrong and cruel. In a family of all boys, I needed to find a way to be a girl and you were safe."

He nodded. "And that just made me fall a thousand times farther."

She sighed and dropped down onto the seat. Her hair was short, but the splashes made the fringes dark and spiked. He barely noticed, being more consumed by the way her breasts floated and those silver dots on the bikini sparkled.

"I can't help how you felt in high school," she said. Then she lifted her chin and waited until he met her gaze. "I never toyed with you again."

Which had made her the unattainable dream. A woman he'd tasted but who was forever out of reach. How he'd jerked off to her fantasy, and with every explosion he'd devised another way that she could become his.

"Which doesn't answer the question," she pressed. "Why are you mad at me now?"

Because she was his biggest disappointment in a spectacularly disappointing life. By all accounts, he was one of Gladwin's smartest, most talented children. He couldn't shift into a grizzly bear, but he could use the law like a weapon to protect or destroy.

He'd been the organizational skill behind his father's and his brother's reigns as Max. And in case legal brilliance wasn't enough, he could fight toe-to-toe with any of the bears. Martial arts training had seen that, if needed, he could survive against most shifters despite their animal advantages.

And what had that amounted to in real life? Jack shit. No one had even noticed when he'd gone missing. Two court cases had gone belly up because he'd been kidnapped, and that didn't include the filings that he'd missed. Not even his own brother had realized he was gone. Why? Because he wasn't a shifter. What he did was in the background where no one saw until the damage was too big to ignore.

Spectacularly disappointing for a favored son.

And now he was a stinking, furry monster with a death sentence, so there was no hope for anything better. No longer could he cut bait and start fishing in the larger, more lucrative waters of Chicago or New York City. Thanks to Elisabeth, all he could do was find the bitch who had murdered him and make sure she got what she deserved. Well, that and fuck the woman who had most disappointed him.

"I would have given you anything, Tonya. But you wanted to be Maxima." She'd wanted to be alpha bitch with his brother. "And when Carl said no, you took my job as beta instead."

He watched her swallow and damned himself for still being aroused by that. "Yeah," she finally said, her voice hoarse, "you got reason."

"You're fucking right I do." And yet hearing her admit it wasn't the victory he craved. If anything, it felt hollow to hear her say that. Like he'd been striving all these years for a brass ring, and when he finally grabbed hold, it turned out to be nothing but a thin piece of aluminum foil. And that pissed him off even more.

"Bend over, Tonya." He was going to fuck her from behind like a beast.

"No." She flashed him a smile. "Let's talk a bit more first."

"Fucking tease," he spat out. The venom in his words startled them both.

"I've never lied to you," she said, her voice cold. Good. Made it easier to hate her.

"Don't care," he said. Then he stood up, feeling the water sheet off him as his chest rippled. He wasn't a vain man. He'd never cared what he looked like beyond making sure he appeared well groomed. But his change had given him muscles where before he'd just been lean. So for the first time in his life, he had a physique to be proud of. Assuming, of course, he kept it to the human normal look instead of hairy monster. So he rose out of the water, letting her see every inch of his chiseled abs and thick boner. And he watched her eyes, feeling both sickened and aroused by the way they widened and her lips felt open.

"Like what you see?" he taunted.

"Yes," she answered. Tonya was nothing if not succinct. Then she tilted her chin, challenge in every line of her body for all that she was sitting down. "We do this, we do it face-to-face."

He snorted. "Like I care what you want."

"Not a want, Alan. It's how it's gonna be."

He took a moment to process her words. Was she really saying she'd spread her legs for him? Now? He couldn't believe it. It had to be another lie like that kiss when he'd been fourteen. "Why? Is it because I'm a shifter now? You don't get off on anyone who isn't a beast?"

She shook her head. "You're not a beast. I wouldn't be with you if you were."

He snorted and held up an arm. "I could prove you wrong." With a single thought, there could be thick fur up and down his skin, not to mention claws where his fingernails should be.

"I don't care what you shift into, Alan. You're not a monster." She leaned forward. "And I've wanted you for a long time."

"Liar." He abruptly slammed forward. One moment they'd been on opposite sides, but he cut through the water fast enough that she didn't have time to protect herself when he gripped her jaw. "Lie again, Tonya. I dare you."

He felt her muscles work under his fingers. A shift and a tension that he didn't accommodate. It took her three tries before she spoke, but when she did, he couldn't believe her words. "I want children. I tried to do it the normal way. Marriage, picket fence, blah, blah, blah. But I'm not a normal girl, so I might as well do it directly." She reached out and gripped his dick, her hand was as firm and direct as his own grip on her jaw. "I want your children, Alan. So fuck me already. Here. Now. Face-to-face. But you damn well better be sure you're set up to provide for them because I'm not going to be another penniless unwed mother for anyone."

Chapter Six

Had she just said that out loud? Tonya felt her entire body blush even as she held her grip on Alan's erection. At least she could blame her color on the heat from the hot tub. But what the hell was she doing confessing her deepest desire to an unstable man? She wanted children one thousand percent. But not fathered by a man who was completely, insanely sexy...er, she meant nuts. Completely nuts. And yet the way he looked at her made her nipples tighten despite the heat.

They stared at each other, and she wondered who would give in first. Alan would, she decided. Alan always gave in to her. So she waited, and a moment later, she felt his hand ease on her jaw. Just like—

He slit open her top, a clean cut between her breasts. She didn't even see his hand move or the second when his fingers became claws. But one second, he was holding her jaw nearly immobile. The next, her breasts bobbed free in the water.

She gasped, startled not by his movement but by the fact that it was Alan who did it. He was so angry that she doubted he had any control of his actions. And then he took hold of her breasts; lifted both of them and stroked them in precise lines as if he'd been planning it for years.

It was so odd the way the man touched her. Both hands surrounded her flesh, moving with undeniable intention. He was going for her nipples, his searing gaze still holding hers. She hadn't expected how large his hands were. That she'd love feeling her ample breasts completely surrounded by the length of his fingers. Against her will, her belly went liquid and her knees slipped open. Oh hell, the way he looked at her—like a man on fire—ignited every lustful cell in her body.

And still his grip narrowed. No rush. And no gentleness, either. He tightened in a steady procession until he squeezed her nipples. Tug. Hard. Enough to make her gasp. And then he twisted. Not enough to hurt, but it shot off rockets of reaction throughout her body.

And then he started it again. A wide hold that steadily tightened to her nipples. And while he worked her breasts, his lips were curled into a snarl. It was an ugly look on him, and yet it didn't frighten her. This was Alan. Angry and brutal, certainly, but underneath, he still seemed like the same Alan who would never hurt her. And while his fingers twisted her nipples, she grinned at the thrill of what he was doing. He took her to the edge of pain—or maybe a little beyond—but made her hungry for more. Probably because she was a shifter. She could take a lot. And this dangerous edge to the love play was making her want him on every level.

"Tit for tat," she said, her voice hoarse as she squeezed him hard. He was large and hot beneath her hand. His thin boxers weren't even a real swimsuit and certainly not enough to stop her from feeling his entire length. Wow, he was thick. Not long, necessarily, but wide enough that he would stretch her to the limit and she would love every second of it.

She reached forward with her other hand. He let her shove down his shorts, and then he leaned forward. The penis reared up through the water. Round, dark red, and weeping. She looked at it and was surprised by the raw hunger she felt. When had she become this lustful at the sight of a man's dick? Never before.

"You want this?" His voice mocked her.

Her gaze shot up to his. "Yes," she answered honestly. "You sticking around, Alan? You going to be a father to your children?" She just had to get him to say yes. If he said it, then he would be true to his word and she could get him back to Gladwin where everything could be sorted out.

He leaned into her neck, and she tilted her head sideways as he inhaled her skin. Just how sensitive was his nose? Could he tell she wasn't fertile? Other shifters would, but that was a matter of experience, not sensitivity.

Pain arced, sharp and startling, at her neck, and she jolted. "Did you just bite me?"

He pulled back and grinned at her. Then he licked his lips, clearly trying to be lewd. Except it backfired on them both. While her mind was still reeling, her body tingled from head to toe, a wave of desire radiating out from the tender spot on her neck. And while she was still reeling from the sensation, he squeezed her nipples hard.

Her belly rippled, the first hard prelude to orgasm. Then she felt her knees widen as he pushed between her thighs. She squeezed back, and he growled, jerking his hips and his dick forward between her hands.

God, that was hot. She felt the power in his thrust as the length of him punched between her palms. The movement also shoved her thighs farther apart. She felt the heat of the water invade her most sensitive places. Holy shit, she was succumbing fast. Lust beat through her body so hard it felt like an assault, but she liked it. Damn it, she liked every part of this angry encounter.

She tried to regain some control, so she squeezed him as hard as she could. But her hands were slippery in the water, the position awkward. All it took was a slight shove from his elbows and she lost her grip. Another shove between her thighs, and she was unmoored. No handhold on him and unable to stabilize her heels on the bottom of the hot tub. Her body lifted higher, half floating, half pinned against the wall with her legs spread.

Then he lifted his hand, raising it so that it was poised before her eyes. Human hand, long fingers, blunt tip. It was Alan's hand and she'd always liked how he kept his nails neat and clean. Except as she watched, hair sprouted along his forearm and the nails became razor-sharp claws.

"Alan—"

"He's gone. You got the monster now."

She shook her head, but he didn't give her a chance to speak. His hand plunged under the water, and she felt the sharp bite of pain as he sliced open the bikini bottom. One long cut across the top of her mound and the fabric floated open.

Then he pushed his fist down between her thighs, rubbing his arm across every hot, swollen part of her.

"Feel the hair?" he asked. "That's not Alan."

She did, and her eyes were nearly rolling back in her head from the pleasure of it.

"Feel my claws?" he asked as he spread his fingers wide.

She felt sharp pinpricks against her most intimate folds. The bite of it had her toes curling in pleasure.

"That's not Alan," he said.

Yes, it was.

Then suddenly, he was inside her. His fingers shoved deep into her center. She bucked at the intrusion, and her belly spasmed again, tightening around him. She feared she'd feel the cut of his claws, but there was nothing like that. No pain. Just him, thick and so very present inside her.

"You like being fucked by a monster?" he taunted.

Apparently so.

"You like it rough?" he asked as he shoved his thumb upward. It was a human hand now, the thick pad of his thumb rolling hard over her clit.

She shuddered, and her head dropped back. She'd meant to fight this. She'd meant to challenge him with her own strength, but this monster-that-was-still-Alan owned her in a way she'd never thought possible. When she'd expected him to back down, he'd cut off her clothes and shoved himself between her thighs. When she'd planned to push him away, her limbs had gone weak and willing. And now he was leaning down and snarling into her ear.

"Scream for me, Tonya. Let Marty know what I'm doing to you."

She'd thought he'd go for her breasts. With her size, every man went straight there. But Alan was between her thighs. His thumb circled hard over her clit, and his speed was merciless—a steady pace neither slow nor fast. Just relentless.

She had to fight back. She had to gather herself enough to show him that he didn't frighten her. "I'm not coming until you do," she gasped, praying she could make it true.

"Bullshit." Nothing else. Just those two words and a wicked grin as he stroked her harder and harder.

She tried to stop it. She gripped his arms, she struggled against the rising pleasure, and she bit the inside of her mouth rather than scream. But she was untethered in the water, her only touchstone the steady thrust of his fingers and the roll against her clit.

Harder.

Stronger.

Against her will, she wrapped her legs around him. It was a way to get purchase, but all it did was shove his fingers deeper inside her.

"Alan, please," she said, wondering what she was asking. *More? Less? Now?*

It didn't matter. Her body shattered. She didn't cry out, thank God. She had that much control, but it was a small thing against the tidal wave of delight that swamped her senses. And he kept it up, damn him. While she arched against him, while she bit her lip trying to keep calm in the middle of a storm of sensation, he slammed her against the wall and drove his hard thickness along her body. He slid across her clit, sending waves of sensation through her that ratcheted up her orgasm. He rolled back and forth against her while she gripped emptiness with each internal explosion. She wanted him to readjust. She wanted him to penetrate her until she couldn't breathe for the size of him. But she hadn't the control to force him. All she could do was hold on as he undulated against her.

It went on forever. Her body detonated a thousand times. And then she felt him explode. His back tightened, his face contorted into a grimace of pain, and he cried out. One single long roar. Guttural. Animal. And the animal in her responded to it, knowing it for what it was.

Possession.

The thought made no sense to her. This was a thing of the body, not of the soul. This was anger and pleasure rolled into a confusing cascade of sensation. And yet in all of that, her bear found meaning.

Possessed.

Alan. Mate.

It wasn't true. It couldn't be true. And yet, there was a locking sensation inside her. As if he'd found something deep within her and written his name on it.

Oh, shit.

She stared at his face. In truth, her gaze had never left his. She'd seen the moment pleasure had overcome his anger. She'd watched as the hardness in his eyes had given way to hunger and then delight. A moment later, his eyes had rolled back in his head and he'd exploded between her thighs.

And then they'd held like that, each riding wave after wave of pleasure. Wet covered her body—from him, from the hot tub, from her own pleasure. Heat was everywhere, too, steam coming off her skin from what they'd just done.

And yet there was a quiet coldness, too. The hot tub still roared with bubbles, and her blood continued to pound, though the contractions were easing. But deep in her heart and in her womb, she felt the emptiness in what they'd done. It was the human in her that felt it. Her bear purred in possessed delight. The rational human part of her watched in horror as he froze against her. His breath came in a harsh rasp, and the hands that caged her on either side curled into fists. When he opened his eyes, she read horror in his gaze. A self-disgust that chilled her.

"Alan?" she whispered.

"Fucking God, Tonya," he rasped. "Don't you get it? Alan isn't here."

He shoved himself backward, grabbed his shorts, and climbed out of the hot tub. He didn't bother wrapping a towel around his hips until he was halfway across the deck area. Tall, muscular, sleek. His swimmer's body with the tight behind that clenched and released as he walked. She watched him go. He was fully human now, no signs of the clawed creature he could become.

Look back at me, she begged silently. If he turned around, then she would know she could still reach him. That part of him still cared about her.

He didn't. He left the deck without turning around. Without

even slowing down. And the shock of that took some time for her to process. Ten minutes. Twenty. She sat in the Jacuzzi. The bubbles clicked off. She was naked and out in the open. The remains of her bikini floated on the opposite side, but she couldn't stir herself to grab them. She was too busy being bruised by her own sobering realizations.

First off, Alan was no longer vulnerable to her sexually. She'd never abused that advantage. Not after what she'd done on his fourteenth birthday. But that didn't mean she wasn't aware of his attraction. She's always known that with one crook of her finger, he'd come running. Except now when she desperately needed him to come home, she'd crooked her finger and he'd walked away.

Second, far from being able to control him through sex, she was the one who'd given up everything. She hadn't even put up a token protest. He'd gone dark and dangerous, and she'd waded right in. She was Officer Tonya Kappes, the coldest, deadliest shifter cop in the state. And yet one dark threat from Alan and she'd turned to mush. Wet, throbbing, hungry mush. And now she was sitting naked in a hot tub wondering what the hell was wrong with her. Hell yes, she wanted kids. She was thirty-one years old and the biological clock was ticking. But she'd never let anyone take her like this. In the open. Without any regard to her feelings or wants.

It was just what he'd promised he'd do. Exactly as he'd warned her. But she hadn't believed him. And when he'd followed through, she'd been both shocked and excited. Which made her the biggest idiot ever. Normally, she demanded dinner and wooing from her gentlemen. No man could so much as kiss her until after a few expensive dates and some genuine courtesy.

Which led her to the most horrifying realization of all: Not only was Alan night-and-day different from the man she knew, but she'd changed, too. Since returning to Gladwin, all she'd thought about was becoming Carl's Maxima. She would lead the female half of the clan by Carl's side. When he'd thrown her over for Becca, she'd been unsettled. Sure, he'd made her beta, but it wasn't the same role she'd trained for. The responsibilities were different, the place in the clan more prestigious and less assured. If she sucked at it—which she did—then the clan itself was at risk. And she sure as hell wouldn't stay beta for long if things continued the way they were now.

Which all spelled disaster of epic proportions for her. She wasn't Maxima, and she was failing as beta. So who the hell was she? This needy woman who spread her legs at the first hot man who beckoned? Absolutely not! And yet her current situation suggested otherwise.

What the hell was going on?

Possessed. Mate.

Absolutely not. Her grizzly was still purring, the happiness at finally finding her mate pulsing in a low beat inside her. Her thoughts drowned it out, which is why she kept thinking. But in the pause between question and answer, the whisper sounded.

Possessed. Mate.

Of all the times, of all the people, why had her grizzly chosen Alan? If the creature had spoken up at any point in the last years, Tonya would have listened. She would have balanced the biological needs with her Maxima ambition and made a reasoned, intelligent choice.

But no, it had been silent. For years she'd waited for a sign, some biological imperative that pointed a big red arrow at a man and said, *This is the one.* But there hadn't been anything, so she'd given up. She'd focused on Carl and becoming Maxima.

But now she'd heard the voice, now her grizzly purred for a man who was angry and sick. Maybe she could work around that, but Alan also hated her. He despised her for toying with him as a teen, for rejecting him as an adult, and forgetting about him in the midst of other crises. She couldn't blame him, and normally she would choose to let him be. He needed to cool off. He needed to sort himself out. And she needed to be patient until he was in a place where she could reason with him.

She sank deeper into the hot water and did her best to think her way to an answer. As usual, she got nothing. Alan was the logical thinker. She was the gut-instinct reactor. But she wasn't just instinct, right? She was a deputy in the sheriff's department. Her brain could sort through clues and solve crimes. She'd just have to look at the situation from that perspective.

A crime involved a perpetrator. In this case, Alan's monster was the problem. Ergo, she had to eliminate that. Once Alan reverted back to his logical, approachable self, then everything could go back to normal. She could talk to him, she could seduce him, she could live happily ever after with him. But only if the monster was gone.

Good thing she'd gotten the key to his room from the hotel manager. It was time to take down a monster.

Chapter Seven

Alan stumbled into the lounge area of his presidential suite. The place was huge and tastefully decorated, everything made out of designer glass: coffee table, decorative vase, even the entertainment system was expensive glass. He'd flipped on the overhead light when he'd shoved open the door, but now the crystal beads beneath the fresh flowers cut into his retinas, and he slammed the light back off.

Why did women only go for assholes?

He headed for his computer, needing a way to focus his thoughts. But on the way, his knees gave out, and he tumbled sideways onto the huge couch. The fabric was lush beneath his fingers, and the overstuffed cushions supported his fall. Beneath his skin, his bones stretched, and his joints crackled. His fever had built to an unhealthy degree, he realized. Every inch of his body seemed to steam, but his thoughts were never more lucid.

Odd how the hotter his temperature ran, the clearer his thoughts became. Or one thought: *Tonya gets off on monsters.*

If only he'd known as a teen, he would have happily treated her like dirt. Except before his change, he'd have lost that fight in a heartbeat. Even now he wasn't sure who would win between them. Monster or she-grizzly. It didn't matter. He wasn't going to live long enough to find out. If the stress of his altered DNA didn't get him, he would likely die at the hands of the bitch who'd done this to him, though he planned to take her out at the same time.

He rolled over on the couch, feeling the brush of silky soft fabric against his skin. He could appreciate the texture as never before, but it didn't come close to the sweetness of Tonya's skin. God, just remembering the sweet slide of his dick across her honey made him rock hard again. And his all-too-lucid brain replayed the way she'd arched beneath his touch. Her skin had flushed rosy, and her lips had gone dark red. Such glorious breasts with dark nipples. Hard, tight berries that he'd pinched. And when he'd twisted them, she'd whimpered sweet, hungry sounds.

A shudder racked his frame, and he knew he was running out of time. At the hospital, they'd given him something to control the fever, but he'd been out of there for a week now. Ibuprofen didn't make a dent. And he'd known the hot tub and the booze were a bad choice from the beginning.

Why couldn't he just die already?

Not before she pays.

It took a moment for him to realize which "she" he was think-ing of. For a moment, it was all shes. Every single woman on the planet. The ones who loved monsters and the ones who were monsters. But in time, his thoughts crystallized. His goal was Elisabeth. He had to kill her before he died. He had to destroy her before she did this to someone else.

So he rolled to his side and stared at his laptop. Maybe Johnny had news for him. Maybe one of the other cougar-shifters had emailed. Maybe waiting in his inbox right now was the bitch's location. But when he extended his hand toward his laptop, another shudder wracked his body.

Oh, hell.

He hated this part. It was the time when his mind slipped away from a body gone insane. As his temperature climbed, his brain stepped away. He thought about life. He sorted through his options. He even wandered through memory. And all the while, his body seized and released. Seized and released.

The first few times, he'd fought with all his will to control himself. To make his limbs obey by sheer mental command. It never worked. So now he settled for option two. He let himself pretend he was a powerful shifter bastard who got back at everyone who'd ever slighted him.

He thought of his uncle who'd tormented him and killed his mother. Alan ripped him apart inch by inch.

He brought up Carl who loved him, but casually disregarded how difficult it was to live as a normal in a shifter community. Alan beat him until the idiot remembered to pay fucking attention when someone went missing for a week.

And the she-bitch who'd done this to him? Well, his imagination knew no bounds for how he'd hurt her.

Eventually, his dark thoughts frightened even him. The blood-lust sickened what remained of his humanity.

That's when he thought of Tonya. Of how her hair turned golden in the sunlight and how her lips went cherry red. Of her taste when they'd kissed on his birthday. And of every damned moment they'd ever been together. That's when he really let go and let his body do whatever it wanted to. Seize up. Stop breathing. Bite off his own tongue. Whatever. He would find out what had happened when it was over. Even if it meant that he died during it.

That was his plan.

He was just accepting the inevitability of it all when his door burst open. He jerked, the motion setting his vision to bouncing. Tonya stood there with a Taser in her hand. She'd dressed in her rumpled uniform, and her wet hair was slicked back so that it formed a dark skullcap. She looked badass in the best possible way, and his mouth pulled into grin. What a woman! Bikini clad one second as she came all over his hand. Then angry cop chick the next. Except as usual, her timing sucked.

"Get out!" he rasped. He still had some pride. The last thing he wanted was for her to witness what was about to happen.

"Fuck that, Alan. You're coming home with me."

"No." That's all he managed to say. A clear, loud denial of everything she wanted. He wasn't going home. He wasn't ever going to be that good guy sap again. And he sure as hell wasn't going to curl up and let her take him like he was a sack of potatoes, either.

He watched her eyes narrow, and then he saw her step hitch as she took in the way he was sprawled on the couch. He tried to sit up, but the tingling had started. Itching first, then tingling, then full-out seizure.

Hell. Only one way to stop a seizure, and even that wasn't hundred percent. One horrible thing he'd allowed only once. He had to go full monster. It was that or let Tonya cart him away into another damned cage.

He never even made the decision consciously. It just happened between one tingling breath and the next. The man on the couch became the monster. His bones lengthened, his muscles thickened. And that mouth that had been so struggling with words? It twisted open to accommodate sharp teeth and a long tongue. Fur erupted in sparks of pain, and he roared as it jerked him and he tumbled off the couch.

He landed easily onto all fours. His nose twitched with the stench, but his claws found purchase in the thick rug.

"Don't make me shoot you, Alan!" Tonya bellowed. Part of him admired her stance. She'd gone pale when she'd first seen him, but now she braced herself. The Taser was up and aimed steadily at his chest. Even if her eyes were pulled wide and sweat beaded on her brow, her gun hand was rock solid.

But she didn't pull the trigger.

Her mistake because as awkward and ugly as his body was, the monster was still damned fast.

He leapt upward, claws extended for her face. Mentally, he tried to pull back. He did not want to rip her apart, but his mind had no control. The man watched from a distance, furious, appalled, and completely impotent.

Tonya ducked, sidestepping his attack. Thank God for her

shifter reflexes or he might have ripped open her throat. He landed in a crouch, his toes gripping the carpet. No claws there. He still had human feet, more or less. Except his right leg wasn't prepared for the weight of his body. Nothing was balanced in this form, nothing worked smoothly or easily.

He stumbled, banging his shoulder painfully into the door. She hadn't closed it, and his weight had slammed it fully open.

Run! Escape!

He willed himself to leave and was pleased when the monster turned toward the open hallway. He had no idea if it could navigate the stairs. An elevator was out of the question.

"Don't do it, Alan." Her voice was hard, but the tone was compelling. Frightened and pissed off. The latter was of no import, but the first caught his monster's attention. Females should not be fearful, and most especially not this female.

The monster turned back to her.

No!

He stalked forward. His knee had stabilized and the tingling had stopped. No seizure. He wasn't sure whether to be pleased or terrified by that. Especially since he could feel the monster's clear intention. It smelled female and the hot cinnamon spice that was Tonya. She'd called him back, and therefore, he would take her. Sexual possession. No matter how much the man screamed to run, the animal side wanted to make more baby monsters.

"Stay back," Tonya said, her voice deeper and more authoritative.

Not going to happen. Even disconnected as he was from any control of his body, Alan could feel the monster's heavy erection.

His nostrils flared, sucking in the hot spice of her. And his lips pulled back into a grin while his muscles coiled to strike.

"Last chance," she warned.

Run away! Alan screamed.

The monster pounced.

Tonya reacted midleap. She pulled the trigger.

Fifty thousand volts slammed through his body.

Pain whitewashed his consciousness. Every muscle seized tight. He couldn't even draw breath to scream. Worse, after the first lightning bolt of electricity, his mind slammed white hot into his form. Instead of watching from a distance, suddenly he centered fully and absolutely in a body still writhing on the remains of the glass coffee table. He felt every sharp stab of the glass pieces. And he knew fury as never before.

"God, Alan," he heard her say. "I'm sorry. I'm sorry, but you have to—"

He rolled to all fours in a jerk of defiance. No thoughts now. Just anger, dark and deadly. Pain burned through his cells and with it came ugly memories.

"Run, Tonya."

His words came out low. More of a growl but he saw her react. She straightened away from him and her gaze shot to the door. He was between her and it. She'd never make it if she bolted.

His muscles had stopped twitching, but they weren't normal yet. Weak and unstable. He still managed to push himself upright. He was hunched, his breath unsteady, but words kept coming from his lips. A reflection of the memories twisting through his brain.

He had no control of himself and no mental distance. It was all him. And he was completely feral.

"No cage," he growled.

She swallowed, the movement drawing his gaze to her vulnerable throat. "You need a doctor, Alan."

Metal bars. Needle stabs. Fever and pain. Memories swamped him.

"No cage!" His words came out loud. The roar of it burned in his lungs, and he lunged forward.

She leapt back and resolve tightened her jaw as she fumbled at her pants. He heard the pop of a button and the grate of a zipper. She was undressing to go grizzly.

He wasn't going to give her the chance.

He rushed forward. There still wasn't enough power in his muscles to make him fast. His motions were as much falling at her as it was an attack. But even so, he made it count. He gripped her arm and slammed her sideways. If she'd been human when she impacted the wall, then he might have killed her. But she'd already shifted even though she still wore her uniform.

Her shoulders were abruptly twice as large. Her head surged forward as the grizzly hump shoved her arms wide and thick fur cushioned her impact. He heard her groan, though. Maybe from landing hard on the wall, maybe from going grizzly while still in clothes. Either way, the moan turned into a snarl. She came off the wall in full bear and he rose to meet her.

She swiped at him, her claws lethally sharp. He was smaller than her now. If she contacted, he would be thrown aside. But every second that passed fed more power to his body. His legs obeyed his commands now, bracing him where he stood and preparing for a leap onto her back.

He could take her down from behind. Then he would mount her.

Feral and still horny. He would laugh if his every resource wasn't aimed at gaining mental control. He had to stop, but it was like trying to halt a careening freight train.

She didn't attack. Her swipe had been to hold him off so she could tear at her clothes. The shirt disintegrated easily, but those pants would take her longer. He had to strike now while she was still easy prey.

He feinted left, then dove right. He scrambled across the sharp remains of the table, then launched himself from the couch. If the thing had been stable, he would have barreled straight into her chest. But the cushions gave way and the furniture slid on the carpet. He caught her, but not with the power he intended.

She grabbed him as they slammed together into the television. The sharp bite as it broke had them both bellowing, but she took the worst of it. He shifted his weight, bringing her around and down. A learned moved he'd practiced a thousand times as a kid, executed flawlessly now.

She hit the ground, and he had her on the floor. But she was larger than him and they were face-to-face. He watched her mouth widen as she prepared to bite him. He slammed her head back with his elbow while scrambling away, regretting the pain he'd given her even as he fought for dominance.

Pain bit into his feet as he stepped on glass, but he hardly cared. She was his target, so he pivoted and leapt again. She caught him easily, her larger size allowing her to grab him and roll with his movements. Back into the television, this time hitting the thing's base. It cut painfully into his shoulder, and his head rang from where she slammed it against the wall.

And then it was full survival. No thought, no planning. Just instinct as he tried over and over to mount her. And she just as determined to fight him off.

Unwilling.

The word echoed in his mind, taking a long time to settle into meaning. His thinking mind latched on to it, but his body wouldn't stop. Dominance was primal. Consideration was not. And while he struggled with the sexual imperative, his arm went numb and one of his legs started bleeding. She was hurt, too, and he could smell the coppery scent of their blood mingling in the air.

It was in a pause to regroup when the word finally coalesced into understanding. *Unwilling.* She was an unwilling female and he was in too much pain. He couldn't best her now.

He should leave.

He gathered himself for a leap. He saw her tense, knew that she was preparing to impale him on her claws. So he jumped. But not where she expected. And certainly not in the path of her paws.

He sprang sideways and then ran around her out the door. There were people pouring into the hallway, probably because of the noise. He swerved around them as they cried out in surprise.

A door was slipping closed, but he made it there first. He slammed it open with his shoulder then scrambled down concrete steps. A huge twisting landscape of concrete, but he jumped and slid his way down. Gunshots reverberated in the narrow space. He heard pings around him and he roared at a hot burn across his shoulder. But then he was down. Dash through the door. Outside.

He smelled the air and knew the sudden openness of outdoors. *Free.*

He still ran. As fast and as far as he could go.

Free.

Chapter Eight

Tonya knew she was in trouble. It wasn't just that she felt beaten to hell and back. She did, but in terms of grizzly fights, this one had been relatively average in terms of physical damage. Scrapes and bruises galore, but nothing life threatening. The presidential suite was trashed, but that's what happened when bears fought indoors.

No, her problem was mental, and it left her so shaken she had to call in reinforcements. Not Carl because she didn't want her alpha anywhere near his brother until she could get Alan in a better mental place. That left Mark, who was a newly bonded feral and a computer genius. She needed to talk to him about both of these things, so as soon as the local cops let her grab her phone, she'd begged Mark to come to her aid.

He'd arrived fifteen minutes ago, but they had yet to be alone so they could talk. The local PD was too interested in grilling her about events. And she'd gotten really tired of repeating the same story.

She and her boyfriend had a fight. She'd pay for the damage to the room. No, she wasn't attacked by a monster. Had the security guard been drinking to suggest that? No, she didn't want to press charges even though her clothes were shredded and there was thousands of dollars' worth of damage to the suite. And *No, no, no!* to the idea that she needed battered woman's counseling, though part of her wondered if talking to a shrink might not be a bad idea. But it would have to be a shifter psychologist, and those were in short supply. Best she just bide her time until she could confide in Mark.

She got the opportunity twenty minutes later when the cops finally allowed her to rest in a separate hotel room. They were still processing the crime scene for clues. Apparently there was a lot of unusual fur to collect. Meanwhile, she could expect them to follow up with her boss. 'Cause she really wanted this disaster all over her sheriff's department—not.

"So that's a new look for you," Mark said by way of greeting.

She was wearing whatever fit from the gift shop since her uniform was shredded. That meant she now sported a parrot tee and ass-hugging yoga pants. At least the spandex wouldn't hurt as much if she shifted, not that she could do that again for another day.

"You look like shit," Mark added.

"And you look like…" Her voice trailed away as she studied him. He'd lost the pinched look between his eyes and the animalistic way he moved. He was still a big guy, but there was something decidedly less bear about him.

"Handsome? Virile? A god among men?"

"Happy," she finally said. "The bond with Julie is holding?"

He grinned. "Stronger by the second."

Which meant he was no longer in danger of going full grizzly full time. For a man who'd been 90 percent feral a couple of weeks ago, that was a miracle of epic proportions. And maybe it was just the answer she needed.

"Great," she said. "So tell me how it happened. Exactly."

He tilted his head, studying her in a very bearlike fashion. His nostrils flared, his shoulders hunched, and his ears seemed to curl toward her, even though he looked fully human. But his gaze—always the most human thing about him—seemed to study her face in minute detail.

"You know this story," he said slowly. "Julie sort of shifted and we locked in on each other. Then…" He gestured vaguely to the bed. "Grizzly tumbling around and done."

"But Julie's not a shifter. She was made into one by that serum. Like Alan."

"Yes." He dropped down onto the bed, making the mattress sag alarmingly. "So what happened?"

Too exhausting to explain in detail, so she gestured to Alan's laptop. She'd managed to keep it hidden from the cops beneath the pile of her shredded clothes. Then she'd secreted it in here. So she pointed at it now and said the only thing she could. "That's Alan's laptop. I need you to figure out what he's doing. I'm going to take a shower." She had to get the blood off. Shifter healing had already closed her wounds, but the smears remained.

"No," Mark said as he grabbed her wrist. "You're going to explain what's going on."

Fine. It's why she'd called him, right? "Alan's crazy, and I bonded with him." Short and sweet. And terrifying.

"Um, no you didn't. No offense, Tonya, but you don't look like a bonded woman."

She snorted. "And what does a bonded woman look like?"

"Happy. Connected. You know, that weird glow women get."

"I think you're talking about pregnancy." She'd meant her words to be sarcastic banter, but an ache accompanied her words. Normally, she could ignore it, but damn it, she was feeling especially vulnerable right then, and she wasn't in a mental place to easily suppress her secret compulsion to become a mom.

"That, too." His expression remained steady. Trust Mark to completely ignore the niceties of social interaction. Sarcastic banter that said loudly, *Don't go there,* flew right by him. "Tonya, why do you think you've bonded with Alan?"

She paced to the window to stare outside. Alan was out there somewhere. She ought to be looking for him. But she hadn't a clue where he was, and, frankly, she hadn't the strength right then for another battle.

"Tonya?"

"We were in the hot tub. Upstairs."

She could see his raised eyebrows in his reflection on the window. But, thankfully, he didn't ask questions.

"We were…um…"

"Playing hide the water dragon? A little Marco poke me?"

She shot him a glare that he completely ignored. Good thing because honestly, his irreverent tone was helping. "Sort of. I said no, but my grizzly…" Her face heated at the memory. So did other parts of her, which was so not appropriate at the moment.

"Your bear went belly up, huh? Begged him to rub your tummy?"

"God, Mark, you do know I carry a gun."

"That's not bonding, Tonya. That's horny."

She shook her head. "It was more than that. She's locked in on him. As a mate."

He studied her again. Nostrils, shoulders, ears. But in the end, he sighed. "She's locked in," he said softly. "He's not."

Tonya turned. "What?"

"I did the same thing with Julie. I picked her long before she returned the favor. And it's not bonding—not like you think—until both sides say yes."

Shit. "He's not saying yes, Mark. More like, 'Fuck you. Get the hell out of my life.'"

"Then you haven't bonded with him."

She leaned against the window, feeling the cold seep into her overheated skin. She didn't know whether to be pleased or upset. "He's important to me," she stressed. "Way more than before. Like…"

"Like a mate. I know. But it's still one-sided." He leaned forward onto his knees. "Just how far gone is Alan?"

She didn't want to go back there. She didn't want to relive the violent encounter with the man her grizzly had picked as a mate. But then Mark touched her arm. A slight brush that had her jolting painfully out of her memories.

"How bad, Tonya?"

"He tried to kill me. He was fully shifted into…" She swallowed. "That *wrong*-smelling thing. And he…" Her gaze went back out the window. "It tried to kill me."

"Kill you? Or mount you? Trust me, there's a very fine line. If he's out of control—"

"Definitely."

"Then maybe it was lust."

It hadn't felt like lust, but then she hadn't exactly gone in with that mind-set. She knew firsthand from her adolescence that shifted sex could be violent. She and her boyfriend had gone at it as grizzlies once and had completely trashed her bedroom. "He's different, Mark." She didn't want to say it out loud, but the word reverberated in her body. *Monster.*

She heard Mark swallow. He knew what she was saying. He'd fought those *wrong* things himself. "Carl said he was getting better. In the hospital, he was better."

"He was stable. And then he left."

"And now he's unstable?"

"I don't know." It was a lie. She very much feared she did know and that there was no hope left for the Alan she remembered. "We have to find him."

"Carl and I have to find him. You're in no shape to do anything right now."

"It has to be me," she said. Her voice was firm, but inside she wavered. He'd frightened her tonight. She was the biggest, baddest shifter cop she knew. Capable of taking down anything. Except tonight, she'd crumpled in every way possible. She'd allowed Alan to seduce her in the hot tub. She'd fought his monster in the suite and lost. What if no one could take him down? What if there was no saving her mate?

Fear cut at her until her knees went weak. She half stumbled, half fell into the desk chair. And all the while, Mark just watched her, his expression steady and sad. So infinitely sad, probably because he'd found his happiness while hers was doomed.

Eventually he spoke, helping her to focus on the practicalities. "Do you know where he ran to?"

She shook her head. "Out. Away. Security guard was shooting at him."

"So he's feral, wounded, and on the run. Not good."

"He's not feral," she corrected. No, he was infinitely worse than feral.

He grimaced. "We have to bring Carl in on this."

"No." This time her voice and her insides were fully in accord. "Alan's his brother. He can't think clearly about this."

"And you can? Your grizzly picked him as your mate."

"I know! But I'm better at, you know, separating my emotions from the situation." That was something she and Mark had in common. They faced facts, no matter how grim. No matter how much they were dying inside.

Mark studied her face again, his gaze seeming to trace every part of her expression. "You really think Alan is that far gone?"

She didn't answer. She didn't want to believe that there was no man left beneath the monster. "Wasn't there a serum or something? To suppress the monster?"

He nodded. "I brought a dose with me."

Her head snapped up. "What?"

"We're making it as fast as we can, but there are no guarantees. And we've never tried it on someone like Alan."

"But Julie's stable. She's like him."

She could feel Mark bristle at the suggestion. It was a measure of how much better he was that he kept his reaction under control. "She only got two shots of whatever that shit was that changed them. We studied the charts. Alan got more than a dozen."

She flinched. She'd guessed as much, but to hear it spoken aloud as fact hurt. "They're working on a cure. They just haven't had enough time. If we can catch him and contain him—"

"Then we can help him." Mark turned his attention to the laptop. "What's he trying to do?"

"You tell me. You're the computer genius."

He nodded and popped open the lid. "Go take your shower. I should have an answer by the time you're done."

She nodded and headed for the bathroom. She trusted Mark to find whatever secrets Alan was keeping in his computer. But even if he managed to ferret out every single digital imprint the man had ever left, it wasn't going solve the basic problem. Mark would figure out what Alan's plans were. Tonya had to figure out how she was going to kill the monster and leave the man.

Chapter Nine

Alan came awake slowly. The aches hit him first. Head throbbing. Kink in his back. And his left arm was numb because he was lying on it. Those filtered in along with derisive laughter from somewhere. Young men being cruel, and the noise didn't fit with the feel of grass on his face and the scent of rich dirt.

Pain flashed bright on his temple, and he recoiled. Something had hit him with a metallic clang, and he came up with a snarl. An empty beer can rolled away from him. His eyes focused with animal intent on two teen boys, not even old enough to shave. But they'd found beer somewhere, and it had brought out their cruel side.

Another can hurtled toward him, and he slammed it aside with preternatural speed. *Oh, shit. Monster in charge.* The air turned foul with his scent, and fur sprouted across his arms and legs. He dug his toes into the dirt and sprang for his attackers. They were standing frozen, their mouths hanging open in shock.

Only one still had a beer can in his hand. Alan slapped that out of a meaty fist, then followed up with a blow to the idiot's torso. His attacker was solid enough to take the impact, but even so the teen lost his feet. His friend was just turning, fists at the ready, but Alan didn't give him the chance. He grabbed the second one by the shoulders and threw him on top of his friend. The two assholes cried out in a terrified tangle of arms and legs.

Alan advanced, watching carefully as he tallied weaknesses. A dozen different way to kill his tormentors. Except his brain was finally coming online, and it was screaming that they were children. Cruel teens who deserved a good spanking, but not death.

Frighten them! Don't kill them!

He slowed his steps, his breath heaving as he fought the adrenaline. That gave the boys time to get to their feet. One took off, his speed good enough for any track team. The other clenched his fists for a fight. Alan let loose a snarl that had the boy paling. He pivoted and sprinted after his friend.

Gone.

The word echoed in his brain, keeping him from pursuing his attackers like prey. It fought with all the other instincts that said: *Kill. Eat.*

He locked his muscles and grabbed the nearest tree trunk to steady himself. As he watched, his claws shifted solidly back into a hand.

The monster receded. Not gone. More like an armed détente. But for the moment, he'd take it.

Alan looked around, his sluggish brain trying to orient itself. He was in the woods near a lake, his feet burned like fire, and he stank. Not just his monster BO, but sweat and tree resin and God only knew what else. And he was *hungry*.

That last information came in the form of a stomach cramp that nearly brought him to his knees. His belly was empty and had been since...

Tonya.

Oh, shit. Memories came flooding back too fast for him to process. He'd attacked her. *Oh, hell.* He'd attacked her as a monster and tried to mount her in any of a billion different ways. He remembered throwing her against a wall and then trying to pin her. She'd been a grizzly, thank God, so he hadn't killed her. But shit, shit, shit what had he done?

He had to call her. He reached for his cell phone only to realize he was just wearing shorts. Nothing else. That was all he'd had on when she'd burst into his hotel room and...

Holy God, she'd Tasered him! He remembered on a visceral level the voltage bursting through his consciousness. The man in him had been struggling to control the monster, but at that lightning bolt, his body and mind had gone white hot. The two of them had fused into one. Then man and monster had gone after the woman, and now he had no excuse. He couldn't just say, "The monster did it." He'd been one person, one consciousness, and all of him had intended to subdue her in the most primal way.

He had to find her. He had to know if she was okay. But he couldn't talk to anyone like this. He headed toward the lake.

He could swim the worst of the stink off and—if he was lucky—catch a fish or something. He was a monster, after all. He might be good at that.

He wasn't. But he was a good swimmer. So he decided to swim the lake looking for help. He also hoped that the exercise would burn off his emotions like they had in high school. No luck there. Every stroke, every kick, echoed with worry for Tonya. Fortunately, he found another swimmer before his head exploded from his fears.

A little girl in pigtails and a one-piece swimsuit covered in ruffles. She looked about eight years old and her mother was calling her in from the water. She was hiding in the reeds, giggling to herself as Mom got increasingly frantic.

Kids could be such jerks. He stroked closer, making sure to splash the child. She squeaked in alarm and that was enough for her mother to zero in on the sound.

"Megan Michele, you get over here this instant!"

Little MM shot him an angry glare, but she obeyed her mother, climbing out of the reeds and skipping over as if she hadn't just panicked the woman who loved her the most. Meanwhile, Alan climbed out as well. He didn't have a towel or anything that could make him look less terrifying, so he simply smoothed the hair back from his dripping face and stood a careful distance away.

"Oh!" the woman gasped. "I didn't see you there."

"I just swam over," he said using his most civilized, lawyer voice. "I'm sorry if I startled you. I'm afraid I'm in a bit of a bind."

The woman frowned, her freckles endearing on her thin, oval face. She was tall and thin, her cutoffs looked ragged but the light tank top appeared new. And she tucked the child close behind her in an obvious show of protectiveness.

"I don't mean you any harm," he said. Then he scratched at his beard in self-conscious awkwardness. "I was…mugged," he finally said, deciding that was as close to true as anything else. "I just want a phone so I can call my friend. I'm not sure if she…" He stopped, unable to speak. God, what if he'd killed Tonya?

The woman's mouth dropped open in shock and suddenly her expression turned into fierce motherly concern. "Oh my God, your feet!" she cried as she took in the raw mess. "Here, take this." She held out a pink towel obviously meant for the girl. "They just left you out here for dead?"

"That's my towel!" little MM cried, but her mother pushed her back up a dirt path.

"Go get another one. And tell Hank—" A fierce wail cut through the air, this one a little boy's. The woman winced as she turned a worried look over her shoulder. "Oh hell."

"It's okay," Alan said. "I don't need—"

"Of course you do," she said as she stomped down toward him and shoved the towel in his hands. "Now come with me and don't argue. I get plenty of that from my kids." She rolled her eyes as the wailing continued. "I'm Gretchen, by the way."

Alan knew next to nothing about little kids, but even he could tell that the boy's scream wasn't a pain scream. This was toddler in full meltdown and he really didn't want to brave that. But Gretchen was in mother-bear mode, so he trudged along beside a sulking Megan Michele wondering if it would be better for him to leave them all alone. Gretchen obviously had enough troubles without him along.

But he didn't. Something in him warmed to any woman in

mother mode. Perhaps it was because he'd lost his own so young, but he found himself reluctant to disobey Gretchen. And so he followed her up a muddy path to where a toddler was red-faced with fury in front of a big guy.

A really, really big guy. Like shifter big. He was fully human at the moment, complete with military tats and close-cropped hair, and he squatted in front of the boy with animal stillness. Then his nose twitched as Alan stepped into the campsite.

Alan froze, knowing better than to startle a shifter. His own nose twitched, but he wasn't refined enough with smells to pick out anything beyond coffee and fried fish. His stomach growled, and he stifled a curse when the woman shot him a pitying look.

"Oh, you poor thing," she said. Jesus, he was a grown-assed man and she was looking at him like he was a lost eight-year-old.

"I just need to borrow a phone. Please." It might have worked if the toddler hadn't started wailing again, throwing himself on the ground as he rolled in the dirt. Nothing could be heard over that, and Gretchen huffed out a breath before heading toward the toddler. She only got a step closer when the crouched man—probably named Hank—held up his hand.

"Let him express himself," he said. His voice was deep and steady. Alan had no idea how anyone could hear the words over the kid's racket, but the message was clear enough. Mom wasn't to interfere while everyone waited on the boy.

Well, everyone but little MM. She rolled her eyes in the most dramatic way possible before stomping over to grab another towel. Mom shrugged and grabbed a thermos that she pushed into his hand.

"Coffee," she said in a pause between wails and she gestured for him to drink it.

Alan did with gratitude, the lukewarm brew going a long way to steadying his thoughts. And while he swallowed, he heard Hank again, his voice steady and low, despite the continued wailing.

"I hear you, little man. You're angry, right? I hear you. I'd be angry too." He kept repeating some version of hearing the boy's anger for another minute. Long enough for Alan to finish the coffee and look longingly around for any remains of the fish. A moment later, he was rewarded with a bagel slathered in cream cheese.

"It's all we got left," Gretchen said.

"It's your food—"

"Eat it. Please. I filled up on the fish and Megan will only eat peanut butter and jelly." Then she glanced over at the man. "Hank's got the only phone that gets reception out here, but we'll have to wait until he's done."

Alan wondered how long that might be, but couldn't frame any question around a mouthful of whole wheat bagel.

Food. Yes. That was the extent of his verbal ability, so he settled on nodding his thanks.

And then, finally, the boy went silent. Everyone breathed a sigh of relief. Everyone, apparently, but the man who continued to squat calmly in front of the boy, still murmuring his same words. And then he held open his arms. Nothing more than that while the child took a gasping breath. Alan watched Gretchen tense and he was right there with her, absorbed in the drama. Would the child start screaming again? Or was it finally over?

A moment later, the child crawled toward Hank, who leaned down, scooped him up, and held him. Just held him, still murmuring that he understood the boy's anger. And then he said quite gently, "I love you, little man. We all love you."

The boy burrowed into Hank's neck, smearing tears and whatnot into the loose tee. Then Gretchen stepped close and the man reached out an arm and snagged her, too, drawing her in close. She wrapped herself around him and the boy while Alan and Megan looked on. Megan had draped herself in a large blue towel and stood pouting as she stared at the group. Hank noticed her, though, and he winked.

"There's room on my other side. You're part of us, too, you know."

And just like that, the towel was dropped and she dashed straight to his open side. Then there was all four of them in a group hug that teetered in fun. Chuckles began soon after that, then giggles and outright laughs. Soon the boy was squirming to get down and the whole clutch fell apart while Alan watched in a choking envy. The love that suffused those four made him ache with a want so tight that he couldn't breathe.

Meanwhile, the boy found a toy truck near Hank's feet and began to play. Gretchen shooed Megan off to get dressed, and life resumed in its usual pace. Amazing. And Alan wasn't the only one who thought so. Gretchen squeezed Hank's arm while she smiled at the boy.

"I don't know how you do that," she said.

"He just wants to be heard," Hank said. "That's all any of us want. To know that someone hears our pain." And with that, his gaze landed on Alan. There wasn't any other message in those words. The man was just looking over in wary curiosity at the stranger, but Alan felt the message all the way down to his core. Was that really what everyone wanted? Half of him agreed, the other half rebelled in angry tantrum. And all of him just sat in confusion as emotions collided inside him. Envy, fury, loneliness, and pain were just a few that banged through his consciousness. There was also hope and quiet, too. And he couldn't process anything except for one thing.

"Can I borrow your phone?" he rasped. He had to call Tonya.

Gretchen nodded and turned to Hank. "He was mugged and just left to die in the woods. We need to call the cops—"

"Tonya is a cop," Alan said.

Hank nodded and pulled out his cell phone, thumbing it on as he went. But as he crossed closer to Alan, his nostrils flared and his brows lowered. Shifter senses. Had to be. And Alan did everything he could to tamp down his *wrongness*. And when Hank slowed his approach, Alan raised his hands in an open gesture.

"I don't want to hurt anyone."

Hank nodded, his gaze taking in every inch of him. "Your feet are pretty cut up. Do they hurt?"

Alan shrugged. "Everything hurts," he said. Then he straightened enough to take the phone, though he kept his motions slow and careful. No sense spooking the huge shifter. He wished his senses were refined enough to know what species the guy was, but though Alan had increased sensitivity, he had no experience with this man's scent. And then, finally, he had a cell phone.

Two seconds later, he was listening to it ring.

"Kappes."

Every part of him sagged in relief. She was alive. She sounded strong and alert.

"Tonya. It's me." He swallowed, stunned at how winded he felt just from hearing her voice. "Are you okay?"

"Alan!" She sounded as relieved as he felt. "Where are you?"

He shook his head and looked around. "I have no idea. Some lake. Are you all right?"

"I'm fine. Alan, find out where you are. We'll come get you."

He frowned as he looked around for a marker. Fortunately, Hank understood his question. "Rand Lake. West side." He rattled off more details of their exact location but Alan's attention had zeroed in on a single word: *we*. Tonya had said *We'll come get you*.

"Who are you with?" he asked.

"Mark. But it doesn't matter. Where are you? Are you feeling all right? Let us help you."

Alan closed his eyes, letting rage wash through him. Irrational feelings were becoming commonplace to him now. Rage that she would be with another man. He even knew that Mark had found someone else, and yet fury boiled through him.

"Why is he there?" he asked, struggling to keep his voice even. But even as the words left his mouth, he knew the answer. Mark was their tech expert and Alan had abandoned his laptop at the hotel. "You've hacked my computer. Tonya, I'm not the bad guy."

"Of course you're not!" she said, her words rushed. "But, Alan, it's not your job to track Elisabeth. Leave that to the police."

She said more, but he didn't hear it over the roar in his blood.

She'd hacked his computer and seen his emails. What he was doing wasn't a secret, but the violation of his privacy was like kicking him in seeping wounds. Elisabeth had already assaulted him in so many ways. To feel this from Tonya and Mark was like getting thrust back into that cage. Every part of him had been stripped away then. And he still had no rights now. Not even from those who pretended to care the most for him.

He didn't speak again. He just thumbed off the phone, then rapidly opened a browser. He had to get to his emails. He had to know what they knew.

He saw it immediately. A single short email from Johnny. It was an address in Pinckney, Michigan, and the words, *There are kids there.*

His jaw clenched, and he felt his arms prickle as fur began to sprout. To the side, Hank jolted. Alan barely noticed.

Kids. Elisabeth had kids with her.

Bad enough what she'd done to him, but now she had kids to work on. Children to twist or destroy according to her whim.

He wasn't going to let that happen. Not while there was breath in his body. And at this point, he didn't care who he destroyed along the way, so long as at the end, the bitch was dead.

Chapter Ten

Tonya slumped in her car, consciously tightening her muscles one at a time as she tried to stay awake. She thought massive guilt for what she was about to do would keep her wide eyed, but apparently not. It had just been too long since she slept, though fear made sure even her quiet times were filled with angst.

It was dusk as Tonya waited at the address asshole Johnny had given Alan. The place where Elisabeth was supposedly hiding out with children. *Jesus. Kids.* The idea that the bitch was experimenting on more children made Tonya's gut tighten with horror. But it was a familiar feeling, one she experienced often in her police career, and so she pushed it aside with her usual practicality. Not so the second-guessing about her decision. They were about to capture Alan, and she hated that with every fiber of her being. But she didn't see any alternatives.

She scanned the area again, searching for either of her quarries: Elisabeth or Alan. Neither was anywhere to be seen. She and

Mark had already cased the crappy cabin and found it empty. Local PD had been alerted to the bitch's location and crimes, which meant the cougar had probably skipped hours ago. Shifters tended to have a sixth sense when they were being hunted. It was the animal instinct side and it was especially strong in loner species like cougars.

That meant that Tonya was here waiting to grab Alan, and Mark hid out in the backyard, being less amenable to sitting in a car for hours on end. Except the whole thing made her stomach clench, and not from the battery-acid coffee she'd been drinking. Alan was the victim here, and she hated tracking him in the same way she'd hunt down a criminal. But he was a danger to himself and others, and she couldn't let that go. She cared too much about him for that.

And still his words echoed in her thoughts. *I'm not the bad guy.*

Didn't he understand? She wasn't tracking him to hurt him. She was on his side, but he was out of control. And when a bear-shifter went off the rails, it was her job as a cop and as the Gladwin Beta to hunt him down.

I'm not the bad guy.

Then stop acting like one. Come home. Let me help you.

She slumped down farther, her gritty eyes drifting shut just for a moment. She'd already tried that tack with Alan to no avail. Which left her precious few options.

She forced her eyes back open before she succumbed to sleep. And in the dim light, she spoke into her mic as another way to keep herself awake.

"You still human, Mark?"

It was a joke…sort of. Barely more than a week ago, Tonya had been ready to put a bullet between his eyes. He'd turned feral and she'd been ready to kill him rather than let him hurt the one woman he treasured above all else. She'd held back—thank God—and Julie had performed a miracle beyond miracles. She'd tamed a feral shifter. Everyone proclaimed Mark cured. Everyone, that is, except anyone with a brain. Tonya didn't trust miracles, and so she kept a wary eye on her friend, who answered her question with an understanding she appreciated.

"Not a grizzly itch to be found," he grumbled. "But I'm thinking of changing that. If one more mosquito tries to suck on my all-too-pink skin, I'm going to go bear on the whole lot."

"Take a blowtorch to them instead. It's safer."

"Fresh out of propane torches. What about you? Any monsters around?"

"Just the Sandman," she confessed. Jesus, she was tired.

Then in the long silence, Mark finally asked the key question. "You rethinking the plan here?"

Yes. "No. Whatever it takes, we have to bring him in. He's sick, Mark."

"Can't cure him if he's dead."

"Last resort. You remember those other infected ones. They weren't sane."

Mark's silence cut her deeper than any words he might say. Neither of them wanted to hurt Alan, but they couldn't let him run amok. He'd attack some innocent and that was the last thing Alan would ever want.

Neither of them said anything more. They just sat in their own misery and waited. And then, she saw him. At first she'd thought her eyes were playing tricks on her. She saw a lanky guy in flip-flops, board shorts, and a blindingly bright tie-dyed shirt strolling down the road. He could have been any one of the summer vacationers enjoying the evening cool. She'd already counted more than a dozen bored teens, not to mention the adults walking dogs. It's what one did on vacation when the heat finally cooled off. She wouldn't have given this guy more than a second glance if he hadn't been walking in that slightly creepy way.

It was something all shifters did. No thumping of the feet, no awkward hitch to the step. The animal in them knew how to walk softly on the earth. And when that animal was on the hunt, he prowled even when he was pretending to casually stroll down the street.

She leaned forward, blinking her eyes as she tried to make out details. Was he hurt? Was he angry? Was that a cut on his arm or a trick of the light? She knew she should say something. Mark needed to know that Alan was here. But the words wouldn't come out her mouth. She was mesmerized by the man she'd known all her life.

She was accustomed to seeing a solidness in Alan when he moved. He'd been a swimmer in high school with the broad-shouldered build typical in such men. He seemed taller now, his bones longer and his joints thicker. But far from making him awkward, he moved with animal precision. There was a grace to him that was altogether new. It was the monster doing that, she knew, but she couldn't hate the beauty of it. He ought to be walking with a jerkiness. Visually, his parts did not completely fit together. But all was smooth hunting.

She swallowed, startled at the realization that she was aroused. Not just her bear, but her human side, too. How could she find the aberration that Alan had become so attractive? She ought to be mourning the man who was, but instead, she was admiring the thing he'd become. He was the monster now, and yet he seemed beautiful to her.

She climbed out of her car, walking swiftly to intercept him from behind. He noticed her immediately. His sense of smell likely picked her up the second she opened the car door.

"Stay away," he growled at her. The words were gravelly and full of threat, and she all but purred at the sound. It was powerful and masculine. She didn't want it to make her toes curl, but it did, and she damned herself for being so unprofessional.

"Elisabeth isn't here," she said. "Probably long gone."

His eyes narrowed. "How long?"

She shrugged. Her own nose said they'd missed the bitch by only a few hours. How refined were his senses? And how close would he let her get to him? She took a step nearer and he tensed, obviously ready to flee.

"Mark couldn't track her beyond the nearest gas station. They were driving."

His lips curled back into a snarl. "They." Not a question.

"Boy and a girl. That's all we know right now, but we're tracking them. We'll catch up soon."

"Email me when you do." His lips curled. "You know the address."

She ached to just touch him, but she didn't dare. "Don't run. Please, Alan, just talk to me a moment."

She knew his speed from the hotel. He could be long gone by now, but he lingered. She hoped it was because he wanted to be near her. Especially given the way he looked at her, his eyes dark and hungry as he scanned her from head to toe.

"I'm glad you're okay," he finally said. "I didn't want to hurt you." There was an odd note to his voice. Guilt and apology were obvious, but there was an underlying agony in his words. As if he hated everything about this as much as she did.

"I Tasered you first." She took another step closer as she noted his cut feet and the welt on his cheek. "How are you feeling?"

He shrugged. "The fevers better. In an odd way, I think the Taser helped. It jolted me more in line." Then he shook his head. "I know that doesn't make any sense."

She smiled, and her fingers twitched as she kept herself from touching him. "New treatment then."

He snorted. "Electroshock therapy has been around for a century. A favorite of doctors and torturers alike."

There was a light note to his words, a clear attempt at teasing. But there was an accusation in it as well, and one she richly deserved. "I'm sorry. I wasn't thinking straight."

"Yes, you were. You were trying to subdue the monster." He lifted his chin, an animal gesture of dominance. "It didn't work."

"No, it didn't," she said as her bear dropped her head and tilted it slightly sideways. Submission. Acknowledgment. "How'd you get here?"

He took a deep breath. "Held it together long enough to convince a very generous family to bring me." He glanced down at his clothes. "Even gave me a shirt and shoes."

She smiled, though the expression felt strained. "So you're Alan again, right?" She gestured to his clothing. "Laid-back surfer Alan—"

"No." He cut off her words with a slash of his hand.

"What?"

"No, I'm not going back with you. No, I'm not going to quit searching for Elisabeth. And definitely no Alan here. Surfer or not."

"Then why are you still talking to me?" She was close enough to kiss him now, and she bit her lips at the desire. Her nose picked up his scent, a cleaner smell than she remembered. Maybe because he wasn't frightened. Or maybe because he didn't care what happened to him. She'd known men who'd crossed into kamikaze mode. They'd already accepted death, so fear became a nonentity in their lives. But as she inhaled his scent, she noted the wrongness was gone. Or maybe she'd just gotten used to it. Either way, her bear clearly liked the scent and she leaned a little closer.

He reached up, his large and callused hand stroking her jaw. She fought the need to close her eyes and lean into his caress. Instead, she watched his eyes go soft and sad. "Why do women only want monsters?"

"You're not a monster." She spoke it firmly. He needed to know she believed that even when the label got tangled in her thoughts.

He stared at her and shook his head. "You think because I'm

not fur and claws right now that I'm tame? That I won't tear right through you if you try to Tase me again?"

She held up her bare hands, spread wide. "I don't want to hurt you. I want to talk to you. Come home with me. Please. There are...things we need to talk about." She'd almost said more. She'd nearly told him about how much her bear was right now pulsing with want. How his scent was oddly compelling even at its worst. About all the confusion that he created inside her. But she was on an open mic with Mark on the other end. She just couldn't force herself to be that vulnerable with another man listening in. So she swallowed the full sentence and settled for pleading.

He was still stroking her jaw, the caress of his thumb gentle and soothing. Hell she was so tired right now, a little tug from him and she'd melt into his arms. It didn't make sense. She was a rational woman, and Alan wasn't the easy man she remembered. He was volatile and dangerous. But apparently that made her grizzly wet and needy. Maybe she did have a thing for monsters.

"When was the last time you slept?" he asked.

She shook her head. "Not until you're safe."

He tugged her closer with just the edge of his nails. They weren't claws just then. There was no pinprick to his touch. Just the blunt edge of his fingers tugging her forward and she went willingly. "I'm not the one in danger," he murmured.

"Bullshit," she answered. But that was as far as she got before his mouth was on hers. Hot. Possessive. Desperate. It was like he was taking everything he could get before it all disappeared.

She met his tongue with her own, arching her neck and dueling with him. Her hands found his shoulders, and she gripped him, dragging him closer or holding on to him for support. She wasn't sure which. And while her heart exploded into a feverish beat, her mind ceased yammering. It had been full of words and strategies, ways that she could convince him to come back with her. But at the first press of his lips, they were silenced. This was what she wanted. This was what they both needed. So she kissed him back, and in the midst of his desperation, she tried to reassure him.

Yes, she said with teeth and tongue. *Yes, I want you, too.*

Then he was gone. He ripped himself from her grip and dashed away. She stumbled at his sudden absence. She gasped and pressed her fingers to her wet, swollen lips as she tried to focus. She saw his flip-flops discarded in the grass. Looked beyond to see him dash between cabins to the backyard. She didn't even have the presence of mind to call him. Just a trapped scream in her belly that she couldn't release.

She couldn't have had him right here again and lose him. She couldn't—

Pop!

She knew that sound. A tranquilizer gun. Mark had it, and Alan had run straight at him. She ran around the corner to see Mark stepping out from behind a tree. Alan was swearing and ripping the pink-tailed dart out of his shoulder.

"Alan, wait!" she pleaded, but it was too late.

She saw him shift, even faster than the last time. His hands became claws, his face twisted into a growl, and he barreled straight at Mark who stood like the Rock of Gibraltar.

"Don't make me hurt you," Mark said, his words almost

growls. He was still human, but with Mark the grizzly was always close to the surface.

"You can't win against both of us," she cried, though God knew it was too soon for her to shift again. She was so tired, she couldn't even manage a good snout. But she could still fight. And, damn it, she could still shoot, though her gun remained firmly holstered.

Alan wasn't listening. He lunged forward, the fury taking him over as he went straight for Mark. But he was slowing down. Even she could see it. His leap didn't take him far and he appeared to be off balance. Tonya thought Mark would meet him. The man had never backed down from anything in his life. But this time, he just stepped to the side. A little slide to get out of the way, and yet still block Alan from running into the woods.

Alan roared in frustration, but Mark just shook his head.

"We can't let you run wild," Mark said, his voice gruff but no less firm. "It's too dangerous. You could hurt someone."

Alan stumbled against a tree, righting himself with a dark curl of his lip.

"We're your friends," Tonya said as she came closer.

He twisted his head to glare at her, and she died a little inside at the hatred in his gaze. He was fully monster now. Every part of him thickened and sharp. She didn't care. She'd seen it before so there was no shock. Just an aching pain at what he'd become.

"You're bringing him out," he snarled. "I'm losing control!"

He tried to dash away. He had a good shot. A path that led into the woods. If he got a head start that way, they might never catch him. But he'd been hit by that dart and Mark was a little too close for it to be an easy escape.

Alan dashed, but Mark stepped into the path. And when Alan tried to strike again, Mark spun sharply, ducking away from the blow even as his leg shot up from behind. He clobbered Alan hard in the back. Alan jolted forward, his face hitting the nearest tree trunk with a sickening thud.

Stay down! Please!

She saw it the moment he went completely feral. Up till now, there'd been a calculation in his movements. A control that kept him from hurting anyone. But then he snapped. He shoved off the tree at double speed. He attacked Mark like a cornered animal. If it weren't for the tranquilizer, no way would Mark have been able to keep him down. Even so, Tonya had to use all her skills to help.

She tripped him from behind. And when he rolled onto all fours, Mark was there to grab him, hauling his arms up and back so that he couldn't fight.

Except he could. Even with Mark's strength holding him back, Alan still managed to tag them both. Hands. Feet. Teeth. He fought with everything. He got one arm free and ripped a long scrape down her calf. He bit Mark twice, though not deeply. Tonya's bear screamed with every impact. Inside, she howled through every second. But she was relentless as was Mark. Until finally, inevitably, Alan wobbled for the last time and collapsed in Mark's arms.

Down.

She stood with her arms raised, her breath coming in gasps

and her mouth bloody from where she'd bit her own cheek to keep from screaming. She waited in taut prayer, watching for any sign of movement. Nothing. Oh God, had they killed him?

No. He was still breathing.

She kept her gaze trained on the steady lift and lower of his chest. It was easier than seeing his battered body. Was he faking? Would he spring back the moment she looked away?

A minute. Two. And he stayed quiet.

Thank God.

And then Mark finally met her gaze with an arched brow. "Now what?" he asked.

"Now we make it worse," she said as she pulled out the hypodermic of suppressant.

"You want me to do it?" Mark asked.

"You have your hands full," she said. With the unconscious Alan.

With shaking hands, she lifted Alan's arm and injected him. Then she abruptly turned aside and threw up every last dreg of coffee and bile that had been poisoning her stomach.

Chapter Eleven

*T*onya.

Alan's first thought as he swam toward consciousness was her name. Over and over, just her name. Then texture came to the word. The scent of her hair, dusty and floral. The feel of her back pressed tight to his chest. And the steady rise and fall of her breath beneath his arm, punctuated by a rumbling snore. He smiled at the sound. He was going to tease her for that.

Other thoughts hovered, black and filled with roiling ugliness that tired him. And he was so damned tired, so he pushed them away. More than anything he wanted to stay in the fuzzy present without thought, without memory. Tonya in his arms the way he'd imagined her so many times. In truth, part of him clung to the idea that this was a really beautiful dream. It had that quality of vagueness that he protected with every part of his being. Mornings were not for thinking but for sweet, special dreams.

He was kissing her hair before he even realized he'd moved.

Within moments, he adjusted to lick her ear and neck. He went by touch and smell. Vision would break the spell, so his eyes remained closed. His mind reveled in the swell of her breast against his forearm and the press of her backside tucked so neatly against his erection.

Her snore softened then hitched as she took a deep breath. She was waking up and he opened his mouth to scrape his teeth tenderly across her neck.

At last. He wasn't even sure what the words meant. They floated so lightly through this dream that was more fantasy than reality. She murmured something deep in her throat. Not quite a purr but close enough that he grinned. The darkness wriggled again, worming into his consciousness as ugly sensations. Aches in his arms and legs. Fuzziness in his brain. He pushed them away in favor of the much more pleasant woman in his arms.

He shifted to her earlobe, tugging on it playfully. She raised her arm, wrapping it around herself enough to squeeze his biceps. That was all the permission he needed. She was wearing a light tank without a bra underneath. That left her breasts soft and so available. He was lying on his right side with her tucked tight. So his left hand burrowed under the fabric, across her rippling belly, and up to her glorious mounds.

Soft. Full. He loved the weight of her breast, and the silky feel. He liked squeezing her nipple and feeling the way she arched into his hand. She pressed back against his erection just when he was thrusting forward.

So good.

He licked her neck again, alternating with light bites. She left her neck exposed to him, and he felt her pulse on his tongue. And, oh, how she trembled when he ran his teeth over that point.

He was harder than a rock, thrusting up through his light cotton shorts. She was wearing something stretchy, so it seemed like she was already welcoming him inside. The crease of her buttocks cradled him, and he wished his shorts gone so he could roll her over and thrust in from behind. Since he was blocked from below, he contented himself with breast play.

So damned good.

"Alan," she gasped as he tugged on her nipple. "Alan, please. We need to talk."

"No talk," he answered. His brain was still fuzzy, and he'd purposely kept his eyes closed. This was a favorite fantasy of his. Waking up with a willing woman. Making love to her without even opening his eyes. He loved diving into his other senses, most especially when she responded so deliciously to his touch. That it was Tonya in his arms took everything to an extra special place.

He moved his top hand, intending to release his shorts so that he could thrust inside her, but he couldn't stop touching her. He slid his hand down her belly then burrowed beneath her underwear. The heat was intense, the pressure delightful as her clothing kept him tight against her slick skin.

"Alan," she cried when he pushed his finger between her folds. All was slick and hot. "I can't think."

He didn't want either of them to think. "Come for me," he said as he pushed into her. He was pulling her more on top of him so he had better access. Her thigh fell open, and he began to thrust inelegantly with his whole hand. One finger inside her.

The others caressing whatever they touched. He pressed against her clit on the upstroke, burrowed inside on the down.

"Alan!" she said. Not an orgasm. Not yet. Just a cry. A wish, maybe, but he ignored it. He could smell her arousal, feel the way she rolled against him. And her breath was stuttered with tiny cries that had his hips pushing in tempo. He wasn't inside her, but she still felt so good. And her scent—cinnamon spice—made him dizzy with happiness.

She reached out blindly with her top hand, connecting with his thigh and gripping it with strong fingers. His entire consciousness was absorbed with the way her body moved. He surrounded her, so he could feel every ripple of her belly, every arch to her back and tremble through her spine. He wasn't working smoothly. His hand was too large, too fumbling, but he knew what she wanted by the grip of her hand on his thigh. She squeezed him when he got it right.

Harder. Tighter. He was right where she wanted it. And he was so close to erupting that his vision had begun to narrow.

He felt her arch hard against him. He rubbed her just like she wanted. Another circle. Another thrust. And then…

She cried out, her body going wild against him.

It was glorious. She was glorious. He held her safe throughout. He cradled her in his arms as her explosion became a pulse, which led to a softer exhale and then a slow, sweet sigh. Beautiful. And way better than any of his adolescent fantasies.

He stroked her stomach as she settled, liking that the caress set her muscles to rippling. Eventually she grabbed his hand, entwining their fingers together. But she didn't speak. He felt her draw breath as if she would. Once. Twice. But she never said a word and he settled her more deeply against him. He was still hard as granite. If ever a man wanted to be planted inside a woman, he was there. And yet, she was so perfect in his arms that he enjoyed holding her. Tonya. Finally in his arms.

He stayed there, appreciating the sweetness of the moment. He thought she might settle back into sleep. She'd certainly stilled enough against him. But he could tell she was anxious about something. He was, too. The aches in his body were starting to intrude on his consciousness. As a way to distract himself, he brought his hand up to his nose and inhaled.

Sweet, beautiful scent. Tonya. He would never forget that smell.

Meanwhile, she twisted in his arms. He relaxed enough for her to move, though his dick throbbed with hunger when her movements tugged on his shorts. Then he felt her stroke across his face, her caress almost intangible.

"Alan," she whispered. "You overwhelm me, and I don't know what to do."

It was the most vulnerable he'd ever heard her. The uncertainty in her tone was so alien to the tough-as-nails cop he knew. Or even the cocksure teen she'd been. He frowned, fighting past the cotton-candy fuzziness in his brain. Something was wrong here. He knew it. But, God, he just didn't want to go there. Unless it was upsetting Tonya. For her, he would face it.

So he opened his eyes. He saw her face first, flushed and pretty. Her eyes sparkled in the streaming sunlight, but it wasn't with joy. He saw worry there, anxiety mixed with tears.

He reached out, touching her cheek. She blinked twice, but held his gaze. And no tears came out. He knew that she was too private to ever let them flow freely. He wanted to kiss her. He needed to taste her as he gently rolled her over. He would make love to her with such tenderness.

But their feet were tangled in a blanket, everything wrapped too tight. So he pulled it aside, adjusting their bodies as he yanked it away from his legs. And in that moment, something rattled. A chain clanked and the weight on his ankle remained though the blanket had pulled free. He stilled, his mind stuttering into a blankness.

He fell back against the pillow. God, his thoughts were so heavy. He couldn't think clearly and so he focused on the sounds.

Birds outside. A kid's laughter out there and the murmur of adults. Closer in, he heard Tonya's breath, tight and quick. He smelled her, ripe and luscious, but there was dust, too. A musty smell that reminded him of a basement or garage.

"Where are we?"

"The cabin that Crazy Cat Lady used. It was the closest, safest place. She's long gone."

He stilled, memories crowding in, but coward that he was, he didn't want to go there. He didn't want to end this tiny interlude of sanity.

"Just hear me out."

Don't think. Don't remember.

"Alan, we had to."

He swallowed, the aches in his body growing more painful, more disturbing. Then he moved his leg again. It was heavier than it should be and that clanking sound filled the space. Worse, it seemed to echo in his head, louder and louder.

No. Nooooooooooooo.

He couldn't think for the screaming in his head. He felt her touch him, then grip tighter, shaking him, but he couldn't respond for the scream. He didn't want to look, but he couldn't stop himself.

An iron shackle around his ankle and a chain trailing down the side of the bed.

A volcano erupted inside him. Fury, hot and corrosive, flashed through his body. Waves of heat poured off him as he shifted to tear the damned thing off. He reached down, but his hands were just hands as they hauled ineffectively at the shackle. His body stretched and pushed with the shift, hoping to pop the shackle from sheer size, but his leg was just his leg. And the hair on his leg remained manlike and without the fur or the coarse oil that was part of the monster.

Nothing on him changed, and that created rage as never before.

He shoved her away from him, but he needn't have bothered. She was already scrambling to her feet. Her mouth was moving, but he couldn't hear her, his own scream filling the space. He tore at the shackle until it turned slick with blood. His fingernails broke against the iron and his ankle ran red from the scrapes.

It took too long for him to realize he couldn't budge the shackle, but when he did he turned on the chain. He hauled on it with both fists, finding it attached to a ring in the concrete floor. They were in a basement with bars on the window and two beds on opposite walls. He saw a bathroom, a microwave, and a stairway up in a minimalist space decorated with pressboard furniture. One slam of his fist and an end table crumpled into shards.

Tonya was screaming his name, her voice sharp and female. He rounded on the sound only because it wasn't his roar. She stood there, her face smeared with tears. Her breasts bobbed loosely beneath her tank and he damned himself for seeing them. For thinking—even on the most base level—how beautiful they were. How much he loved touching them, smelling them. That even in the midst of a scream that filled his entire universe, he still wanted to kiss them.

And that made him even angrier.

He lunged for her; he didn't even know why. She scrambled backward. He leapt after her, but within a few feet, the chain yanked tight. Pain flashed up his leg, and he whipped back around in a snarl. He would bite the damned thing off, but he couldn't. He was a man, not a beast right then. And he both hated it and was absurdly grateful. He couldn't be the slavering monster he wanted right then. Not in front of Tonya. She wouldn't see that, and yet she was the one who had done this to him. Chained him like a dog. Teased him with her body only to cage him as a monster.

He collapsed to his knees. He couldn't break the iron chain no matter how much he hauled on it. He knew it, and yet still he tried. He fought it with everything he was until it was too much. And still the scream continued in his head.

On and on he fought until he had no strength left. Futility

curled in on him, compressing his spine and his breath. He knew this place. He remembered the moment when strength abandoned him. His tormentors would come soon. Petty cruelties as they kicked at his cage or threw his food in his face. They were bad enough. But the shit they'd shoved into his body was worse. The violation of serums injected, of joints on fire, and his own blood and piss everywhere.

He remembered this, and it crushed him.

Chapter Twelve

"What do I do? What do I do?"

Tonya whispered the question over and over. Her voice was a hoarse rasp from trying to reach Alan. All she had left was doubt and pain, reverberating in her question. She was crouched on the concrete floor, just out of range. She'd tried to go to him over and over, but each time he'd lashed out with teeth and claws. It hadn't made any difference that he'd stayed human. All the serum had done was suppress the change. The animal was still there, fighting in blind panic to survive.

"What do I do? What do I do?"

The agony of what she'd seen—what she'd *caused*—would haunt her for the rest of her life. She'd watched the fight go out of him then. His body had betrayed him. She had betrayed him. And now his mind was gone, too. At the very end, he'd finally focused on her, his eyes bleary with defeat. He'd blinked twice and took a breath. She'd straightened up, thinking that perhaps rationality had returned. But before she could draw breath, he closed his eyes.

Unconscious.

So now she crouched just out of reach and sobbed. She'd done that to him. She'd destroyed him. And now what was she supposed to do?

The answer was obvious, and she hated herself for questioning her choice. She had to unchain him. She couldn't put him through that again. She couldn't.

But what if he woke up violent? She wasn't able to shift to grizzly yet. She was too tired. And since the adrenaline of the last hour hadn't made her sprout fur, she guessed it would be at least a day before she could go bear. That meant she would be defenseless against him. Even before his change, Alan had trained hard as a martial arts fighter. He'd needed the skill just to maintain some safety when messing around with his shifter friends. Add to that his new strength and speed, and she would be hard pressed to defend herself. Hell, they'd already tangled once monster against bear, and she'd barely survived.

If she unchained him and he woke able to shift? He could kill her. She had her gun outside in her car. Mark had wanted her to bring it inside, but she knew that shifter speed made guns a liability in a small basement space. Too easy for him to knock it out of her hand. Too easy for the wrong person to get a hold of a weapon.

So her pistol remained locked in her car. And since Mark had left to get more of the suppressant, she was alone with Alan. It was what she'd wanted. She had to explain why they'd locked him up. Why they'd chained him like an animal. Why they were treating him this way.

Idiot.

She had to set him free. If she had any hope of reaching him, she had to do it in a way that made him feel safe. And since she'd had Mark padlock the door to the basement, the only person she risked was herself. She just hoped the suppressant lasted long enough for her to talk rationally to him.

So she straightened out of her crouch. Her muscles burned as she forced them out of her taut position. She walked on bare feet to the opposite side of the room and pulled out the key to the shackle. Its weight was repugnant in the way it sat cold and cruel in her hand. But she held it tight, knowing that was a fraction of what Alan felt.

All her fault. What an idiot she was.

She crept closer, moving by inches and watching for any reaction from Alan. He remained still, his breath quick and shallow. As if even when the rest of him had collapsed, his breath still fought. His body still knew he was chained.

Why was this so hard? Having decided to risk it, she should be quick and decisive with her actions. Part of her trusted Alan implicitly, and it urged her forward. But her logical side kept flashing images of rabid animals, of addicts who needed a fix, of women who believed in their abusive husbands because their hearts couldn't accept the truth. Was she one of them now? One of those foolishly, hopeful women that she'd sneered at all her life?

Yes.

Finally, she just did it. She opened the lock on the ankle band. She popped the piece apart, cringing at the drying blood everywhere. The chains fell with a heavy *thunk*, and she froze, watching to see if he would react.

Nothing. Had his breath steadied? Was it slower? She couldn't tell. She stepped backward, watching him carefully. Did he know that he was free? Would he understand that she was sorry?

She watched him for another ten minutes. Fifteen. But the more she stared, the more she despised the sight of the heavy iron. There was rust on it, and she didn't like it that close to his open wounds. A little late to be worrying about that now, but she did. So she crept closer again. This time she grabbed the chain from the ground. She unfastened it from the bolt in the floor. Did she move him enough to take the shackle away? She might wake him.

First she dealt with the chain, setting it back in the closet where they'd found it. Then she stared at him. She had to risk it. She couldn't stand seeing the heavy band there, even open. It was still touching him, and she hated it.

So she crawled back. As gently as possible, she lifted his leg. If he woke, one good kick would give her broken ribs. But he didn't react. She grabbed the slick iron and hauled it away. Five minutes later it was out of sight, but certainly not out of mind.

And then she waited with the same question burning through her thoughts.

What do I do now?

Chapter Thirteen

His nose woke first. Alan smelled food. Meat. Cheese. Hot.

He didn't want to wake. This twilight where the ache was muted felt like enough consciousness for the moment. If he could sink back down, he would. But his nose smelled food, and his belly cramped in hunger.

Consciousness came at him whether he wanted it or not. He was hungry. Thirsty. Cold. And the floor was fucking hard.

He opened his eyes first. He saw her at the same moment he saw the food. She was sitting against the wall, her eyes red and swollen. She chewed something, chasing it with a drink from a bright red plastic cup. But her gaze remained trained on him.

"Yours is in front of your right hand," she said. "It's probably cooled off enough by now. It's a Hot Pocket. Not gourmet cuisine, but it's food." Her voice was hoarse, her tone soft, but it took on strength with her next words. "I'm so sorry, Alan. I was scared and stupid."

He waited in silence, slowly recruiting his faculties as he watched her. It looked like she would say more. Her mouth was open, but then her expression faltered. She went from earnest to awkward. Her gaze dropped to the floor, and eventually, she shoved another bite into her mouth.

He wasn't going to move. He knew what he felt like after spending hours on a hard floor. But the scent of melted cheese was too alluring. So without him consciously willing it, he stretched out a hand for the Hot Pocket. But as soon as his hand came into his line of sight, his mind stuttered to a halt.

His fingers were covered with dried blood. His nails were cracked and black. He couldn't tell if there were wounds on his hands. There was too much filth. And the idea that those hands would touch his food made him slam his eyes shut while revulsion rolled through his thoughts.

He was a disgusting monster.

"There's a bathroom to your left. The hot water takes a bit to kick in, but the showerhead is pretty strong. Mark left his spare set of clothes for you. They're in there, too."

Mark's clothing would hang like a sack on him. The man was bigger than a bulldozer.

Alan lay still, his mind at war with himself. He was a monster, and so he ought to look like one, too. But that was the attitude of a sullen child. Lying on the floor in filth was only hurting himself. So he gathered his strength and pushed himself upright.

He was weak, his arms trembling as he levered himself onto hands and knees. But this time when he opened his eyes, he saw the iron bolt in the floor. He saw the dried blood and remembered his chains. Automatically, his lips curled back in a growl and his joints seemed to swell, but that was as far as it went. No thickening in his muscles. Just a gnawing ache in his bellow.

"No chains," Tonya said, her voice breaking on the words. "I'm so sorry."

He shot her a glare. "I'm free?" he rasped. God, his voice sounded and felt like a rusty saw.

He watched her flinch, but then her gaze steadied. Tonya always told him things straight out. No hedging. "The door at the top of the stairs is locked. Mark has the key. Shouldn't be a problem for you when you can shift again."

His chin jerked up. "What did you do to me?"

She swallowed. "There's a serum for suppressing the shifter. Mark had it with him in case he started slipping. We gave it to you while you were unconscious."

"I've had it before," he said as he tried to shove the memories away. Evil Einstein had told him it would ease his transition, but that had been a big fat lie. "It started the seizures."

He hadn't thought she could go paler, but she blanched to a ghostly shade of white. "We hoped…I thought it would give us time to talk." She took another breath. "Einstein has a theory. He believes that people like you—the ones who have been activated—go from normal to feral in weeks instead of years. That explains the sudden aggression."

"And the crazy," he said. Ferals always went crazy. That's why they were so dangerous. Their human minds just couldn't handle being all animal, all the time.

"So we thought the suppressant would help. If we knock back

the shifting ability—give your mind a break for a time—then you can figure out how to manage better. How to control—"

"The monster?" he interrupted. He shook his head. "Even if I can't shift, he's still there. He still…owns me."

"No, he doesn't!" she snapped. Then she moderated her tone, though part of him warmed at her passionate defense. How wonderful to know that someone else would fight for him when he'd lost the strength. "They're still adjusting the serum. We'll figure it out."

He dropped back onto his heels. He didn't want to figure any of it out. He just wanted it to end. But again, that was the tantrum of a child. He had to remember. He had to know what had been done to him.

"Did I convulse?" he finally asked.

"No," she said rapidly. "It seemed to quiet you. Though that might have been the tranq dart."

He did remember that. The thud that knocked him back on his heels. Mark stepping out from behind a tree. And then…Jesus, Mark had held him in a headlock while he'd fought like a crazed animal. He abruptly scanned Tonya, not seeing any injuries but it was hard to tell.

"Did I hurt you?"

"No. It was the other way around."

Monsters deserved to be hurt. He flexed his calves then pushed to his feet. He was surprised he wasn't crippled. But then shifters—even monsters—seemed to heal quickly.

Tonya looked up at him, her expression wary. "I'm so sorry, Alan."

Yeah. He got that. Didn't mean he forgave her. All he had to do was look to the iron ring in the floor and emotions churned furiously in gut. But he didn't exactly hate her, either. He looked away rather than face the roiling emotions whenever he thought of her. Lust. Anger. Affection. Fury. He couldn't make sense of it.

"Any coffee?" he asked. Damn, he hadn't wanted to talk civilly yet, but some things were paramount.

"I wish," she drawled.

Not half as much as he did. Whatever drugs they'd given him—tranquilizer or monster suppressant—were still swirling around in his body. Food would likely help, but he had to clean up first. He just couldn't stomach anything else.

The bathroom had the bare essentials. Tonya's go bag was there, complete with a toiletry kit and disposable toothbrush and paste. It was part of being a cop, he supposed. Or the fact that Tonya liked to be prepared for any eventuality. He stared at it for a long moment, seeing her in her things. Her scent in the travel-sized deodorant and shampoo bottle. Her light blond hair in the compact brush. Even a small tube of lipstick in a soft rose color.

Conflicted.

He turned away rather than think about the woman who had drugged and chained him. Especially since she was also the woman who had orgasmed around his hand and held him while he slept.

He lingered in the shower longer than he intended, but eventually hunger pushed him out of the cleansing heat. By the time he put on Mark's oversized basketball shorts and a too wide Detroit Tigers tee, he felt ridiculously human. As if he'd stepped back in time to his awkward adolescence when nothing ever fit right on his rapidly growing body. He ate like one, too, gobbling down two Hot Pockets without tasting them or even caring when the second one seared his tongue. He noticed that the third had chicken in it, but that was all that registered as he washed it down with tepid water.

And then he was cleaned, fed, and alone with Tonya without any decision on what he would do next. He was just glancing up the stairs, flexing his hands to see if he could shift yet when she spoke up. Her words were rushed, as if she had to force herself to say them. But once her words registered, everything in him stilled to a frozen silence.

"I've bonded to you."

He turned to look at her. She was standing next to the microwave with her shoulders back and her chin lifted. It was a defiant posture, one that he knew she adopted whenever she felt vulnerable.

"I know you're thinking about leaving, and I don't blame you. But you need to know that. Just in case you care."

He cared about everything she said. Always had. But her words made no sense and so he stared at her and wished—again—for some thick, black coffee.

"It's insane, I know. But I can't think of any other reason for me to do the things we've done."

He snorted. "Because you like whack jobs?"

"Get your head out of your ass!" she snapped. "God damn it, Alan, you're the smartest man I know. You're pissed, with reason. You're off balance for damn sure. Join the fucking club. I've got a situation here, and I'd appreciate it if you gave me five minutes of your time to help me deal with it."

He arched a brow, his sense of humor kicking in. Trust Tonya to tell a dangerous, unstable person to get his head out of his ass. "Fine," he said. "You're wrong. Get some sleep and some real food, and it'll all be gone by morning."

"Fuck you," she snapped. Then her gaze went to the bed they'd shared. "My bear picked you and now I haven't a good goddamned idea what to do about it."

"You're *wrong*," he said, stressing the word as loudly as he could. "When was the last time you slept? Ate a decent meal? Tonya, you just started as beta and that's a nightmare of a job. You're not thinking straight."

"And you're not listening. My bear picked you. All you have to do is enter the room and she's wet and spreading for you. Even if I wanted to let you walk out that door, she'll follow you. She's yours and you need to get your head out of your ass to deserve that kind of devotion."

He stared at her, seeing her anger and frustration. Jesus, she believed what she was saying, which set off all sorts of reactions inside him. Flushed pleasure was the most obvious. Hell, the idea that his high school crush couldn't help herself sexually around him had him sporting a thick chubby of pubescent delight. But the rest of him felt a dark anger churn in his belly. She'd *chained* him to the floor, for God's sake. He wasn't sure he could forgive her for that.

"You're *wrong*," he said again. And he turned away, heading for the stairs.

She was on him before he'd realized she'd moved. She was at his side, gripping his arm and whipping him around to face her. And then when he was still snarling at her, she grabbed his ears, holding him steady as she slammed her mouth against his.

God, he didn't want to react. He wanted to shove her away from him with all his monster strength. But when he gripped her arms, he couldn't do it. She was pressed against him. Her tongue was pushing at his lips and teeth. And when he opened to bellow at her, she invaded his mouth.

Well fuck that.

No kissing. No touching. No...

He arched her back and pushed her tongue aside as he thrust into her mouth. He devoured her mouth like the animal he was. And she fought with him with the ferocity of any she-bear. Tongue to tongue. Breasts to chest. Pelvis to dick.

He didn't want this. And yet, he so obviously did. He tried again to shove her away from him, but he ended up pushing her up against the wall instead. And once there, she wrapped a leg around his hip, opening her crotch to the hard ridge of his cock. Jesus, basketball shorts did nothing to dull the sensation of her softness. Of the way she cradled him between her thighs.

"No!" he bellowed as he tore himself away from her. He stumbled sideways, his breath heaving in and out like a great bellows. He wasn't a beast to be controlled by his lusts. To take a woman against a wall.

Except, of course, he was. He wanted to. And it was taking all his willpower to stand gripping the handrail to the stairs.

"See?" she gasped, her voice flat. "*See?*"

"No," he lied. Because he did see her problem. This wasn't the Tonya he remembered. The one who kept bears and cops in line with a single icy stare. This wasn't the girl she'd been, either, the one who seduced him mercilessly at fourteen, then headed straight for his brother.

"Don't be an asshole," she snapped. Then she took a rasping breath. "Mark said it was the same for him the minute he saw Julie. It took her longer, though."

He'd heard the story, but he still didn't fully believe it. "It's too soon," he said. "It might not last."

"He says it's real." She lifted her chin and turned to face him. He couldn't match the gesture, but he watched her out of his peripheral vision. "I believe him because I feel the same way."

He took a breath, finally doing what she'd demanded and brought his brain online. He didn't know much about the bonding process except that it was one of the few ways to save a feral. He knew that when grizzly-shifters locked in on someone, it was usually for life. He'd known a few bad marriages where the woman hadn't been worth the shifter's devotion, but the grizzly hadn't let the poor SOB end it. He supposed it was possible that Tonya had landed herself in a similar situation. Bonded to an unworthy man. Which really sucked for her, but there was nothing he could do about it.

"You've got to find a way to break it," he said. "This isn't going to end well for you."

She dropped her head back against the cheap wood paneling. "Don't you think I've tried?"

He straightened off the railing, doing his best to attack the problem logically. Problem was, he was rusty on using his logic circuits. He'd been one raw nerve of impulse and fury since the day he'd been abducted.

"When did it start?" he asked.

She sighed. "When we were going to rescue you. I couldn't breathe. I was so afraid for you that it nearly crippled me."

Ugly hatred twisted in his gut. It was the cold shot he needed to kill any sympathy he had for her. "You mean when you were going to rescue Julie. You didn't even fucking know I was there."

She shook her head. "We knew. We were trying to get a hold of you and we heard."

"You were looking for *Julie*! The rescue was for *Julie*!"

She didn't flinch from his bellow and her gaze remained locked on his. "Not me. Not from the very first second we realized you were there."

He didn't want to believe her. The rage inside him was that strong. It wanted to hold on to his fury at his abandonment by everyone who'd ever pretended to love him. But she didn't waver and she didn't lie. Which left him speechless with an incoherent rage that kept flaring and dying beneath her steady regard. Hatred quieted into agonizing pain.

"I'm a monster," he said.

She shrugged, the gesture filled with defeat. "If so, it doesn't matter."

He stared at her, finally allowing everything she'd said to sink into his brain. It made sense, in a twisted way. The things she'd allowed him to do to her at the hotel. Here. And even before that, she'd gone without food or sleep as she chased him all over

Michigan. Any normal woman would have cut her losses long ago, but she'd Tasered him, drugged him, and even chained him to the floor.

"Jesus, Tonya, you're a fucking train wreck."

She gaped at him, but then her lips began to twitch. A moment later, she was chuckling, though there was an edge of hysteria to the sound. Soon her knees went out and she slid down the wall to squat on the floor. And still she laughed. He did, too, because, really, what else could he do?

She stopped first, wiping the tears away with the back of her hand. And then when she had sobered enough to draw breath, she looked up at him, her heart in her eyes. He saw desire and fear, swirling in those misty blue depths. And then he watched her tuck the emotions away as she squared her shoulders and pulled out her cop persona, though she remained squatting on the floor.

"One more thing," she said, her voice firming with every word. "I know you want to kill Elisabeth. We all do. But you're not trained for this. You're a vigilante running on rage and it's going to get you killed."

Her voice broke on that last word. He'd expected her to go the other way. To tell him that a scorched-earth policy destroyed the innocent as well as the guilty. That was his only fear right now. That his suicidal rampage would have collateral damage. But the tremor in her voice told him she'd just voiced her greatest fear. That he'd die as part of his kamikaze mission. But she didn't understand the truth, so it was up to him to tell it to her as baldly as possible.

"I'm dying anyway," he said. "Not one of Einstein's creations has lived a month."

"That's because we shot them."

"Because they were insane." He looked at her, trying to force her to accept what he'd felt on a subconscious level from the very beginning. "I'm going feral, Tonya. You said it. Weeks, not years, remember?"

"We'll suppress it. We can—"

"It doesn't work that way. Even if I can't shift, the mind..." He gestured vaguely at his own brain. "I'm still going crazy."

"Every shifter goes through this at adolescence. They all have to learn to control the beast. It's just compressed for you. All happening at once."

He glared at her, not wanting to feel hope that he could survive this. It was an insane reaction. Who didn't want to believe? But he'd accepted that this war in his mind would end soon. The idea that he would have to conquer it was like ripping the Band-Aid off a mortal wound. At least before he couldn't see it, he didn't have to face his inevitable loss or try to battle against overwhelming odds. But she wasn't letting him get away with that. She was forcing him to gird up and face the war again. Part of him hated her for that. Almost as much as the part that adored her.

"What do you want me to do?" he asked, honestly wanting to know. "Elisabeth has children with her. I can't let her do this to someone else."

"I know. But can we do it smart? Can we hunt her together?"

He snorted. "I don't intend to let her live. You're a police officer—"

"I'm off duty."

"Like that makes any difference to you." Tonya was a cop through and through. No one was surprised when she went straight from college into the police academy. They only wondered what had taken her so long. "You have the law written on your bones."

"Says the lawyer."

He thought, really thought, about what she'd just said. He barely noticed when he sank down onto the lowest stair step as he processed it all. Once he'd revered the law. Once he'd pledged himself to uphold the truth of it even when he knew "truth" and "legal" were often entirely separate things. Where had that gone? He didn't even like comic books because the heroes operated by their own code instead of the law. In the end, he only had one explanation.

"I'm a monster."

"I'm so sick of hearing that." She pushed up from the wall but she didn't approach. She just used her superior height to emphasize her words. "Really hear this, okay? You're off balance because you've lost control. You've been so fucking smart your whole life that you've never felt this wild. You think you've become a monster and I even believed you for a while. But what if this is you going through normal shifter adolescence? Just speeded up. Then it's all you, Alan. It's just the dark side that everyone has but that you've never let yourself see before."

He gaped at her. Did she really think that was true? That deep down was the same old Alan that she'd always known? "Bullshit!"

he said as he exploded upward. "Alan's gone. I keep telling you that—"

She slapped him. Hard and fast enough that his head whipped around. And while his ears were still ringing from the impact, she pushed up on her toes so she could bellow straight in his face.

"Alan's *changed*, you moron. He's not gone. He's *different*."

Which brought them right back to where they were before the conversation began. His face stung and his blood pounded with adrenaline. He grabbed her arms before she could hit him again. And when she tensed, he slammed her back against the wall.

Was she attacking him to get to this place again? This wild, violent place of lust? God help him, he kind of liked that about her. He watched her nostrils flare and in that thin tank top, he could see the hard tight points of her nipples.

"Is this what you want?" he rasped. "Are you goading me into this?"

Her expression tightened, shifting rapidly through emotions he was too pissed off to read. "I don't know," she said.

"Yes, you do." He lowered his head until they were nose to nose. Until their breath heated the space between them to nearly boiling. "You know exactly what you want."

She did. He could see the realization in her eyes. He knew when her conscious mind latched on to the truth of her actions. She was doing anything to keep him here. Anything to get him inside her. And God help him, as angry as he was, part of him knew that he was holding on to fury as a way to keep away from her. Better to hate her than complete the bonding process. To tie her irrevocably to the monster he'd become.

Then she proved that she was braver than he was. More honest than he could ever hope to be. She looked him in the eye and said the words aloud.

"Make love to me, Alan. Please."

Her words hit him low and deep. Not just his gut but his soul, so deep inside him that he hadn't even known he'd needed those words. She wanted him. He'd been nothing but brutal and cruel to her, and she still wanted him. He didn't know whether to worry about her sanity or be eternally grateful for her insanity. Both. Definitely both.

"I don't have a condom," he said, startling himself with his own words. When had he decided to do this? Or perhaps, when had he stopped fighting the inevitable? He'd never been able to refuse her anything since the day he turned fourteen.

"I don't care," she said, though her voice shook.

He did. He wouldn't saddle her with his child. Not when he had no idea what was going on with his biology. But before he could say anything, an image flashed through his brain. It was of her toiletry bag. The one in the bathroom that was stocked for all possibilities including thing one.

"You have condoms in the bathroom," he said.

She nodded. "So go get them." That was it. No hesitation, no coy girlishness. Not from Tonya.

He eased off her slowly, straightening as he watched for any doubt in her expression. She remained as true to her word as ever. And so with a weird kind of satisfaction, he headed for the six neatly folded foil packets. Given the way he felt, they were going to need every single one.

Chapter Fourteen

Tonya held herself excruciatingly still. Had she just asked…
Actually, had she just *begged* a man to make love to her? *Yes.* And
given how much her body was tightening in anticipation, she
didn't regret the decision. She felt like a lit firecracker just waiting for the flame to hit gunpowder.

He was quick in the bathroom, coming out with the strip of six
condoms in his hand. But it was his expression that worried her.
They'd known each other all their lives. They often knew each
other's thoughts without even saying a word. And yet, right now,
she couldn't even guess at his emotions. He was certainly horny.
The huge tent in his sports shorts told her that. But there were
more feelings there than just lust.

She saw it in the way he moved toward her, prowling in a way
she'd never seen on him before. Slow, measured, and not exactly
direct. Her belly rippled at the sight, feeling the excited stir of her
own animal. He lowered his chin, flared his nostrils, and watched

her with eyes that seemed to burn straight through her. Her nipples tightened in reaction. Her fingers curled into her palms, and her breath shortened in anticipation.

Unable to stay still, she stood before him, tightening her thighs to keep her knees strong. Adrenaline hummed in her blood, and she readied herself for a chase. There was nowhere to go in this basement, but some pursuits were less about speed and more about dominance. She might have asked for this, but she'd be damned if she just rolled over for it.

"You're not naked," he said.

Her lips curled. "Always with the romantic talk."

"I tried that, remember? Silver-tongued compliments and all, and you gave me exactly jack shit."

She snorted. "You seriously think you were witty at fourteen? That I would get all wet and wanting at your Christmas ball jokes?"

His eyebrow quirked. "They made you laugh."

They had done that. And she'd secretly treasured every one because he'd helped her relax despite the constant stress of the Gladwin shifter politics that always surrounded them. "Still doesn't make it romantic."

He prowled closer. She held her ground. Only prey ran at this point. "What about later? Flowers on your birthday, chocolate at Valentine's Day."

"From your family."

He snorted. "Like my brother ever thought of that shit."

And right there was the Alan she remembered. The one who did all the work, let everyone else take the credit, and secretly resented how abused he was.

"If you wanted to be romantic, you had to sign your name and no one else's."

He paused. "Would it have made a difference?"

She wanted to say yes. She wanted to tell him they could have found a normal romance in the usual way, but she didn't think so. And after the disaster of his fourteenth birthday, she'd sworn to never lie to him again.

"I was focused elsewhere."

"On my brother." The words were snarled.

"On being the Maxima. After my dentist boyfriend freaked, I just couldn't handle a real relationship. Maxima was a political position, not a romantic one." She shrugged. "You don't get to corner the market on stupidity." Truth was, she'd taken missteps with him way more than he had with her. She was about to say more. To express again how sorry she was for all the different ways she'd screwed up, but he never gave her the chance. While she was lost in the wish that she'd been smarter, he pounced on her. Not slow. Not subtle. A simple, predatory pounce.

He pinned her against the wall.

She fought on instinct, but he was stronger. And smarter, which startled her. She fought with power and shifter speed. She might not be able to go grizzly yet, but she had muscles and rapid reactions. She twisted out of his hold, she knocked his arms away, and she writhed out of his control. But in every action, he had a counter. He let her twist only to use the motion to push her sideways toward the nearest bed. He let her knock his arms wide, but that only gave him the momentum he needed sweep her legs out from under her. And when she writhed in his hold, he tightened his grip so that she felt every hard ridge on his body. Most especially the one that thrust against her.

And then, she was on the mattress, facedown, while he stripped her yoga pants away. She was panting from her exertion and wet from desire. He was rough as he jerked her clothes off, lifting her feet high in the air. She let him do it, knowing she'd get her chance to retaliate in a second. He had to take off his shorts at some point. And God only knew where the condoms had gone.

But just when her feet were coming down to earth, just when she was gripping the mattress for purchase for her next move, right then, he shoved her knees wide and set his mouth to her spread legs. It was fast and awkward, given that she was facedown. The slap of his tongue startled her, but within a second of his lips connecting with her groin, he began to suck.

Fire sizzled in her blood and she cried out at the sudden rush of sensation on her already sensitive flesh. She been trying to pull herself away, but then the strength in her arms disappeared. What he was doing felt too good.

She arched her back and pressed her mound on his mouth. Then he began to lick her and all she could think was, God, what a wicked tongue. He knew what he was doing down there and she was powerless to resist.

And then suddenly he stopped. His hands still gripped her thighs, keeping her spread open before him, but his mouth was gone.

"Tell me that you want this," he said, his voice hard and demanding.

"You know I do."

"Tell me you want *me* to do this."

He needed it graphic? She had no reservation about speaking as filthy as he wanted. "I want to orgasm all over your tongue. And I want your dick shoved so far inside me that I taste your come."

She felt his hands spasm on her thighs, but he didn't go back to what he'd been doing. "So romantic shit isn't what turns you on."

Nope. "You've got the silver-tongue part down."

"Yes, I do." Male satisfaction rang in every syllable. And then, thank God, he went right back to her. He drew it out. He pushed her to the edge a half dozen times, then cooled her off enough to have her screaming in frustration at him. And then, abruptly, he sucked her clit hard. Twice.

Detonation.

Her body spasmed around nothing, her womb pulling at the emptiness inside her. He hadn't even thrust his finger inside her, but the pleasure was beyond intense.

Until it eased. Until she realized she was lying boneless on a mattress while he'd apparently stripped out of his clothes and put on a condom. How did she know? Because he told her.

"That was the tongue part," he growled right before she heard the rip of the foil packet. "Now it's dick time."

Crude, but damn she wanted it. She made no resistance when he pulled her up onto her knees. She still had no strength in her arms, but it wasn't necessary. She felt him at her opening, poking lightly.

"Say it again, Tonya. Say you want me again."

"Alan, yes." Both words came out in short gasps. Her heart was still hammering, her breath barely recovered. She arched, waiting for the impalement. It didn't happen. She was open and vulnerable, he was right *there*, damn it, and he still—

"Me? Now?"

"Alan Wilson Carman, fuck me now or so help me I'll—"

He thrust. All the way in, in one slamming rush.

"Oh God, you're big." He was. It wasn't just that he stretched her passage. She felt like her womb was being crushed up against her diaphragm.

He froze, fully embedded within her. "Problem?"

God, no. It was just going to take her a moment to adjust. Fortunately, he gave her the time, and in the pause, she found her way to take back some control. She stretched herself along the bed, arching her back to give him more room. And then she began to squeeze.

Never in her life had she been more grateful to have studied tantrism. In truth, it had been her college roommate who was the aficionado, but Tonya had taken the time to master some of the basics. Like a rolling squeeze from base to top.

"Fucking God!" he gasped.

Music to her ears. So she did it again. And that appeared to be all the encouragement he needed.

He grabbed hold of her hips and began thrusting. Hard jerks that smashed him against her. Again and again, while she gasped and held on. She tried to maintain control of how she squeezed him. She tried to retain some sanity in the wet slam. But there was no controlling this ride. Within moments, her body convulsed again, but this time she squeezed all of him. This time she was filled with Alan. He cried out, jerking against her. And she pulled him all the way in.

Fireworks.

Chapter Fifteen

Alan came back to himself with a satisfied smirk. Hard to avoid given how absolutely, frigging amazing Tonya was. Never in a million years would he have guessed that she liked dirty talk. Or that she could do whatever-the-hell that had been when he'd been inside her. Controlled rocket launch? Stair step to mind blown? He was so exhausted, he'd just collapsed sideways, taking her with him. They were still joined as they spooned on the bed. And though her breath had steadied, she seemed as bonelessly pleasured as he was.

Except, hell, that wasn't exactly how he'd dreamed of making love to her. Over the years, he'd imagined thousands of scenarios but all of them had involved tenderness. Sweet caresses and joyous kisses. Never had he lifted her hips and slammed himself home like a…

Like a monster.

He groaned as he buried his face in her back. She still wore her tank top and the light cotton shamed him. He hadn't even taken off her shirt.

"Oh hell," she sighed. "You're thinking again."

What? He didn't even say the question aloud, but she answered it anyway.

"You may have changed, Alan, but some things will always be you. I've never known anyone who could examine a situation from so many angles, even after the deed was done."

"What?" This time he did say it aloud, and she chuckled at the confusion in his voice.

"I'm not complaining," she said. Actually she was. "It's what makes you such a good lawyer. I can't tell you how many times you've made me or Carl run through scenarios."

"Carl does that, too. So do you."

"Yeah, but when we decide, it's over. You keep searching for what we missed." She gripped his hand, pulling it closer. "It's also why you're a great beta." Her voice was quiet, the words filled with quiet acceptance.

But he couldn't let her doubt herself. Not in this. "You just got the job. It takes a while to settle in."

"It takes a different temperament. Attention to detail and organizational skills. That's you."

"Strategic thinking, military precision," he countered. "That's you." He levered himself up onto his elbow, suppressing his groan of regret as he slid out of her. But this was too important for her to be distracted. So he pulled out, then turned her so he could look in her eyes. "Carl is used to me doing the job. Don't let him act like you're a replacement for me. You're not. You've got your own strengths, your own skills. Own the position, Tonya. Make it yours. Trust me, you're more than capable."

She stared at him, her blue eyes widening as he spoke. He didn't know if the message sank in or not. If she'd really take it to heart. In the end, he could only hope that her slow nod meant she would do what was needed. What the Gladwin grizzlies deserved.

"You're going to be terrific at it," he said as he pressed a kiss to her shoulder.

"Does that mean you forgive me for stealing the job?"

He lifted his head and frowned at her. "You didn't steal anything. Carl gave it to you."

"But—"

He pressed his finger to her lips, silencing her as he tried to find the right words. The most honest words. "Yeah, I was pissed at first. That was my only standing in the clan."

"Not true!" she spoke past his finger and when he tried to stop her, she grabbed his hand and pulled it away from her mouth. "You're part of us."

"Because I can shift now?" he asked, his words harsher than he intended. "Or at least half shift."

"Because you've grown up with us. Because your uncle, father, and now brother are our Maximums. Because the only one who ever felt he didn't measure up was you."

Well, that was bullshit. They both knew that there was a quiet prejudice against the nonshifters in a grizzly family. They were called normals and genetic losers in the game of shifter offspring. It didn't matter that they were included in the clan picnics before the wild run through the park. The pecking order was blindingly clear. The Maximus shifted first, then the others followed into a tumbling, rumbling bit of fun through the park. And when the shifters disappeared into the park, the normals cleaned up the leftover potato salad. They grabbed the children too young to shift and helped the grandparents get home. They were the maids of the clan, and everyone knew it.

But rather than argue, he pulled away from her and headed to the bathroom to clean up. And typical to her stubbornness, Tonya didn't remain quietly on the bed. Nope. She rolled up right after him, pacing him to the bathroom and talking the whole way.

"Sure, there are dickheads in every group. But you look me in the eye and tell me that your brother didn't know your worth. That Mark didn't go to you with his biggest problem. That I didn't see what you did every day and thank you for it."

He swallowed. He couldn't because she was right. The ones who counted had known his worth. That's one of the reasons he'd stuck around so long. That's why it had been so hard to leave Gladwin in favor of other dreams. But she deserved the truth.

"I got a job in Chicago."

She jolted, her entire body stilling. "What?"

"That's what I was doing when they grabbed me." He took a breath, pushing away the memory of his abduction. "The day after Carl offered you the job as beta, I put out my résumé to some of the big firms in Chicago. I was coming back from the interview when they got me."

"And you got the job." A statement not a question, but he answered it anyway.

"At a great salary." Then he looked away. He would have gone. He knew that without a shadow of a doubt. He would have taken the job and driven off to a great new future in big city law. Except Elisabeth had found him. Einstein, her partner in evil, had shoved poison in his arm. And his entire future had burned to the ground.

Meanwhile Tonya absorbed his words, her eyes widening even as she leaned heavily against the door frame. "You were leaving us."

He sighed. She still didn't get it. As much as she was the queen of facing facts, she still hadn't sorted through all the possibilities. But with his silence, her quick mind figured it out.

"You still are leaving," she said heavily.

"Shall we sort through every possibility?" he asked.

"You get healthy. We either figure out how to change you back—"

"Fat chance."

Her lower lip pushed out mulishly. "We fix what they did to you," she repeated firmly. "Or you get a handle on controlling it." She gestured to his body. "You're already there. You're looking and acting fully human now."

On the outside. He still knew he was crazy on the inside. "There are lots more job opportunities for me outside of Gladwin, and not enough for me to do now that you're the beta."

"You can have the job back," she said. Firmly. Like she really meant it. But he knew how important the clan was to her. And once the kinks got ironed out, she and Carl would be a seamless unit.

"I'm not going back to being the beta. I don't want it." Which turned out to be true. And no one was more surprised than him.

"But you could work nearby, right? In Bay City or Lansing."

"Maybe," he said slowly. But half measures had never worked for him. He either left the clan or he didn't. Living an hour away was still gone because once he left, there would be nothing to bring him back. Nothing but memories that he already knew were going to be too painful to revisit for a long, damn time.

"So that's settled—"

"Look at the other probabilities," he said quietly. "We don't know the serum's side effects. We don't know if I can survive a month much less a lifetime."

"We all live with that."

Not like he did. This change was a ticking time bomb inside him. No way could he live like this without some part of him destroying itself. But he couldn't explain that certainty to her. He couldn't put words to the knowledge. So he said the one thing guaranteed to end all her hopes.

"I'm going to kill Elisabeth."

She actually ground her teeth together. He heard it loudly. "We're going to get her, Alan. She'll face justice. I promise you that."

Would that be enough for him? Seeing her in handcuffs? Going through the agony of trial so that she spent a lifetime behind bars? Would that satisfy the black hole in his gut that demanded vengeance?

It might. Except he knew the criminal justice system. He knew about prison overcrowding and the sympathy juries had for older women. Evil Einstein had been caught red handed, but thanks to a shifter-aware district attorney, he was now working for the Gladwins. The bastard's only punishment was an ankle monitor as he worked in a secret, shifter-backed lab. All in all, it was a good thing. The serums the dickhead developed could really help the ferals in the community. Which is why Alan hadn't put him as target number one on his hit list. That and he knew that Elisabeth was the one who'd pulled the strings. She had found and manipulated the crazy scientist. So Alan was focused on her, not her whacked-out flunky.

"Not enough," he said, his words dropping like a wall between them. "She's evil, Tonya. And I'm going to end her."

"You're not trained. Alan, you'll more likely die in the attempt."

He nodded. "Or succeed and go to jail." Because he wouldn't fight that. No point in committing the crime if he wasn't going to take responsibility for his choice.

"Do you even hear yourself?" There was an edge of fury in her voice. A shrill note that got stronger with every word. "Alan, think this through! Your life is different. It's not over."

She said more. She argued a dozen different angles, and he patiently listened to each one. But he didn't really hear them. He didn't truly consider any of them. And in the end, he had to tell her why. So when she finally sputtered into silence, he told her the raw truth.

"I can't live like this, Tonya. I won't."

She wanted to slap him. He saw her fingers twitch and her

hand raise. She was that furious with him, and he presented his face for her use. It was the least he could do when she was trying so hard to save his life. But he'd died the moment they'd slapped a chloroform rag over his mouth and thrown him into a van. He'd died the first time they'd shoved a needle up his arm and changed his biochemistry forever. And just because his body had come out of that cage, just because he had experienced moments of pure bliss with her, didn't change the fact that he was a monster intent on murdering Elisabeth. In defiance of his entire life's work as a lawyer. In complete disregard for the woman who stood before him radiating frustration. And in total disgust of who and what he'd become.

"I hate myself, Tonya," he said, his words filled with venom. "I hate the oils that stink when the fur sprouts. I hate the knobby joints and the need to rut like an animal. I hate the casual violence and the danger to everyone around me. It needs to end."

She stared at him. "You're talking about you, Alan. You were kidnapped and tortured. You've been changed against your will. What you're feeling is all normal, and it's all you."

Finally, she understood. Finally, she'd arrived at the understanding he'd hit before he left the hospital more than a week ago. He hated everything about who he was now, and he refused to live constantly at war within his own mind and body.

"I know," he said. Then, when she was going to fight him again, he pulled her tight. He tucked her into his arms as gently and as reverently as he'd wanted to from the very beginning. She resisted him at first, but he was determined, and in the end, she melted into him. He pulled her close, tucked her head against his chest, and pressed a kiss to her forehead. "I know it's all me. And I despise it."

"I won't let you do it," she said. "I won't."

He had no answer. The argument was moot since he wasn't likely to survive long enough to fight with her about it. So rather than reach for words, he went for action. He stroked her jaw and lifted her face to his. Then he kissed her. He pressed his mouth to hers and gently, slowly, sweetly seduced her into opening for him.

"Let me make love to you," he whispered between kisses.

She chuckled, the sound both funny and achingly defeated. "I think we've already done that."

"No, we haven't. Not like I been dreaming of since I was fourteen."

She pulled back enough to arch a brow at him. "That wasn't my fault. If there's something you want, buddy, then—"

Her words stopped on a squeak of surprise as he swept her feet out from under her. This, at least, was something he could thank his newfound strength for. Not only did he lift her up, but he tossed her slightly in his arms, just because he could. She grabbed on to his shoulders in alarm, but laughter spilled from her lips.

His steps hitched when he heard it. She was such a no-nonsense woman that he'd rarely heard her laugh. This was a low sound, like brass wind chimes on a lazy summer day. It was so delightful that he had to capture it with his mouth. So he held her over the bed and pressed his lips to hers.

She kissed him deeply. Wrapping her arms around his neck, she pulled herself higher in his arms then opened herself completely. He plundered her as thoroughly as he possibly could.

Eventually even his shifter strength gave out and he set her gently on the bed. She didn't let go of him, and so he went down with her, their mouths still playing. He took his time at this because, damn it, some things should be enjoyed completely, leisurely, and with a lot of joy.

He nipped at her lip, and she returned the favor. The kisses became sloppy because they were playing, teasing each other and smiling as they licked. Turns out her ears were unexpectedly sensitive, and he made her moan as he tugged on the right one. By the time he'd given attention to her left, she was shuddering as she pressed her breasts into his chest.

Thank God it took no time to strip off her tank top. That left no impediment to his hands, which enjoyed every boobalicious inch.

"You have the most glorious breasts," he said as he dropped low enough to give his full attention to them. "I've fantasized about these since I first noticed girls."

"You and every male this side of puberty," she growled. But then she curled her hand around his neck and into his hair, drawing him back to her nipples.

"But I'm the only one who gets to do this," he said as he sucked a dark berry into his mouth.

The appreciative rumble that went through her chest filled him with satisfaction, especially when she murmured his name. As if she were branding him on her body. That idea had his hips jerking in hunger.

God, he loved this woman. Always had, always would.

The thought filtered through his brain even as he worshipped her breasts and belly. She was the one who pushed him over before setting her tongue to his penis. He groaned in delight. Shifters had the best tongues and he fell backward in delirious pleasure. But pretty soon, he wanted more. Her hips were beside his shoulder, so it was an easy move to lift her over his head before burying his own tongue between her thighs.

And there was her happy rumble again. She made such perfect noises. And then she startled him. He never thought a couple could roll in sixty-nine, but she pulled him sideways and the abrupt shift had him chuckling. Except she wasn't done yet. The bed wasn't quite big enough for the rumble tumble she initiated, but they managed anyway. And then, she was sideways across the twin bed, her legs and head dangling off opposite sides. She clutched his shoulders, trying to stay upright, but he wasn't having any of it. Especially since her legs had fallen open and his hips had dropped right into her cradle.

Wet heat, giggles, and a thrust. The sensations and actions merged together in a seamless tapestry. He stroked inside her while she wrapped her legs around him. He nibbled on her neck while she tugged on his ear.

So good. Every part of this, so absolutely good.

When orgasm came, it was almost an afterthought. Every second of this had been bliss. Every kiss, every stroke, every contraction and release. She cried out when she came. He felt like every cell of his body shot into her. Fireworks. Oceans. Infinite space. All those words applied and none of them. Because it was seamless, beautiful love.

And when they finally collapsed together, when he pulled

them both straight on the bed so neither would fall off, he tucked her close, kissed her temple, and closed his eyes so that he could better remember the feel of her body, the scent of her skin, and the sweet warmth that she gave straight to his soul.

This, he thought. Just that word. *This.*

This moment, this feeling, this everything. He would cherish it for the rest of his very short life.

Chapter Sixteen

*B*liss.

Tonya stretched, luxuriating in the delicious feel of having Alan holding her, petting her arm, and pressing tiny kisses to her forehead. There were problems, she knew. Dark in her mind was his clear intention to commit suicide by vengeance. The man was a lawyer, for God's sake, not a vigilante. But she had faith in her ability to make him see reason. Especially after the amazing sex they'd just had. He'd asked to make love with her, and that's exactly what they'd done. Created, shared, and reveled in love.

No man gave up on something that good. And no woman, either. She just had to get his head out of his ass. And that was item number one on her to-do list.

She rolled over slowly, curling into his arms so that she could lick his neck. He chuckled and leaned in for a long, slow kiss. Which lasted about a half second before a thumping on the door jolted them both upright.

"Tonya! Alan! I'm coming in!"

Carl. Alan's brother and alpha to the Gladwin shifters. And just the person she really did not want to see right now.

"Don't you dare!" she bellowed right back. "This is an active crime scene!"

Alan pulled back with a frown. "What?"

She shrugged, her face heating. "I'm a cop. I get to declare crime scenes. It's part of the job description."

He snorted, then jumped out of bed heading for the bathroom, though he paused long enough to toss her clothes at her. Meanwhile, she could hear Carl futzing with the padlock on the door. She glanced at Alan, worried about his reaction to the sound. She knew he heard it by the way his shoulders stiffened. Then, even worse, his gaze cut to the iron ring in the floor. But he didn't say anything, and she didn't have any way to make it better, so they both pretended it never happened as they hastily dressed.

Then the door opened, but Carl didn't come down. Instead, he waited out of sight at the top of the stairs.

"How we doing down here?" he called

He knew exactly how they were doing because the idiot had a nose. "We're fine," she snapped, sarcasm dripping from every word. "How are you?"

She actually heard Carl swallow anxiously before he spoke. "I've got a change of clothes. For both of you. Mark's back at Gladwin PD working with them on…I don't know. Computer shit. Tracking the cat bitch."

Alan had been washing up in the sink, but he flipped off the water at that. "Any leads?"

"One. Maybe." He hesitated. "Can I come down now?"

"No," Alan answered before Tonya could say yes. "Toss the clothes down first."

A duffel bag landed with a heavy thud. Tonya grabbed it, unzipped it and pulled out an impressively complete set of clothes and toiletries. "No way did you pack this," Tonya said as she pulled out shorts and shirt for herself. Then she slid the bag across the floor to Alan.

Carl answered, still from the top of the stairs. "Becca did it. I was chasing a dead end in Detroit."

There were probably other reasons he'd been in Detroit, but Tonya didn't go there. They had plenty on their plates right here, right now.

Alan held pressed khaki pants next to his hips. Even Tonya could see that they wouldn't fit though they'd been his typical summer attire for years. His legs were longer now, his hips wider, and the crotch would likely be uncomfortably tight. He must have come to the same conclusion because he dropped them with a sneer. Instead, he grabbed a pair of dark blue Dockers with the tag still on it. Trust Becca to guess that he might need larger clothing. The woman had an eye for detail that Tonya admired.

Alan snapped off the tag with a quick jerk of his wrist, then pulled on the shorts. Tonya couldn't help but watch the flex of his body as he dressed. The man had muscles, that's for damn sure. The change had cut his body fat down to zero, and she was woman enough to admire the result.

Sadly, she couldn't stand there gawking. Not with her alpha grumbling under his breath at the top of the stairs. "I'll be two seconds in here," she said as she headed for the bathroom. She'd meant her words to be just for Alan, but shifter ears heard everything.

"Take as long as you need," Carl said. "We've got a town, not an exact address. Mark will text as soon as he knows something more."

Alan hauled her close enough to whisper into her ear. "Do you want a moment? A shower or something?"

Hot water and a couple of minutes to regroup? That sounded like heaven. "God, yes," she murmured. "But—"

Alan turned his head toward the stairs. "Go get us coffee," he ordered. "You know what we want."

"Jesus, Alan, I'm not your—"

"Not negotiating. Go."

That was harsh. Not the words, but the tone. Alan had always been polite, even when angry. He could make a "please" or "thank you" sound like the biggest middle finger, but he hadn't even attempted that here. Instead he'd snapped out his words and underpinned them with a growl.

Damn. It was sexy in a disturbingly different kind of way.

Carl must have heard it, too. She could almost feel him trying to suss out the situation from the top of the stairs. But in the end, he decided on prudence rather than a show of power. With alphas, especially ones as testosterone-filled as Carl, one never knew when temperament would overcome good sense. But Carl was a logical thinker, and so in the end, he made the correct choice and headed back out. After a parting shot, of course.

"I'm not getting any froufrou shit."

Good, because she didn't want any. It was Alan who usually preferred the gourmet stuff. But one glance at his face told her he didn't give a good goddamn what his brother did, just so long as the man left.

"Go on," Alan said as he nudged her into the bathroom. "The convenience store is just up the street. He'll be back quick."

She nodded and headed in, but she kept her eyes on Alan until he shut the door for her. He was acting strange. Certainly great sex tended to mellow a man, but Alan was being almost genial. Calm. Contained. Nothing alarming in word or deed. Given the roller coaster of emotions of the last twenty-four hours, that seemed too good to be true. Sadly, there was nothing she could do about it except worry. And take a really fast shower.

Would he even be here when she got out? The door was open now. There was nothing keeping him here. Hell, what if—

"I'm not leaving," he said through the door, obviously reading her mind. "Take your time."

Did she trust his answer? Yes. Did she still take the fastest damned shower in her life? Absolutely. So much for grabbing a few moments to regroup. She was so worried about what Alan might do in her absence, she rushed through everything. But at least she was clean, though even that gave her mixed emotions. She'd hated washing the scent of him off her skin. Without that lingering smell, it felt like the last twenty-four hours had been a dream.

She wondered if Alan felt the same way. Was his every other thought a reliving of their encounter, too? Did his heart squeeze in excitement because he hadn't used a condom? The odds were slim, but she might become pregnant. She'd known the moment he'd thrust inside her that they'd both forgotten protection. She hadn't had the breath to say anything at the time and, frankly, she hadn't cared. Right then, she'd wanted his child more than just about anything. So she'd gone with it, and now they would both have to live with the consequences.

She pulled on light jeans and a clean tank, stepping out of the bathroom even before she'd zipped up. The room was empty. Her breath nearly choked her as it froze in her throat. It took her two tries, but she finally managed a semblance of calm as she started climbing the stairs.

"Alan, so help me God—"

"Upstairs," he interrupted. And he was. Prowling around the main floor, poking his nose—literally—into every corner. He was using his shifter senses to learn what he could about the house.

Smart. She and Mark had done the exact same thing before settling in to wait for Alan.

"There's not much to learn," she said, pleased that her voice was steady though her heart was anything but. "Elisabeth and two shifters were here. All cougars, we think, but—"

"Altered," he said. "The kids. They're altered. Like me."

Well, at least he hadn't called them monsters. That was progress, she hoped.

"Yeah," she agreed.

"You and Mark find anything else?"

She shook her head, but he wasn't looking at her. "Nothing except for really a bad taste in cereal." She gestured to the kitchen cabinet. He opened it to find healthy high-fiber stuff that tasted like shit.

"Diarrhea is a side effect of the drugs," he said. His tone was flat and hard, and she shuddered at the image. To be trapped in a cage while that was going on? Nightmare. Especially for the usually debonair Alan. As if to prove his point, he popped open the refrigerator and saw a mostly finished bottle of Pepto-Bismol. There were also a rather impressive amount of vegetables and a half dozen eggs.

"Think we have time for an omelet?" he asked.

Her stomach growled in response, and he flashed her a smile.

"I'll take that as a yes." He pulled out the food and set it on the counter. A moment later, he'd found a frying pan and breakfast was begun. Tonya eased forward, leaning against the counter as she studied him, unease coiling in her chest.

"How are you feeling, Alan?"

He didn't even look up. "Fine. How about you?" He shot her a look as thorough as it was quick.

"I'm great," she said, though inside her instincts were starting to scream. The more normal Alan acted, the more she thought of a volcano. Just when and where would he erupt? "So no fever, no GI problems?" *No seething underbelly of violent intent?*

He looked up at her, his expression steady. "Wondering when I'm going to explode?"

She nodded. "You've had a turbulent few weeks." And wasn't that the understatement of the year?

He didn't disagree, but his eyes grew a little distant. As if he were looking inward rather than outward. But a moment later, he shrugged and turned back to making their breakfast. Er…late lunch. "I feel calm, Tonya. Like everything has settled into place." He took a deep breath. "No fever or seizures, either, so I think the Tasering did something good there. Shocked everything into working together."

That was good…maybe. Calm and settled was really good. Unless he meant the last final pieces before the suicide run. Which, given what he'd been saying before, made way more sense.

"We need to talk," she said as she settled on a stool. Though God only knew what she was going to say that she hadn't already. Except for, are you aware that I might become pregnant? That I've just done what I swore I'd never do? Risked becoming a mother with an unstable man?

He looked up at her, clearly about to give her a glib answer. But at her serious expression, his eyes narrowed and he straightened. The sight reassured her. When other people fobbed her off with a glib answer, he'd always taken her seriously. He'd always known when to pay attention, even if they ultimately didn't agree on whatever the topic. She smiled at him and thought that now maybe they could talk meaningfully and still keep their clothes on.

But just as she drew breath to speak, Carl stomped in, balancing three cups of coffee and a bag of Danishes. "Help me," the man called, "before we have a caffeine tragedy."

Alan shuttered his expression and turned back to the eggs. Tonya sighed and went to help her alpha. She might have had some choice words for the man about his terrible timing, but the smell of coffee hit her nostrils and all was lost amid the need to drink. She grabbed two of the cups, slurping from one and handing the other to Alan. He took it quickly, flashing his gratitude to her with his eyes before drinking his.

"You're welcome," Carl said, his tone grumbly. Tonya glanced at the man, her brows arched. The three of them had known each other all their lives. They'd lived in each other's houses, shared food, family, and childhood idiocies. Alan had been two years younger, but he'd kept up for the most part. He'd only pulled back when the natural separation happened. Shifters on one side, nonshifters on the other. The first went wild in the woods. The others went to college prep classes and science camp.

Even so, the three of them had always seemed like a unit. When Carl was grumbly, the others shouldered more of the minutiae of the clan. When Tonya was bitchy, they gave her space. And when Alan got sullen, they teased him and bought him spa shit or gourmet foods. It was their rhythm, or it had been. Because the new Alan refused to play that game. Instead of asking Carl what was going on, Alan shot him a glare.

"Didn't ask you here. Not going to thank you for interrupting."

Carl's eyes widened at the unusually cold tone. "I'm trying to help."

"So tell us the lead."

"Tell me how you're feeling first."

"Hungry." He scooped an omelet onto a paper plate, which he pushed at Tonya. Then he grabbed a Danish out of the bag before starting the next omelet.

"That's not what I meant," Carl said.

"Too fucking bad. What's the lead?"

Carl glared at him, not out of anger but frustration. Tonya could relate. They both wanted to help him, but weren't sure how. And Alan wasn't giving them any clues. Carl tried to wait him out, but it was a losing game. Had been since they were six and eight. Alan could out-patience a rock, and no shifter would ever outlast him in that department. Though, apparently, Carl wanted to try.

How did men ever get anything done around such monumental stubbornness?

"Just tell us the lead," Tonya said as she dug into the omelet.

Food. Sweet heaven, it was really good food, and Tonya had to stop herself from inhaling it like a starving child.

Carl turned to her, studying her with his serious dark eyes. "You okay?" he asked, his voice lower. Less disgruntled.

Alan looked up, and both men waited for her answer. She swallowed quickly, then nodded. "I'm fine. He's fine. We're all fucking fine. Now what the hell is the lead?"

Both men arched their brows in identical expression of surprise because one, they were brothers and two, no one was anything close to fine. But since nobody was talking, it was up to her to keep them on track. And that meant glaring at Carl until he spilled first.

"Fine," he said before taking a moment to drain his cup of coffee. "We think we've spotted her at a Walmart outside Grand Rapids. She had a boy with her and was buying school supplies."

Alan paused in the middle of flipping his omelet. "School supplies? For the kids?" His voice was tight with disbelief.

"Yeah. It was one of Tonya's spotters who called it in." He looked at her. "Left a message at the station."

Tonya immediately reached for her phone, which was downstairs. Damn it, she'd been so busy with…She shut off that thought rather than get distracted. She'd been so busy that she hadn't even checked her phone. She pushed off the stool to get it, but before she'd done more than stand up, Alan slid it over to her.

At her surprised look, he shrugged. "I haven't invaded your privacy. Don't know the code."

"Yeah you do." It was his birthday. Because…well, because some dates stuck in her head. His fourteenth birthday was one of them.

He shrugged. "Okay, maybe I do, but I didn't check."

She wanted to ask him why not. She wanted to know if he'd just hadn't gotten a chance to look or if the old Alan—the one who was considerate and law abiding—was coming back to the fore. But no way to easily express that, so she swallowed it down and thumbed on her phone. A moment later, she was listening to a message from Samantha, a shifter-friendly mom of three who lived in Grand Rapids. The woman said exactly what Carl had already relayed. A cougar-shifter buying school supplies. That was it. Then she took another five minutes to scroll through all her emails. None of it helped.

Meanwhile, Carl kept talking. "Mark got access to the security tapes. It looks like her."

"But you don't know where in GR she's staying," Tonya asked as she set her phone down.

"Not yet."

"So sniff her out," Alan said, his voice calm.

"We're talking a major city, not some backwoods town. Even our noses can't pick up her scent when she's in a car among thousands of other cars."

Alan took his time, dropping his food onto another plate before setting the pan in the sink to soak. "She's not in a car."

Carl frowned. "How the fuck do you know that?"

Alan gestured with his fork toward the garage. "Go in there. See if you can smell a car."

Carl started to turn, but Tonya held him back. She and Mark had gone through there as well and the whole place had smelled of hot summer dust. "Alan's right. No car. Hasn't been one in there for months."

"Then how the hell did she get from here to Grand Rapids so fast?"

"Greyhound?"

"No," Tonya said, finally putting it together. "She's got a friend who drove her." They both turned to look at her, their expressions once again identical.

"Who?"

"Think. She's on the run with two cougar kids, but she stops in a major city and starts buying school supplies."

Alan leaned forward. "She plans to settle down. Raise them."

"She's been trying to repopulate the cougars after the wolf–cat war. That's been her whole goal from the beginning, hasn't it? That's why she brought in her relatives from Arizona."

Carl took up the thread and kept going. "But they're dead now. Worse, she can't experiment anymore because we've got Einstein and all his serums."

Tonya nodded. "So what's her only choice?"

Alan released a low grumble. "Activate whatever kids she's got and raise them. Pick a metropolitan area like GR and just be quiet. Who will notice her?"

Tonya tapped her phone. "My spotters will." She had a network throughout Michigan of shifters or shifter-friendlies. She'd alerted them months ago about Evil Einstein and the Crazy Cat Lady. And once they'd gotten the bitch's real name—Elisabeth Oltheten—she'd had pictures and everything. "Plus, she only had one kid with her at the Walmart, right?"

Carl nodded. "The boy."

"So where's the girl? Someone has to be watching her."

"Unless she's dead," Alan said, his voice flat.

Carl shook his head. "She was buying school supplies for two."

Tonya looked around the kitchen, remembering the food here. "She's trying to settle down. Healthy vegetables in the refrigerator, nutritious cereal—"

"Chains in the basement," Alan added.

Tonya blanched, unable to respond for the momentary flash of what was down there and what she'd done to Alan. But Carl didn't know, and so he kept thinking out loud.

"So the kids are fighting her."

"Of course they are," snapped Alan.

"Which means she's definitely got someone with her. Someone—"

"Johnny." Alan's voice was tight with emotion. And when she and Carl looked at him, he closed his eyes in frustration. "Why the hell didn't I realize that earlier?"

Because he'd been drugged, chained, and then...And then other things had happened. She reached out to touch him, hoping to connect in some way, but he slammed his fork down and turned away in disgust. "He's the one who told us to come here. He has to be the one who told her to skip, too."

Tonya nodded. "We checked Johnny. That's part of what Mark's been doing all day—combing through his phone records and the like, but we haven't found anything yet." She looked to Carl for confirmation and the man nodded.

Alan glared at her. "That's because I wasn't the one to question him."

Carl shook his head. "You can't question him. He's in jail. Picked up late last night in a bar fight and has been sleeping it off ever since."

Tonya arched a brow at him. "And you were holding this information back why?"

Her alpha snorted. "It's not a lead yet. Mark hasn't found anything and—"

"Where is he?" Alan interrupted.

"In jail," Carl stressed. "You can't just barge in there and beat the crap out the guy. That's not the way to get a man to tell you where the bitch is. If it was, you'd have found her by now."

"I got it," Tonya said as she stood up. When the other two

moved, she pinned them both with a glare. "Look, boys, I'm the only one here trained in interrogation techniques. I'm the only one with a badge and as much as amateur hour has been fun, can you please—for the love of God—let me deal with this?"

Neither man answered at first. Carl's jaw clenched, but she already knew he wasn't the problem. The man had learned to delegate years ago, though he still struggled with the concept. It was in an alpha's nature to take charge, but when he didn't say anything, Tonya knew he'd back off. Not Alan, who stared at her without flinching. Who folded his arms across his chest and finally drawled his response.

"So much for working together."

"So come with me," she said. "Just don't expect to go at Johnny like a battering ram."

"Or come home," Carl said. "Becca will make lasagna and another cake, and we'll talk. Or not."

Alan addressed Carl first, his voice low but no less powerful. "I'm not coming home. Ever."

His brother huffed out a breath. "It's your home—"

"Remember Mrs. Morales from down the street?" Alan interrupted.

Carl frowned. "The old lady who always smelled like sour cream? The one who hated us?"

Alan snorted. "She hated *you*. She liked me. She paid me to weed her yard, and we used to talk legal ethics while she fed me chocolate chip cookies."

Carl blinked, waiting for the rest. "Yeah, so?"

"Yeah, nothing. I was just thinking about her."

The two brothers stared at one another while Tonya rolled her eyes. Lord, spare her from man-speak. "He's telling you that you have different lives."

"I know that," Carl snapped, but Tonya rolled right over him.

"Did I ever tell you that I had boyfriend in college who was an art student? I let him paint me. Like really paint on my skin."

Alan was about to say something as well, but at her words anything he was going to say was choked off. Carl blinked as well, and then one of them managed a garbled, "Wha—?"

"And that's it for the *completely irrelevant* part of the discussion, boys. I'm heading out to talk to Johnny. Alan, what are you going to do? With him, with me, or are you walking somewhere?"

"You're letting me go? Just like that."

She hated the idea that he might just walk away now and she'd never see him again. Her belly clenched and her palms sweat, but she had to show him he was free. Within the confines of the law, of course. "You planning to steal any motorcycles or rearrange Johnny's face?"

"Not today."

"Then you're free." She turned to Carl. "Go home. You've got shit to do there."

"So do you," Carl retorted.

She sighed. "I know. I'm the world's crappiest beta."

"You haven't been around enough to be the crappiest."

"Well, either give me a few more days or appoint someone else. You know—" Her words cut off when he held up her hand.

"I trust you with this, Tonya." His gaze settled heavily on Alan. "I trust you with my brother, so take all the time you need."

She exhaled in relief. One crisis averted.

"I'll come with you," Alan said to her, his tone excruciatingly neutral.

"Great," she said as she pushed away from the counter. "Let's—"

"One more thing," Carl said as he pulled a pencil-length hard case out of his back pocket. She'd seen it there, had even guessed at its contents, but hadn't wanted to think about it. Carl wasn't giving her the choice as he set it quietly on the counter and popped it open. A filled hypodermic needle flashed in the sunlight. "It's the only dose we've got for now. We're working on more, but it's a complicated process."

Alan's eyes narrowed. "What is it?"

"The shifter suppressant. Worked great on Mark. Knocked back his bear for almost a day."

Alan leaned forward and picked up the syringe. Inside was an innocuous-looking liquid the color of light beer. "Great. Thanks." Then he crossed to the sink and squirted the thing straight down the drain before smashing the needle in half.

Carl jerked forward, his voice sharp. "Wait!" Then he rolled back onto his heels. "You could have just said no," he growled.

"Could I?" Alan challenged, clearly not believing it. Then he did the one thing he'd always done to piss off his brother. He turned away as if the alpha meant absolutely nothing. "How long for you to get ready?" he asked her.

"Alan!" Carl snapped, his voice coming out like a drill sergeant's.

Tonya stepped bodily in front of her alpha, blocking him from doing anything stupid. "Quit being a dick, Carl."

"Me!" he exploded. "He's the one—"

"Let him go," she hissed. "He's doing this so you let him go. So you quit feeling like you're responsible for him."

"He's my brother!"

"And you love him. But let him make his own damn choices."

"Even if he's got his head up his ass?"

"Even if." She pressed on Carl's chest, trying to push him back. He didn't move an iota, but at least he didn't barrel forward. "You said you trusted me with him."

Carl exhaled loudly. "I do."

"So go home. I'll keep you up to date."

The man clearly didn't want to. He wanted to use his force of personality—or his body—to muscle things into his version how things ought to be. But no way was Alan going to allow that to happen. After what Elisabeth had done to him, she doubted Alan would listen to anyone right now. He had to reestablish his independence, even if that meant finding creative ways to tell his own brother to fuck off. And if Carl kept pushing, Alan would create a breach between them that could never be repaired. Why the hell couldn't Carl see that?

Men!

Eventually Carl gave in. He stepped back with a frustrated huff. "Okay," he said. "I'll go home." Then he looked at his brother, his heart in his eyes. "If you need anything, just call. Day or night. I'll do whatever—"

"I know," Alan said, and there was warmth in his tone but also a huge well of sadness. "I know."

Carl waited a moment longer, his gaze locked with his brother's. It was a communion of sorts, one that seemed to ease the tension between them, so she did nothing to interrupt it. And then Carl gave her a quick nod and left.

Tonya exhaled, ticking off *Stop Carl from ruining his relationship with his brother* on her mental to-do list. Which brought her front and center with the next item: *Tell Alan to quit being a dick, too.* And oh goody, she now had a couple of hours in the car to do just that. Assuming one of them didn't go monster or grizzly and crash their asses along the way.

Chapter Seventeen

Alan's thoughts were murky at best. He blamed it on the monster. He'd always been clearheaded before, right?

Wrong.

Tonya had always stirred up the muck from the bottom of his brain. It wasn't just that she challenged him intellectually. From the moment she'd become a cop and he a lawyer, they'd argued different sides of the law just for fun. Usually after a few beers, but sometimes not. But she also stirred up feelings that were all the more confusing now that he'd been changed. Love, hate, want, rejection—it was all churning inside him in a confusing mass. He wanted her, but he had to push her away. A relationship with a *wrong* shifter was just too psycho to contemplate. He loved the way she made him feel but hated it, too, because it tempted him to think that he was normal. That he could function when the truth was he couldn't even imagine a life after Elisabeth was dead. How did he walk into a courtroom when any moment he could turn into a stinking, hairy beast? How did he go to the grocery store or pick up the mail when he might run into a shifter who scented him for the *wrong* thing he was?

He couldn't. Jesus, it freaked him out that he'd made love to her. How had she allowed him to be inside her? He was repulsive! And yet no part of him regretted that. In fact, his little brain was all about doing it again as soon as possible.

He just had to focus on his task. Get rid of Elisabeth. Save those kids. End the bitch so that this nightmare never spread to anyone else.

"You want to keep brooding or do we talk now?" Tonya's voice jerked him out of the black soup of his brain enough for him to stare at her. She was driving her patrol car, her long fingers tense on the steering wheel.

"I don't brood," he said, the words a reflex.

"Are you kidding?" she snorted. "Between you and Carl, it's your family crest."

"That doesn't make sense," he retorted. "You sure you went to college? Or did you just spend all your class time getting painted by art students."

She shot him an arch look. "It was a *student*, singular. And I was wondering if we'd wander over to that."

He came back with a lascivious look. "If I'd known you were into paint-fume highs, I would have bought out the hardware store years ago."

She turned back to the road, her expression blasé. "You wish."

He did, actually. A lot. Just like he enjoyed the banter between them. They'd been doing this horny guy–standoffish girl thing for a couple of years now. He wasn't even sure how it started, but it was familiar now and grounded him firmly in territory labeled "before." Of course that was dangerous ground to walk, so his lips had barely finished curving into a leer before the humor faded again.

He really needed to commit to feeling one way or another. This back-and-forth shit was messing with his brain.

"And there you go," she mocked, "right back to brooding."

She was so right and that made him cranky. "What do you want from me, Tonya?"

"So many things," she said, her voice unusually wistful. "But for the moment, I'm going to settle for a serious conversation. What are your plans, Alan? After I arrest Elisabeth?"

And wasn't that exactly what had set him to brooding in the first place? That he had no plans at all? "Let's cross that bridge when we get there."

She shook her head. "And to think I used to wish you could go more with the moment at hand."

"What?"

"Your brother thinks things to death, looking at military and political strategies until I want to shoot him. And you're always a half step behind him with a dozen legal arguments."

"Good thing, too," he retorted, "because you're the one who usually wants to go in with guns blazing. Where's Miss Action now?"

"Trying to keep you from committing suicide by cougar bitch." She turned to look at him, her light blue eyes almost transparent from the sheen of wetness there. "Alan, talk to me. I'm kinked up eighteen ways from Sunday, and you're all about saying good-bye to your brother like you'll never see him again."

He jolted, horrified as much by her tears as by her words. Damn it, he needed to focus, but like always, she was stirring up things that he'd rather kept quiet.

"Start at the beginning," he said.

"Fine," she huffed out. "Your whole story to Carl about Mrs. What's-Her-Face."

"Mrs. Morales."

"Right. Her. You think I didn't understand that story? You were pointing out how different you and Carl are."

"Yeah. We are."

"That you make your own choices."

"We do."

"And that sometimes you got the bigger stick, sometimes he did."

"Yes! What of it?"

She huffed out a breath. "You were absolving him of guilt about your death."

He frowned. "That's a stretch."

"Is it? Tell me I'm wrong."

He stared at her, feeling acutely uncomfortable. Self-reflection wasn't something prized in the shifter community, mostly because grizzlies never thought deeply about much of anything. Among the Gladwin grizzlies, Alan was known as a supersmart man because he'd gotten a law degree, but that had nothing to do with self-awareness. It was his own inclination that had gotten him to a comfortable level of self-knowledge. Until a month ago, he knew himself as a good lawyer who had a thing for the woman who'd wanted his brother. Now that was all turned around, and he couldn't find his footing.

Meanwhile, Tonya took his silence as agreement. "For a smart man, you sure can be a fucking moron."

"For a smart woman, you sure have lousy instincts on when to push a man."

"Bullshit. Seems to me we're in this problem because I've been too easy on you."

Easy? There was nothing in this situation that was easy in any way, shape, or form. But he knew her well enough to let her have her say. So he leaned back, folded his arms, and prepared to tune out an earful.

"You don't say," he drawled, just to prod her into talking. Best to get it over with quickly.

"You've been hurt bad. Not just the torture and stuff, but even before. Losing the beta position and all."

"We already talked about that. Best thing for everyone."

She nodded. "Maybe. Eventually. But that doesn't mean you weren't hurt by it. That I didn't feel like a shit for taking that from you."

"Best. Thing—"

"Whatever. So with everything, I've been trying to give you space."

He snorted. "You chased me down, shot me with tranquilizer and suppressant, then—"

"I was trying to keep you from hurting yourself or anyone else." She shot him a glare. "I should have just told you to get your head out of your ass."

He wanted to be annoyed with her. She was absolutely talking bullshit, but it was familiar bullshit. Tonya was a straight shooter. If she thought you were being a dickhead, she said it. Usually in colorful language. That's what she was doing now, and it was yet another return to the landscape of before.

"While you were telling your brother all about Mrs. Bakes Cookies—"

"Morales."

"Do you know what I was thinking about?"

He couldn't begin to guess.

"How you used to wear Axe body spray. To the point that our eyes would water."

"That was once. I spilled the bottle."

"That was your entire freshman year of high school. And that your hair was always just so. That you gave yourself manicures."

Now he did scoff. Loudly. "Never."

"Neatly groomed nails, Alan. Always."

Well, that was true though it was a far cry from a manicure. "Nothing wrong with clean hands and nails."

"Nope. I always liked that about you. And that you wore tailored clothes instead of baggy jeans and hoodies five sizes too large."

That was because he wasn't a shifter. Every Gladwin teen in the know about shifters wore baggy clothes. Nobody wanted to change into a bear in skintight clothes. They'd all heard stories about a first shift in jeans that refused to tear when the sudden bulk occurred. For boys especially that was a nightmare.

But by the time he was fourteen, he'd known it wasn't in the cards for him. He'd still held out hope for a while, but in the end, he'd embraced the lack of hairiness. The ability to speak his mind rather than growl. And that left him free to wear clothes that showed off his swimmer's body without the fear of an accidental castration from an unexpected shift.

"Your whole life, you've dressed and acted classy. You spoke clearly. You kept your life organized. Hell, even your sock drawer is tidy."

"You have no idea what my sock drawer is like."

She rolled her eyes. "I extrapolated. Am I right?"

Yes. Not that he was going to admit that.

"Exactly." Again, she took his silence as agreement. "So then suddenly you're abducted. They shove shit into your veins and, bam, you're a shifter."

"I'm not a real shifter," he stressed. He was a laboratory experiment gone ugly. Like in *The Fly*.

"Of course you are. You walk around human looking, then when you want, you shift into something different."

"It's not just when I want," he snapped. It happened whether he wanted it or not.

"Welcome to shifter puberty." She turned and pinned him with her own hard stare. "Get your head out of your ass and figure it out. Like all the rest of us did."

Jesus, she did not just say that to him. "It's not the same! I don't change into a bear or a cougar. Or even a fucking dog. I'm…" His throat closed up and it was hard to repress a shudder of revulsion. He became a stinking hairy monster that wasn't man or beast but some hideous combination of the two.

"You hate it."

"Yes!"

"Get over it."

Nausea rolled through his body. He wanted to scream at her. Hell, part of him wanted to slam her mouth shut. And for damn sure his BO started clogging up the car. And right here was why he couldn't just fucking *get over it*. And all the while, she kept talking, her voice as bracing as it was uncompromising.

"Go ahead and scream. If you want, we can pull over and you can try to beat the shit out of me."

"I don't want to beat you!" he bellowed.

"Bullshit!" she countered as she angled the cruiser into a rest stop. "Every single one of us had to deal with our violent side. The tear-apart-whatever-the-fuck-is-pissing-us-off side. Every one of us except you."

"Because I'm not an animal!"

She slammed the car into park and turned to him, her eyes shimmering even as her tone flattened to cold. "You are now. And you hate it."

"You're fucking right I do!"

She nodded, then leaned across him and shoved open the door. The sudden press of her body made him want to slam her straight into the dash. The other part of him want to drag her sweet-smelling flesh right up to his face so he could lick every inch. Fortunately, he didn't have time to do either one because she was shifter fast.

"Get out."

He wanted to tell her to fuck off, but that would mean he'd

have to sit still in her car when he wanted to tear into something. So he popped the seatbelt and stomped his way toward the picnic benches. It was a good thing that they were in a mostly deserted rest stop. A car was just pulling out and a single truck was parked far down the lot. That meant nobody was going to interrupt their screaming argument. And since they were outside, the BO could be mistaken for a pissed-off skunk.

It was late afternoon, the heat hanging in the air. His skin already slicked with sweat. That was annoying enough until he realized that it wasn't sweat but the oils that preceded the fur. He was shifting, and he hated it. So he clamped down on his emotions. He went to the picnic bench and gripped the weathered wood hard enough to leave dents. And he just stood there breathing hard while Tonya locked up the car and sauntered over to him.

"See?" she said. "You can keep it under control."

"I could also kill you where you fucking stand."

She rolled her eyes. "You could try."

They'd had this argument already. He was tired of it. She was a badass. He was a monster. Goddamn it, didn't she get it? He was a real-life, honest-to-God *monster*.

Then he frowned, abruptly tired of his own thoughts. Even in the privacy of his own brain, he was really sick of the M word. And screaming it at himself or her didn't change that. And while he struggled with that, she settled onto the top of the picnic bench right in front of him and casually kicked her feet back and forth as she turned her face to the sun. God, how could she be so damned calm when he was screaming inside? He shut his eyes rather than look at her. But even with his eyes shut, he remembered how the sun made her skin golden and that there were so many different colors in her hair. Not just blond, but light brown and a reddish white.

But as he sealed himself in blackness behind his eyelids, she started speaking. Worse, he felt her stroke her hand across his jaw while the other casually touched his oily forearm.

"You keep calling yourself a monster, but damn it, Alan. I like it."

"You're sick."

She chuckled. "Maybe. Ever wonder why we never got together before your change?"

"Because you have a thing for—" He choked off his words. He couldn't say "monster" again. It was getting repetitive.

"Because you were too prissy for me."

"Bullshit." He glared at her.

She shrugged. "Maybe 'prissy' isn't the right word. Too classy, maybe. You always have it together when I'm constantly stopping myself from putting a bullet between some dick's eyes. Being next to all that perfection is intimidating. Especially since I'm half grizzly. Who would want that in a woman when you could have a hairless runway model?"

"I did."

She studied his face. "Remember that girl you brought home for Christmas your sophomore year in college? What was her name? Brittney? Whitney?"

"Eleanor."

"Oh. Well, she was tall and blond with boobs so perky they

almost strangled her. Not a hair on her forearms, and, worse, she was some ancient philosophy savant. Already working on her PhD. Jesus, I wanted to claw her eyes out."

He stared at her, unbelieving. "She was a pale copy of you, you idiot."

"And then there were all the law school babes. The Chinese girl with so little hair she had to pencil in eyebrows. And the brunette who spouted law like diarrhea of the mouth."

He laughed, though the sound was strangled. How could she get it so wrong? "I was trying to make you jealous. All you did was congratulate me on the good catches."

She rolled her eyes. "They were good catches. Way better than me."

He shook his head. "Not a one of them understood the law like you do. None of them came close to your badassery. And let's be honest, none of their boobs could hold a candle to yours."

She groaned. "Why is every man fascinated by my boobs?"

"Duh. Because they're great boobs." He shifted until he stood right in front of her. Then he let his hands stroke down her thighs. "Besides, I'm really more of a leg man, but you shine in that department, too."

She stretched out her leg, obviously enjoying the way he stroked down its length. That was another thing he loved about her. Not a coy bone in her body.

"So there you go, Alan. I like the new you because it doesn't intimidate me."

"I've wanted you since I was twelve, well before my birthday kiss. How the fuck could I intimidate you?"

She shrugged. "Exactly because you've wanted me so long. How could the real me compete with your idea of me?"

He sighed as he dropped his forehead to hers. "The real you blows my mind. Every single time."

She stroked his jaw then angled her mouth to meet his. "So there you go," she said as she pressed her lips to his. "We're perfect for each other."

He didn't answer. He wasn't sure he could. The lust was pounding in him so strongly that he wasn't sure he could form words.

And right there was the problem. A man could form words. A monster could not.

Or a beast.

He drew back from her, self-awareness forcing itself into his consciousness. "I hate being uncontrolled. It makes me feel like an animal."

She nodded. "And you hate being an animal."

"It's smelly and filthy. It's a bull in a china shop—"

"Or a bear squatting in the woods."

He swallowed. He didn't want to say what he was thinking. What he was feeling.

"You've always thought of yourself as a little better than us shifters, haven't you, Alan? You were civilized, we were animals. You make love with precision, we grunt and heave—"

"And destroy bedrooms." He hadn't wanted to bring up how she and Carl had once shifted in her bedroom and nearly tore down the house.

She turned her face away at that, but that didn't stop her words. "You think of me as an animal, and it disgusts you."

"No!" He touched her face, forcibly bringing it back to him. "I've wanted you since I was twelve. I think we both know that."

"But did you want to?" She frowned, struggling with her words. "Didn't you think it was a weird aberration or something? You didn't want to want me, did you?"

"Because you were hung up on my brother."

She shook her head. "I was hung up on being Maxima."

"Either way."

She sighed and pulled his hands away from her face. Then she pressed her lips to his hands, gently kissing them. "Here's the question, Alan: Can you find a way to love the animal? To see that it's part of you? Because it's part of me, and I like it." She suddenly looked up at him, her eyes large and so intense it stole his breath. "I love it."

He heard the unspoken question. Felt it vibrate from her body into his. She was asking if he could love her. The answer was obvious. Of course he could love her. He did love her. Except…

"You can't love me, Alan, if you don't love the animal. The one in you, and the one in me."

Chapter Eighteen

Tonya held Alan's gaze while inside every part of her tightened to an agonizing pinprick. Despite her badass reputation, Tonya didn't take many big risks. She calculated the odds, weighted the possibilities, and then went with her gut, which had rarely steered her wrong. The one notable exception being when she'd pursued Carl instead of Alan. Dumb-shit thinking is what that had been.

And this right here was mega dumb-shit thinking.

It was too soon to push Alan. The man was still in so much pain it made her ache to even look at him. He was a civilized man who had abruptly been shoved into kidnapping, torture, and now a body alien to himself and everyone else. So what did she do? She forced him to look at his beast and gave him an ultimatum. Accept it or lose her forever.

Dumb-shit thinking because, honestly, she belonged to him no matter what he did. Grizzlies mated for life, and, apparently, her bear had picked him. For life. Because that was her kind of luck.

Meanwhile, Alan's expression went through a dozen different emotions. She saw fury and confusion, but also tenderness and fear. A lot of fear. In the end, he took her hand. Calluses caressed her palm and his jagged fingernails scraped her skin in a pleasing kind of way.

"I've never had a problem with your bear," he finally said. "She's part of you and she's wonderful."

"Uh-huh." She did her best not to give anything away with that, but he knew her too well. He knew that part of her was calling him a fucking liar, so he released an annoyed snort.

"Okay. Maybe I really liked not ripping through my clothes or randomly getting hairy."

"Maybe?" she taunted.

"Definitely."

"Can you even imagine a time when you'd appreciate it?"

He shrugged. "Not that part."

She sighed. "Didn't you read *The Hulk* as a kid? That part where he bursts through his clothes and kicks ass is pretty cool." Personally she'd enjoyed him more than She-Hulk, but they both worked for her.

"You're asking me to take a comic book as a role model." His expression was droll in the most posh way possible. And it was exactly a before-the-change Alan look. Which meant he was finding his way back to himself, or so she hoped.

So she leaned back into a fading sunbeam and gave him a teasing look. "Afraid you can't pull off the big and green look?"

He leaned into her, crowding her personal space in the best possible way. "Would that turn you on?"

Everything about him turned her on, but she wasn't going to admit that. "You'll just have to try it and see."

He held there, close to her face, and she narrowed the distance even further. He had to know he didn't frighten or disgust her. But as their breaths mingled, the heat curling around her mouth in a delicious way, she realized that what she thought didn't really matter. It was what he thought about himself.

"Alan, try to imagine something good about you now. Use that big ol' brain and think of an advantage. I'll even start you out. You're stronger, faster—"

"I stink and frighten anyone with a nose."

"You can shift more often than the rest of us. I'm stuck with every other day at best."

"My joints ache all the time, and I notice shit that I really don't want to see."

She hadn't known about the pain. "Young shifters get that a lot. It eases after a while. And if you don't like what you see, look somewhere else. There's plenty of pretty stuff in the world."

He closed his eyes and let his forehead drop to hers. "It just isn't who I am, Tonya."

She touched his jaw, feeling the hard angle and the scrape of his five-o'clock shadow. She smiled at that. She liked his stubble. Before his change, he'd had a bit of a baby face.

"It's who you are now, Alan. And I like you a lot."

She kissed him then, gentle and tender. He responded in the

same way, but it wasn't the commitment she wanted. It didn't have the passion she craved. He was holding himself back from her and that really pissed her off. Patience had never been her strong suit.

In the end, she pulled back, fighting the frustration inside her.

"Tonya—"

"We need to get to the police station. They might have let Johnny go by now."

That snapped him to attention. His eyes narrowed and he cupped her elbow as she jumped off the picnic table. "I'll drive."

"Bull—"

"You're tired and cranky. It's been a rough few days for you. Let me drive."

It had been a rough few months for her, but it had been a hundred times worse for him. Still, she appreciated the consideration. Even more, she realized he was right. She was tired on a bone-deep level and it would be nice to rest while someone else took the lead. "I'm still a badass," she grumbled as she passed him the keys.

"Never thought anything different."

But the moment she climbed into her car, her phone rang. The news was short and frustrating. Johnny had been bailed out by his wife and was in the wind, probably getting wasted at the nearest bar. She knew Alan would want to burn rubber to find him, but she needed to delay that. As important as it was to find Elisabeth, Alan was still her top priority. And that meant slowing the man down so he had time to adjust to his new body. And that gave her an idea.

She thumbed her phone off and turned to him. "Johnny's out on bail. Our best chance to catch him is in the morning when he's half awake."

"Not a chan—"

"So we're going out to dinner tonight because I have *needs*."

That got his attention.

"You have *needs*," he drawled in his bedroom voice. The one that made her toes curl even if part of him was mocking her.

"I do. Real food in a real restaurant." She lifted her chin. "Like on a date. Saginaw isn't far, and there's a great Italian restaurant I know. Homemade pasta, locally grown vegetables, and the owner really does serenade each table."

"You *need* homemade lasagna?"

"It's your brother who loves lasagna. I want—"

"Mushroom ravioli," he said, proving that he did know what she liked.

"And a serenade. He's got a great voice."

Alan frowned at her, obviously figuring out that she was stalling. But would he go for it anyway? "Work with me, Alan," she pleaded. She arched her brows. "I promise to make it worth your while."

His eyes shifted to blazing in an instant, but he held it back. In the end, he nodded. "Fine. Ravioli and serenades. But then we're going to work on some of my *needs*."

She felt her body heat as he turned the ignition. When all else fails, appeal to a man's basest desires: food and sex.

* * *

Dinner was amazing. Alan even seemed to enjoy the serenading or maybe it was the expensive bottle of wine. Or maybe it was the company. Tonya certainly hoped so because she had a great time. They'd always been able to talk to each other. They could argue the finer points of police brutality or discuss cheese with equal passion. And with the promise of sex tonight, the dinner held an extra edge. An excitement that showed in the banked hunger in his eyes or the slow way she licked the tiramisu off her fork.

He didn't let her pay, and she didn't let him drive since he'd consumed most of the wine. Her shifter metabolism kept her sober even when she wanted to be tipsy. She had no idea what his metabolism did except allow him to eat three times more than usual. Even he commented on it as they wandered out to the car.

"I should feel stuffed."

"You don't?" She was practically waddling.

"I do. But…" He looked at his hands, stretching them wide in the moonlight. "I think I needed that."

"Shifting burns a lot of calories." She touched his face, bringing it around for a kiss. "You still have that lean, hungry look."

"Like a starving wolf?" he taunted.

"Like a man who has *needs*." It was an invitation and he took it, pushing her against the car as he owned her mouth. She'd parked in the back corner of the lot under the shadows of a couple of old oaks. Plenty of darkness for what she had in mind.

So she sank into his kiss, feeling the burn in her blood as he thrust into her mouth. She loved the lean strength of him and the hot press of his cock against her pelvis. And when he lifted his head just for a moment, she pulled off her shirt.

He drew back, startled, his gaze automatically sweeping the parking lot. No one was around. She'd kept them late at dinner on purpose. Even so, there was a tiny thrill in her belly at the thought that they were exposed. That someone might see them.

"I never pegged you for an exhibitionist," he drawled.

She wasn't. Not really. "I told you," she said slowly. "I have a need."

He frowned. "To fuck in public?"

She shook her head and popped her bra. His eyes went straight down as her breasts bounced free.

"Tonya?"

"Ever run as your animal, Alan? Ever played in the moonlight with a grizzly?"

His expression tightened down. "You know I haven't."

True. It was too dangerous for a normal person to rumble tumble with a bear. Even if the bear was a shifter who tried to be careful. But he wasn't normal anymore. She pointed behind her at the trees. "That's Shiawassee National Wildlife Refuge back there. The river is fabulous this time of year."

His eyes narrowed. "I knew you didn't like being serenaded."

She chuckled. "Not really, though he does have a nice voice."

"Tonya—" he began, but she tugged at his shirt.

"Let's try it now. Shift."

His expression locked down and his body tightened with anger. "No."

"Why not? Afraid I'll hurt you?" She could remember a dozen times as a teenager that he'd claimed he could go toe-to-toe with any of them as a grizzly. It had been pure bravado, but she used it now to get what she wanted. "Afraid you can't keep up?"

"You wish."

"So prove it." She stripped out of her pants then tossed everything inside the trunk of the cruiser. The only thing she kept out were the car keys, which were strapped to her arm on an elastic coil large enough to fit her grizzly body. Then she stood there, stark naked with her eyebrows raised. Could she taunt him into joining her? Tempt him? At the moment he was just staring at her naked body. God, it was good to be wanted like that. To induce lust that tented his shorts and made his hands reach for her.

"Catch me," she said with a laugh. Then she shifted and ran.

Chapter Nineteen

God, he hated her. With a fury that startled him for its boiling intensity. She just wouldn't freaking let up. *Love the animal. Imagine the good things.* Blah, blah, blah. Did she think he hadn't tried? That part of him hadn't been searching for a way to make peace with his monster?

Goddamn it, she was getting away. Her grizzly was a golden brown she-bear with liquid eyes and a pert behind. A freaking pert behind. *On a bear!* But it was cute and it wiggled in a completely feminine way as she pranced about in her animal form. Apparently even grizzlies could prance.

He wanted to bellow at her. He for damn sure was growling deep in his throat. But damn it, he *wanted* to run with her. He'd been wanting to run with the bears since his first Gladwin clan picnic. He'd sat with his mother while they watched man and woman strip naked and leap into their grizzly bodies. Like the most amazing magic. Pink flesh shifted to brown or black. Faces lengthened, and the roar that echoed through the forest was the most joyous thing he'd ever heard. Laughter inside a roar. Even he'd felt the happiness inside the normally terrifying sound. And he'd been excluded.

Until now.

So why was he fighting this? Why wasn't he already with her, running amok in a national park?

Because he wasn't going to be a full bear. He was going to be a half-shifted bizarre thing, and he didn't want her to see it. Except that was stupid. She'd already seen him shifted. Hell, they'd already fought. Which meant, why not? Why wasn't he grabbing what joy he could when he could?

He toed off his shoes and stripped off his shirt, tossing both inside the open trunk. Did he go full commando? Put some new life into all those Big Foot legends?

Again, why not?

"Fine," he bellowed as he shoved down his shorts. "But if I catch you, I'm not going to be gentle."

He stopped long enough to slam down the car's trunk, and then he took off, shifting fully before he left the parking lot.

Sensations abruptly became clearer as his thoughts skittered away. No more complex sentences. No more thinking and re-thinking his decisions. All those things became too hard or simply unimportant when compared to the wind on his skin. Coolness through fur. Soft ground to grip with toes and claws.

He scented her easily. Cinnamon spice even as a bear. He heard her, too, a low murmur almost like a purr. Definitely not human, but all Tonya.

He cleared the brush easily and spotted her scratching herself against a tree. Her back was arched and her eyes seemed to dance. She turned her head and bared her teeth. Was that playful or was she reacting to him?

Both, he realized, because as he closed the distance between them, she reared up enough to swat him. He swerved, but not fast enough to evade the other paw. She caught him on the shoulder and he stumbled, dropping to one knee. She dropped down onto all fours, sniffing him uncertainly. But that was exactly what he wanted.

He sprang up, jumping on her back. She reared up, obviously startled, but she recovered quickly. Before he could settle, she slammed him against the tree. Not hard enough to break anything. Just enough that he felt the impact in every bone.

She paused a moment, obviously concerned as she twisted her head to look at him. He grinned at the liquid beauty of her golden brown eyes and the sweet contours of her face. He saw so clearly in this form. Even though the moonlight ducked in and out of the clouds, he could still pick out the individual strands of her fur. The way her nose bunched when she sniffed. And the bright pink of her tongue as she licked him.

Wet. Hot. The roughness of her tongue on his leg was like sandpaper, and it made him laugh as he pushed her away.

She nipped as his fingers. He punched her nose. She hip-checked him and sent him rolling. And while he was still finding his feet, she started running. Bears didn't look like they could move fast, but even the most ordinary bear could outrun a human. Make the bear a shifter, and suddenly she could chart the terrain quickly, crossing distances with remarkable speed.

He couldn't catch her, except when she tired. Good thing at her size, she tired relatively quickly. So began a wild romp through the park. She would outdistance him quickly, lengthening their separation by inches, then yards. But then she would slow, turning to watch him as he came at her. At some point, he was close enough to launch himself around her neck and then they would fight or roll for a while just for the sheer joy of touching each other.

He loved the feel of her fur against his coarser hair. He loved her bulk because it gave him something to grip. And he loved that he could squeeze her with all his considerable strength and she would growl at him but not break.

And then came the time when he caught her just right. She'd been stepping over a rock and he'd leapt at just the right moment. His arms wrapped around her middle and pulled her sideways.

Got ya!

He'd meant to say it out loud, but he'd long since lost the ability to use words. She roared in response, but she didn't throw him off. Instead, she nuzzled into his neck, licking his torso. A lot of poundage in that nudge. But then she raised her head.

Eye to eye, he saw her. Not just the golden liquid of her eyes or the jut of her nose. In that moment, he felt like he saw her soul. Open. Loving. And completely at one with his own.

How beautiful she was. And then she shimmered. Right there

in his arms, he felt the prick of magic, the sudden burst of heat as she released her grizzly form, and suddenly he held a naked woman.

He started to draw back. He needed to match her, man to woman. But she touched his face. "You're beautiful just like this," she said. She stroked her hand across the hard jut of his mouth and nose. Then she stroked through the fur that thickened his back.

He tried to speak, but his jaw wouldn't work right. He could force garbled words if he needed to, but she stopped him.

"You're just fine like this." Then she pushed him onto his back and straddled him. His hips, his dick, even his thighs were the most human part of him. His feet had never fully shifted. But like this, he couldn't kiss her. Not like a man. And if he grew too impatient, he could hurt her.

He scrambled to pull his thoughts together but coming back wasn't easy. The wild tumult still gripped his soul. And when she rubbed herself against him, his thoughts splintered away. He only felt her. Wet. Hot.

Open.

"Stop thinking," she said, jerking his shoulders enough to startle him. He focused on her face. Smelled the sweetness of her hair and the spice of her body. "Just feel."

No other choice. Not with her so beautiful above him. So strong. So…

Tonya.

* * *

Alan woke to the sound of birds and the rustle of a squirrel inches from his face. He was snuggled around Tonya. Even in August, night in the woods can be chilly and the heat of her body was especially delightful.

She stirred when he did. Then he felt her stretch. All woman. All naked. Caught in his arms.

"Good morning," she said against his chest.

"Yup." It was all he could manage as he rolled her on top of him. It took him less than a moment to realize he was as fully human as she. And that it was daylight and they were naked somewhere in the middle of a national park.

Even so, certain parts of him didn't seem to care. Neither, apparently, did she.

She slid down on top of him, and suddenly he was engulfed in sweet, glorious Tonya.

Impossible not to thrust. Inconceivable to slow down. Not when she squeezed him in that slow roll of inner muscles. Not when she arched up and played with her own breasts. And certainly not when he slid his thumb between them to stroke her clit.

He knew now when she was about to come. Her breath caught. Her head arched back. And everything stilled for a split second before she went wild on top of him.

Then his own climax roared through him, and he poured everything he was straight into her.

And the entire world seemed to join them in a single, glorious, *yes*.

He barely noticed when she collapsed down on him. He was

still partially blacked out, still boneless and milked dry. He had enough energy to cradle her with one arm. To press a kiss to her forehead. And to smile when she licked the side of his neck, right below his ear.

They lay like that forever. Or maybe it was two minutes. Hard to tell given the situation. She stirred first, stretching up and off of him as she lifted her face to the morning sun. Gloriously naked. Amazingly unconcerned.

"We should get back before it gets too hot."

"Or some hikers stumble across us and get an eyeful."

She waggled her eyebrows at that. He flushed as he rolled over. It wasn't until he felt the wet on his dick that full memory kicked in. They'd made love so many times last night. Shifted, unshifted, he didn't even know. But one thing was abundantly clear.

Neither of them had thought about a condom.

"Um, Tonya…are you on the pill?"

She stilled, then slowly turned to look at him. She didn't speak while he struggled to tell her what he was thinking. And then slowly her brows rose.

"We've been humping like bunnies for three days, and you're just now thinking of birth control?"

Of course not! He was the man, damn it. It was his responsibility to remember these things, and he took that seriously. Except he hadn't. Which meant…His gaze dropped to her belly.

She rolled her eyes. "Relax. I'm not fertile." And at his surprised look, she chuckled. "Shifters know these things." Then she hedged. "Well, I know these things. Don't know about other women."

"You're certain?"

"Which way you hoping, Alan? That I'm wrong or that I'm right?"

He didn't know. Damn it, a baby wasn't exactly in his plans right now. But hadn't he warned her how many nights ago? Hadn't he told her that he was going to fuck her without a condom and not care about the results?

And she had said okay. *Okay.*

He gaped at her. "You want my child?"

Her expression softened into vulnerability. "Yes."

"But they screwed with my DNA. It could be born with fur and claws."

She shook her head. "They activated your DNA. No gene splicing. No fundamental change. Just a turning on of the DNA you already had."

"And if the kid is born turned on?"

"Then we'll love him or her just as much."

God she was insane. Completely insane. "That's a fucking huge risk to saddle on a child."

"Is it? Any bigger than any of the other risks with a baby? There's no guarantee that any child will be normal." She said normal with her fingers doing air quotes.

He swallowed. "But it's my child. My…" He held out his hands, feeling the prickle of fur and sharp spike of his claws.

"And mine. And I want it."

God, it was too much. How could she be so casual about such a huge thing?

"Relax, Alan. I told you. I'm not fertile." Her words were tight, her shoulders slightly hunched. Then she started walking away. How she knew what direction to go, he hadn't a clue. Was that a grizzly ability or just one of her special skills? Either way, he fell into step behind her, his thoughts spinning in on themselves until he felt dizzy.

"You want a baby?" he finally said, not really asking as much as trying out the feel of the words.

"I told you that days ago."

"You want *my* baby?"

She shot him a glare. "Did you see me rolling around the woods with anyone else?"

No. But…his? "Why?"

She sighed, the sound coming from deep in her belly. "Goddamn it, Alan, you're such an idiot sometimes." Then she broke into a run, streaking through the woods. But instead of catching up to her, he held himself back. He ran a step behind as he tried to process the truth of it.

She wanted his child. The idea thrilled him down to his toes. Almost as much as it terrified him.

Chapter Twenty

*M*en = *Idiots.*

Tonya knew this, of course. She worked with cops, for God's sake. Some of the most boneheaded people wore a badge. And any female in their ranks had to be smarter than the average man just to survive. But, really, Alan was the bright brain in Gladwin. Valedictorian, lawyer, and Carl's right-hand man for years. What the hell was wrong with him that he couldn't figure out she was in love with him? She'd even told him that her grizzly had picked him as her mate.

She'd told him!

But—if she were honest—she'd never actually said she loved him. Never told him that in addition to their shared childhood, she'd grown to appreciate the man. Hell, he'd played a starring role in her favorite fantasies. But when had lust shifted to love? When had desire kicked into please be the father of my baby?

Tonya sighed as she crossed into the parking lot. She popped

the trunk of the car and started dressing with efficient movements. Alan was a step behind. Silent and sure as he did the same.
And neither of them said a word. After the most magical night
of her life, she couldn't freaking manage to speak to the man she
loved.

So who was the real idiot?

Rather than face that question, she checked her phone. Plenty
of messages, none of them helpful. Not for the first time, she
wished crime fighting was like it appeared on TV. Fingerprints
processed in seconds. Email and phones hacked between pauses
in dialogue. If only. Which meant that in the absence of any
other leads, it was time to go wake Johnny.

She turned to head to the driver's seat, but Alan was there before her. His expression was troubled, his body language tense.
She thought for a moment he was going to demand that he drive
for some macho reason. Instead he just stood there, his face in
shadow and his hands awkward as he stroked her arm.

"I'm sorry, Tonya," he said.

"For what?"

"For not being the man you need."

She tilted her head in confusion. "What do you think I need?"

"You need…" He cut off his words. "You deserve a man who is
in control of his mind and body. You deserve someone who will
protect and provide for you and your children. Someone who can
be there whenever and however you need him."

God, he was trying so hard. She could feel it in his entire body,
and she sympathized. She was pretty damn sure that whatever
she wanted, he would struggle to provide. To his very last breath.

"That's not a man, that's an ideal. And in case you hadn't noticed, I'm pretty good at providing for and protecting myself."

He nodded and then he stroked her cheek with his knuckle. "Why me?" he finally asked. "You could have any man you want."

She snorted. "I wish." Then she tried to express what she was only now just figuring out. "And maybe I want a man who makes me laugh even when we're both fucked up. Who fights with words instead of fists. Who sticks around because he cares. Not just about me, but about the Gladwins and the world."

His hand dropped away from her. "Now who's talking about ideals?"

She pressed a hand to his chest, wishing she could push her words into his heart. "You want specifics? Answer me this. Will you hold me at night when I'm scared?"

His eyes widened at that. "Of course."

"Will you help me figure out shit when I've got no clue?"

"Tonya—"

"Will you fuck me into screaming orgasms and then love the babies we create?"

His eyes blazed at that and she could feel his abs ripple in response. If nothing else, they had chemistry. But she wanted more than that. She wanted him invested in their life together.

"I want you, Alan." She took a deep breath. Could she actually say the words out loud? Could she take the leap even knowing that he wasn't ready to say it back? She'd never thought herself a coward, but this was *big*. Still, she forced herself to do it. "I love you. I want to build a life with you. I want your children." There. All said. And when his mouth opened and no words came out, she sighed. "I know you're not ready to hear that. It's okay." She pushed past him. "Let's go get Johnny."

He stopped her just before she opened the car door. His hand was gentle on her arm as he turned her toward him. But then he surprised her. She'd barely looked up at him when he swooped down. He kissed her hard. Not sweet. Not kind. Not even romantic. He just took her mouth like a man would take a weapon. With need and possession. As if he wanted to draw its power into himself.

She opened for him immediately. She let him thrust inside and take what he needed. And while he pressed her against the car, she wrapped her arms around him. She lifted a leg and ground against his dick. And every part of her grew wet and needy for him.

He broke away before she was ready. He ripped his mouth from hers and leaned against the car while both their breaths came out in quick pants. God, no one else could take her from zero to a hundred so fast. And no one else left her aching the way he did. Because he wanted her just as much as she wanted him. But he was still lost and there was nothing more she could do to help him come back. Nothing but wait and pray that he found himself. And her.

"Jesus," he moaned. "I'm screwed up, Tonya." She was about to ask why, but then she saw he was looking at his hands where they pressed against the car. Sharp points of claws were there on hands and forearms dark with fur.

"You'll learn to control it. Even if you can't love the animal inside, you'll learn to control it."

He looked at her, his eyes stormy. "I love your animal. She's beautiful and fun."

Her grizzly purred in delight, but her thinking mind knew that loving her wasn't going to be enough. Because if he continued to despise himself then he'd tear himself apart and her along with him.

She searched for something to say, but words had never been her strong suit. In the end, she just gestured to the car. He nodded, not even needing her to explain. Twenty silent minutes later, they pulled into the gravely disaster that was Johnny's driveway. The man had inherited a small farm that grew corn, and that was his only contribution to supporting his family. His wife, Holly, ran it and raised their children while he drank himself into a stupor most nights. As they crossed the weedy front yard to the run-down porch, Tonya wondered if the woman thought it was worth it. She had children and a farm, but had to spend most nights sleeping next to a drunken ass.

Tonya knocked firmly on the rickety door. School hadn't started yet, so it was no surprise when a girl about ten pulled open the door. She had pigtails and freckles, and she looked at them with narrowed, suspicious eyes.

"Hi, there," Tonya said with a gentle smile. "I'm Deputy Kappes and I need to speak with your father."

The girl rolled her eyes. "Good luck with that. He won't get up for hours."

"That's okay. He doesn't need to be out of bed to talk."

The kid wasn't going for it. Her chin jerked up and she kept a hand on the door, probably planning to slam it in their faces.

"Mom's working, and I'm not allowed to let anyone I don't know inside."

"You have to. She's a police officer and I'm a lawyer. We're here on official business to talk to your father." Alan voice had a gravelly edge. Almost animalistic, and Tonya shot him a quick alarmed look. Was he on the verge of going monster? She didn't see it, but her nose twitched searching for his scent. Clear so far, but damn it, suddenly she was on edge, unsure of her partner in this escapade.

"Want to see my badge?" she offered, going with Alan's lie. The child didn't have to let them inside unless they had a warrant. The girl nodded, and Tonya held it out. The girl had to let go of the door to inspect it, which she did with a thoroughness that suggested interest.

"It's pretty cool to have one of these," Tonya said casually. "Gives me the right to force people to talk to me. To make them treat others right."

"And to shoot people," the girl said, a bit of envy in her tone.

"Only if they're going to someone." She waited until the child looked into her face. "I'm not going to hurt your father unless he tries to hurt me first. Or you."

"Or Mom?"

Well, wasn't that a telling question? "Or your mom."

She nodded slowly, stepping back to let them inside. "He's upstairs." Then she grabbed a cell phone off the table. "I'm calling Mom."

Tonya nodded. "Good idea." Then she and Alan mounted the steps and headed for the sound of heavy snoring.

The man was disgusting, and that had nothing to do with the smell of cat piss that wafted out from the master bathroom. That was one of the negatives of being a cougar-shifter. Didn't matter how fastidious the homemaker, cat pee stank. But Johnny was just gross. Naked, reeking of cheap beer, and sprawled across his bed in a sad room decorated with yellow wallpaper that had once been pretty. Tonya was still studying the scene, trying to pick up clues as to how violent the man might get when Alan stepped past her. His hands were claws, his jaw already jutting forward, but still free of fur. That meant he was worked up, but not out of control…she hoped. It certainly looked like he was gaining mastery of his shifter abilities, so she stepped to the side to give him room to work.

He started with a hard slap to Johnny's face. "Wake up."

Johnny came up swinging, a meaty fist striking out. Alan blocked it easily, slapping it away hard enough to slam Johnny back into the mattress. Which is when the man finally opened his eyes.

"Good morning," Alan said, his voice low with threat.

Johnny blinked his eyes about a dozen times, his mouth opening and closing twice before he formed words. "I gave you what you wanted! I emailed you!"

"Yeah, we know. Now we want to know where you got that information and who else knew."

Johnny's eyes darted around the room, pausing for just a tick on Tonya's face. He was probably looking for a weapon, but Alan didn't give him a chance. He jerked the man's face back to his, though how he could stand to be that close to Johnny's breath, she hadn't a clue.

"Who'd you tell, Johnny?"

"Think I'm stupid? I didn't tell no one!"

"Then where'd you get the information? How'd you know she was there?"

"What does it matter? If you got her—"

"Who?" Alan's claws were extending, drawing little pools of blood where they pressed hardest into Johnny's jaw. Tonya kept a close eye on that. Pinpricks, she could ignore. No way was she letting Alan kill the mangy cat.

Meanwhile, Johnny's eyes were getting wild. "You got no right," he whined. "I ain't done nothing wrong."

"How did you know?" Alan pressed.

Johnny didn't want to say. His mouth was turned into a mulish line and Alan's scent was getting thick. Damn it, she couldn't let escalate any further. If Alan and Johnny went off the rails, no way could she contain the situation.

"Don't piss him off," she pleaded with Johnny.

It might have been the earnest panic in her voice or Alan's scent up close and personal. Either way, Johnny spilled, though every word held angry venom. "I got it from Holly, you fucker! She knew."

Tonya stepped forward. "How did your wife know?"

Johnny tried to spit at her, but he quickly stopped the motion when Alan tightened his claws. "They were tight, okay? Holly was best friends with Elisabeth's daughter."

Okay, one connection explained. Tonya was about to ask more, but she heard the back door open and close. Holding up a hand to Alan, she backed out of the bedroom to stand at the top of the stairs. She heard a woman tell someone to take the kids outside and then footsteps. It wasn't until she heard the pump of a shotgun racking that she pulled out her weapon.

Just what she needed. A trigger-happy wife added into the mix. Jesus, could this get any worse? Hoping to head off disaster, she called loudly down the stairs.

"Damn it, Holly, we're not here to hurt you. Don't be stupid." *Please, don't be stupid.*

Alan abruptly appeared at her back. He was tense and his gaze split evenly between the bedroom and the stairs.

"You got no right to come in my house," called a woman— presumably Holly—from below.

"I'm Officer Kappes. We just wanted to talk to Johnny," Tonya returned. "I'm coming downstairs. Don't shoot."

She started to move but Alan was there before her. He wasn't letting her walk down the stairs first. Stupid and macho, but there wasn't time to argue. A quick look showed that he appeared mostly human. Good. But the situation was too volatile for her to let appearances mean anything, especially since Alan's scent was still strong. So she nabbed his elbow.

"Keep it together, okay?"

He gave her a sharp nod and kept descending. By all accounts, Holly wasn't a shifter, so she couldn't judge Alan by his smell. Then he held his hands out to the side, and Tonya saw the sharp points of his claws. Damn. Not fully human.

She moved forward, keeping a half step behind him and her gun out as she aimed over his shoulder. If Holly knew to look at his hands, she might freak. But there was no time to stop Alan as Holly came into view.

"Who the hell are you?" she demanded. Tonya couldn't see her, but she'd obviously gotten an angle on Alan.

"This is Mr. Carman, my partner," Tonya answered. Even in this tense a situation, a tiny thrill went down her spine at those words. Alan as her partner. It felt right.

"What the hell do you want?"

Alan put his hands down and curled them into fists. It helped to hide the claws, but the aggressive stance was unmistakable. "Elisabeth Oltheten. Where is she?"

Bam!

The shotgun. *Shit!* Tonya had barely made the last step when the noise deafened her. She whipped around, gun at the ready, but all she saw was Alan gripping the barrel of the weapon and holding it high. Tonya frantically scanned him, but there wasn't blood anywhere and no coppery scent either. Good. Though now they had the scent of gunpowder further clogging the air.

Meanwhile, Holly struggled to retain control of the weapon, but Alan had a good grip and he wasn't letting her aim anywhere but at the ceiling. Which, now that Tonya looked at it, had a shotgun hole in it.

"Settle down!" he growled. Oh hell, fur was sprouting on his forearm.

The woman jerked at his tone, letting go of her weapon as she jolted backward. Unfortunately, she backed into a cheap coffee table that teetered under the sudden impact. Alan caught her with his other hand, gripping her tightly to keep her from falling.

And then he was standing there with a shotgun in one hand and a terrified woman in the other.

"A little help please?" he growled as he looked at Tonya.

She holstered her pistol and stepped around to face the woman. "Holly? You're Johnny's wife?"

"I won't tell you shit!" the woman bellowed.

Meanwhile, heavy footsteps clunked down the stairs. Tonya turned to face Johnny, but his eyes were all on his wife. "Don't argue, you stupid bitch. You don't know what he is!"

Alan couldn't do anything but keep a hold on weapon and woman. It was almost funny the way he glared over his shoulder at Johnny and her, but Tonya liked that two of the four people in the room were effectively immobilized. And she had no trouble dealing with Johnny.

"Sit your ass down," she snapped and was thrilled when Johnny obeyed, dropping heavily onto the nearest couch.

"You, too," she said to Holly. The woman wasn't going to obey, but Alan twisted her around by her arm then abruptly let go. She dropped with little grace onto the couch beside her husband. Then he was free to pop open the shotgun and set it aside.

She had let Alan take lead with Johnny, but a furious woman was her province. So she stepped up to Holly and looked hard at her. "How did you know where Elisabeth was?"

"I'm not telling you shit!"

Johnny shot his elbow back, right into his wife's chest. "Shut up, you idiot."

Tonya reacted on instinct. She grabbed Johnny's arm, twisted it, and threw him to the ground. Within a second, she had the bastard facedown with her knee on the back of his neck while she twisted his arm with increasing strength. He howled in reaction, but she just kept going. Well, somewhat. Eventually, she eased off. And about a minute after that, he stopped bellowing.

"Nice move," Alan said from over her shoulder. He was standing with his hand out in front of Holly, presumably to keep the woman from joining in.

"I have my moments," Tonya responded. Then she turned to Johnny. "I promised your kid that you wouldn't hurt her mother. Don't make a liar out of me." Then she glanced at Holly. "You okay?"

The woman didn't answer, clearly too furious to speak. But whether she was mad at Tonya or Johnny was anybody's guess.

"We just need to find Elisabeth," Tonya said. "Before things get worse."

"She ain't done nothing."

Tonya stared at the woman. "What makes you think that? Because she raised your best friend? Do you know what kind of shit Elisabeth's been doing?"

"Yes! She's saving the cougars." She lifted her chin. "She's making new ones and you fucking bears don't like that."

"We fucking bears don't give a shit about you cats. Except when you decided to have a war with the wolves right in our backyard."

"We ain't warring with anyone!"

No, they weren't anymore. But that's because the populations of both species were so decimated there wasn't anyone left to fight. "So you think Elisabeth is just making new cats. Just whammo, bammo, she pops out another one?"

"Idiot," Holly snarled. "She's too old for that."

Which is when Alan spoke, his voice as quiet as Holly's was loud. "She promised to change you, didn't she? She said she'd figured out how to activate your cat DNA and you'd become a shifter." He glanced at Johnny. "Maybe become equal in strength and speed to this asshole."

Holly glared at Alan, her voice sullen. "It ain't for me. I'm pure human, through and through."

Oh hell. "It's for her kids," Tonya said. Jesus, what people would do to get an advantage for their children. However misguided the thought, Tonya understood the impulse. "It doesn't work, you know."

"'Course it does! I saw one. Her cousin from Arizona. He shifted perfect."

Alan stepped back, his eyes dark. "Big guy, thick knuckles? Doesn't speak?"

Tonya recognized that description. It was one of the guys who'd been guarding Alan and Julie. The one who'd been shot but got away. Meanwhile, Holly nodded.

"That's him."

"Already a shifter. That's why she had to bring him up from Arizona."

"You're lying," Holly snapped, but her face said she wasn't so sure.

Alan squatted down in front of Holly. His movement were jerky, but his voice was anything but. When he spoke, it was with a silky softness all the more frightening because of his smooth tone.

"Do you want to know what she's doing? Do you want to see what she's going to turn your kid into?"

Suddenly Johnny started writhing, panic in his voice. "No, Holly. No!" Tonya had to press down hard to keep him from escaping.

Meanwhile, Alan stretched out his hands in front of Holly. "I was one of her test subjects. I'm half bear. She was gonna make me into a full shifter."

Alan made it sound like he'd wanted this. Made Holly think they had that in common when the truth was the exact opposite. But the suggestion worked. Holly's eyes were fixed on Alan's hands.

"This is what she did. And this is what she's going to do to your kids."

He went full out. The claws came first and then the fur. But seconds later, his face had changed and his back hunched and thickened. And then the BO hit. Lord, Alan was really laying it on.

Awful. But it didn't really bother Tonya. In her time as a cop, she'd smelled tons worse. But she understood the effect on someone who hadn't. Someone who'd expected to see and smell a normal animal.

The woman choked back a scream. She scrambled backward on the couch even though Alan hadn't moved an inch. And Johnny started gagging. Oh hell, all that booze last night, it didn't take much for the man to start retching. Bile and God knows what else came up, and Tonya jumped out of the way.

Well that didn't help the smell in here. *Ugh.*

Meanwhile Alan stood up. His jaw wasn't constructed well for human speech, but he got out words better than Tonya could when in her bear form.

"Is this what you want? For your kids?" he asked.

Holly shook her head, terror in her eyes.

"Where is Elisabeth?"

It took three tries before Holly managed to speak. And when she did, it was with a quavering voice. "I don't know. She called me. When she got to the new place."

Tonya spotted the cell phone and picked it up. "You're the one who told her we were coming?"

Holly nodded.

"And did you help her get to Grand Rapids?"

She shook her head. "The guy did. I…uh…I let him borrow our car."

Johnny shot a weak glare over his shoulder. "You said it was getting fixed."

"It is getting fixed!" Holly snapped. "He's doing it because you can't stop a fucking oil leak."

Okay. This was rapidly descending into domestic-dispute territory and no way did Tonya want to be in the middle of that. So she scrolled through the phone history and pulled up a number. It didn't take long. It wasn't like many people wanted to talk to these two. Plus it was the only number that didn't have a name attached.

"This it?" she asked, showing it to Holly.

The woman jerked her head in a shaky nod.

Tonya pulled out her phone and texted it to her police partner Steve. "We should have an address in a minute," she said to Alan. Then she grabbed the shotgun. "This is a registered weapon, right? All legally obtained with the proper paperwork?"

Johnny didn't answer except to glare.

"Yeah," she said as she set the gun on her shoulder. "Thought not." Then she turned to Alan. "We can go now."

He nodded and started to move for the front door, pausing long enough to glare at Holly. "If you're lying—" he began. Tonya interrupted.

"She's not." The terror on the woman's face was pretty clear. She'd told them everything she knew. Meanwhile, Alan made it to the front door, but Tonya kept him from opening it. "You can shift back now," she said in a low voice. The kids were out there somewhere and maybe a neighbor. No sense in terrifying them, too.

He looked at her, his expression bleak. "I'm trying," he said in a low tone. "It's not going away."

Still on the floor, Johnny let out a low moan of fear. With his shifter ears, he probably heard Alan's comment clearly.

"Well," Tonya said with a shrug, "you'll figure it out in the car." Then she hauled open the door. Might as well expose the kids to the idea that the world held many strange and unexpected things. And that some of the good guys had really bad BO.

Chapter Twenty-One

It took him twenty minutes to return to human. Twenty fucking minutes of breathing exercises, Zen mantras, and reciting the Constitution in his head before he could look at his hands without seeing the horror on Holly's face or feeling the seething satisfaction of when he'd slammed Johnny into the floor. Twenty minutes of remembering why he was a monster now and could never, ever live in a civilized world.

Tonya tried to help him. She talked about ways young shifters find to settle the beast inside, but every time she spoke, he grew angrier. This wasn't supposed to be his life. He'd nearly become a constitutional scholar. He read poetry just to appreciate the eloquence of words. And in his spare time, he did crossword puzzles. Such a man did not relish terrifying people, even if they were ignorant rednecks who had made some really piss-poor choices in their lives.

Eventually Tonya fell silent, though she'd ended with the words, "Everyone has to find their own way."

Maybe. And maybe his way was to end Elisabeth however possible, including his own death.

But what if he survived the bitch's capture? What if he lived beyond the woman's end? Tonya was right now coordinating with local law enforcement to raid Elisabeth's house. That would likely end in an arrest, not murder. A few days ago, that would not have been an acceptable outcome. But now he wasn't so sure. Now he was thinking like a lawyer again—sometimes—and revisiting all his views on vigilante justice.

It came from sitting in a cop's car and watching the most beautiful deputy in the world do her job. She was a law-and-order kind of girl, and he wanted desperately for the happily ever after she believed they could have. But how could she possibly love anyone who gleefully embraced killing? And it would be gleeful for him. It would be positively delightful for him to end Elisabeth once and for all.

He was still brooding as they made it to Grand Rapids. Brooding and trying not to stare at Tonya's belly and imagine his child growing inside her. Their child, their life together. It wasn't possible...

Was it?

She pulled her car over in a middle-class suburban neighborhood. The kind that had front porches, curtains on the windows, and basketball hoops attached to the garage roof. But only some of the lawns were mowed, a few sported sunflowers in brilliant yellow glory, and a few more were entirely choked with weeds. A neighborhood going to seed. Or maybe struggling to build into better. Hard to tell.

Tonya parked the car and turned to him. "We're waiting for the search warrant. It'll come soon. Just stay with me and don't go off half-cocked."

"Which half? Cock or doodle?"

She rolled her eyes. "You know you're not half as funny as you think."

"Yeah, but you like me even at fifty percent."

"Yeah," she agreed softly. "Yeah, I do." Then her expression turned serious. "We're doing this the right way, Alan. It's how it has to be."

He shook his head. "She's a cougar-shifter and a violent psychopath. There's no way the normal justice system can handle her."

"We've got plenty on her without bringing in the shifter stuff. We just need to keep it together for a little bit longer." Her eyes pleaded with him. "It's time to choose, Alan. You've spent your adult life working inside the justice system. Tell me you remember that now."

"Of course I remember it." The question was whether he was still believed in it or wanted to live entirely outside of it.

She heard the subtext. Of course she did, and she released a heavy sigh. "You're a pain in the ass, you know that?"

He wiggled his brows. "We haven't tried that yet. Want to?" It was comfortable to drop back into sexual banter, however lame. It gave them a sense of preabduction normalcy. But Tonya wasn't fooled.

"God, Alan, please be the man I love. Please."

His leer faded. "Shouldn't you love your man no matter what? Isn't that what love is?"

She nodded, not even hesitating. "There's love and there's the real world. Hear this clearly. You go off the rails now and I will put you in cuffs."

"That won't stop—"

"I will go full bear in front of all these people, Alan. I'll expose the whole fucking shifting thing if it keeps you from doing something you're going to regret for the rest of your life."

He grimaced and stared at his hands. "That's the problem, Tonya. I don't think I'll regret it. Not one tiny bit."

"Then trust me," she said, her expression fierce. "Trust that I know you better than you do right now. I know you'll find your balance. And I know that when you do, you won't want a murder on your hands. Not even of the one person who most deserves it."

He nodded because she wanted him to. Because when she had that peculiarly Tonya look—half pleading, half commanding—he wanted to give her whatever she asked.

"I don't know that I can control it," he abruptly confessed. "I want to. I'm trying. But…" His voice trailed away, but in his mind, the words kept spilling out. But what if when he sees the bitch, he rips out her throat out? He'd imagined that and worse a million times. What if he couldn't be the man she wanted because the monster was stronger?

He expected her to be sympathetic, to say something encouraging. Instead, she hit him with a hard glare.

"Work harder, Alan. Or go home." She pressed the car keys into his hands, the message clear. She needed him to be a man not a monster. And for the first time since this entire disaster began, he felt a fierce, bright light kindle inside him. Hope? Determination? Love? Whatever it was, he grabbed it with both hands. He would be the man she wanted or die trying.

He squeezed her fingers, but before he could speak, a few police officers pulled up in a Chevrolet Impala.

Tonya glanced over her shoulder, then shot him a quick smile. "I think they're going to tell me they got the warrant. Give me a sec." She climbed out of her car and went to speak to the big guys in suits. Probably GR detectives.

Alan remained in the car, watching the quick conversation. But as the discussion went on and on, his attention wandered to the house where Elisabeth was supposedly holed up. The phone number from Holly was a landline to this address. Coupled with the sighting of Elisabeth nearby, they might get a warrant. Except looking at the nicely maintained two-story home, Alan began to wonder. It all looked too good. No toys cluttered the lawn, the hedges were trimmed, and the flower bed was pretty. There was a decorative flag hanging next to the door and whimsical flowers with solar lights along the front walk. It didn't make sense that a woman on the run with two children would be in a place so charming. Unless she had some connection to whomever lived inside.

With that thought in mind, Alan got out of the car. Tonya was arguing with the two GR police, her gestures tight and her expression fierce. Bet she didn't get the warrant after all. Legally speaking, that was probably the correct judicial response. Fortunately, he wasn't a police officer, so he had more latitude than Tonya in what he could do, starting with walking right up the front walk and banging on the door.

He got about five feet before Tonya grabbed his arm.

"Jesus, you don't listen to a damned thing I say, do you?"

"Get the warrant?"

"No." She blew out a breath. "The place is owned by an older couple with no obvious links to Elisabeth."

"So I'll just have a chat—" She put her hand on his arm, gripping him with her shifter strength.

"Alan. You promised to let me handle it."

Actually he hadn't, but once again, she gave him that look. Fierce and pleading all at once. He raised his hands and backed up to the car. "Fine. Ten minutes."

"Twenty."

He snorted. "Fifteen and then I'm coming in."

She shot him an arch look. "Twenty, and you'll text before you enter." Trust Tonya to not negotiate. Then before he could argue, she gestured to the local cops. All three of them climbed onto the porch, then rang the doorbell. Alan hung back, watching from the car as an elderly woman answered the door and sweetly gestured them inside.

Too easy.

Alan narrowed his eyes as the door closed behind Tonya. He stood quietly fuming in the late afternoon light and wondered at his compliance. It was almost as if he were bowing to her greater experience and wisdom in crime fighting. That he was returning to his place as a lawyer. And yet part of him itched right beneath the skin. Part of him wasn't going to delay a damned thing in his search for vengeance. And that part—the monster part—wasn't staying down.

He looked around the neighborhood and tried to think of options. If he were a psychotic cougar-shifter, where would he hide? They already knew what the bitch wanted. She was working to repopulate the cougar-shifters. That meant activating the two kids she had and raising them as best she could. In quiet. Probably with the help of her big, beefy, and stoic cousin from Arizona.

He looked around the street, picking out houses that would work for that. Something defensible and without toys in front. Toys encouraged moms and their kids to visit. The yard wouldn't be ultra neat or gone to seed. Something in the middle without any extra decoration. No American flag, no bumper stickers on the car, and certainly a closed garage. Elisabeth definitely wouldn't want anyone to see inside her home. Curtains were a must.

There.

If he were trying to raise shifter kids in quiet, he'd pick that house. It was a few doors down on the opposite side of the street.

He crossed over, strolling with his hands in his pockets and his senses dialed up to maximum. Not a lot of people out right then. It was dinnertime for most families, though he noticed a few houses with the kids still running around in the backyard. He could smell a couple barbecues going and he was struck again with a longing that made his breath catch. Kids in the yard playing fetch with the dog while he grilled and Tonya took care of the baby. God, it would be so perfect.

And then he smelled Elisabeth's cousin. It was an acrid scent that brought back nightmares of his captivity. Chewing tobacco held too long. It poured out of the bastard's skin, and Alan felt his hackles rise.

Unless he was confused. Unless it was some other guy who just liked chaw. But it sure as hell didn't feel that way. Especially since suddenly his monster was flashing on all the ways the bastard had tortured him back when Alan had been locked in a cage.

He stalked forward, feeling his nails grow into claws. Fur sprouted on his forearms and his joints thickened. Muscles, too. He was familiar enough with the process now to not be revolted by it. Or maybe he was just too focused.

He slipped through the rusty gate into a fenced backyard. Weeds were thicker here as was the scent of cougar piss. This was a smell he knew well from tracking Johnny. Definitely the right place.

Suddenly, he was in full predator mode. His joints loosened, the muscles twitching as every movement became more fluid, more animal. Sight, sound, smell, even the texture of the air on his skin became a wealth of minute information fed straight to his monster brain.

His human side forced him to pause. He needed to text Tonya that she was at the wrong house. This had to be where Elisabeth was holed up. Unless this was just another shifter family. There could be an innocent cougar-shifter here. It was possible.

His predator side rebelled at the very idea, but his mind was in control. At least for the moment. He had to know if this was really where Elisabeth was hiding out so he stalked forward. He slipped around the corner and peered into windows. He got enough of an angle on the kitchen to see Pepto-Bismol on the table and fiber-based cereal on the counter. That was enough proof for him.

Time to text. He started to pull out his phone, his hand shaking as he warred with the monster inside. It was literally screaming in his head, but he would not give in—

Wham!

Pain exploded in his shoulder as the world suddenly flew sideways. His mind splintered as the monster took over, prioritizing information that flew at him too fast too process consciously.

Bastard shifter man. Baseball bat.

Alan thrown sideways. Secondary impact on the air conditioner.

He used his claws, digging into the vents as he swung around midair. His feet hit the siding and pushed off.

Attack.

The human in him was scrambling to keep up. He recognized the stoic bastard from before. The one Julie had shot but who'd escaped. He had enough time to snarl, "Remember me?" before he landed on the thug.

The Arizona Diamondback ball cap went flying. So did the two of them, rolling past the concrete porch onto the patchy grass. He couldn't let the bastard shift into a cougar. He was much less dangerous as a big man with a bat.

Total instinct now as his monster stink poisoned the air. Rapid swipes from Alan's claws took out the muscles of the guy's wrist.

Coppery smell. Bright color. *Blood.*

Good.

Bastard still barreled forward.

Impact. Grappling, their strength relatively equal. But bastard was bleeding, therefore weakening.

Unless there were more. Where was Elisabeth? Where were the kids?

Another quick attack. End it now.

Shit!

Sucker's bet. Bastard had been ready.

Spun around. Choke hold!

His breath was cut off. Squeezed tight and nothing he did with his claws made any difference. So he poured everything he had into his scent. Let the bastard choke on it.

He did. To Alan's utter shock, the man started gagging and his hold slackened. Alan twisted the moment he felt the bastard's first cough. This time his claws did damage and—a scream cut through the air. It was muffled, coming from the upper story, but with his shifter hearing, Alan identified it clearly.

Young male. Fury. Alan knew exactly what it meant. He'd raged just like that when he'd been the one in the cage.

He responded without thought, the need to get to the child overriding everything else. He leapt away from bleeding asshole and headed inside. His nose led him through the house. Past the kitchen, but not upstairs where he'd planned to go. Instead, he pushed through a door that looked like a closet. It wasn't. It was actually a stairway to the garage attic.

More screaming. The boy. "Take her to the doctor, now!"

Alan raced up. His nose told him *she* was up there. Also the children, but he didn't care. *She* was his only focus.

His nose and jaw lengthened, his vision narrowed, and when his claws wouldn't work on the doorknob, he slammed his way through it.

Where was she?

There.

The bitch was standing over the children, her back to him. She wore baggy sweats, the kind she could shift out of at a moment's notice. The girl was lying down, her face flushed with fever, her breath coming in short pants. The boy stood beside the cot, fury burning through his entire body.

All of them looked to him.

Alan wanted to launch himself at her. His beast screamed to attack, but he held himself back, though his belly quivered at the restraint. The children were too close. He couldn't kill her while they were there so close.

Meanwhile, the bitch's eyes suddenly widened. "The bear," she said, her words almost a hiss. "Alan, right?" Her gaze ran over him, clinically detached in her perusal. It was just like when he'd been in a cage, and he felt filthy just from the memory. "You're looking well."

It was hard for him to form words, so much monster burned in his blood. But he forced the words out, using all his focus to keep some measure of control. "Get away from them."

"No. They're my children." Her lips curled into a creepy smile. "Just like you are. And you won't hurt your mother."

His monster roared, but a scent filled the air. Something strong and distinctly hers. What the hell was that? It made his mind reel. Memories flooded him from when he'd been feverish and she'd sat beside his cage watching him. How could he have forgotten that smell? It choked him until he felt like he was under water.

Focus!

It took all his will to push away the nausea. Part of him understood that this was just memory. Her scent bringing back the trauma of his captivity. All perfectly normal, maybe even expected. But he couldn't let it win. He couldn't let what she'd done to him cripple him now.

"You can't hurt me," she repeated, her scent and her words seeping into his consciousness. The monster in him went crazy. It flooded him with memories of what she'd done to him. Of fever and seizures that never ended.

No!

Pain real and remembered burned through his joints. His body at war with itself again. His knees weakened. His hands shook.

No!

His mind shoved forward. He wasn't trapped in a cage. He wasn't at her mercy. Not now. Not ever again.

"Get. Away. From. Them."

He saw a grimace of distaste flash across her expression. Horror at the monster she'd created? Good. Because it was going to be the last fucking thing—

Her body shimmered and the air turned cold. The shape of a cougar superimposed on the woman, then solidified in the blink of an eye. Human clothes drifted to the floor as the cougar leapt free.

As she leapt *at him.*

Chapter Twenty-Two

Tonya knew within seconds of entering the house that Elisabeth wasn't here. No cougar-shifter stink. No animal wariness from Grandma and Grandpa who opened their home so easily. And certainly no young children running around unless it was one of the many grandchildren who visited every Sunday, according to the elderly couple. But Holly had gotten this phone number somehow, and so Tonya had to flash the picture and hope that one of the two had a good memory for faces.

The good news was that Grandma remembered Elisabeth right away. She even remembered the quiet boy who'd hung back in the shadows seemingly too afraid to speak. Elisabeth hadn't even wanted to come inside, but had said that her cell phone was broken. Of course Grandma had offered her landline and that was how Holly had gotten a call from this phone. But when asked where Elisabeth was living, neither grandparent had a clue. The woman and boy had gone on bicycles to the grocery store.

All of that added up to exactly what they already knew. Elisabeth and her charges were somewhere in the neighborhood. Tonya thanked the couple and stepped out. She asked the local detectives to chat a little longer and get details on the neighborhood. Meanwhile, Tonya would update Alan and start scouting. Together, their noses would go a long way to narrowing down options.

Except when she stepped outside, Alan was nowhere to be found. Too soon to start panicking about what he was doing. He could have simply gone for a walk to scent the neighborhood. But fear started clawing in her gut. Elisabeth was here somewhere, as was her bastard cousin. What if he came across them? What if he lost control and attacked them? What if they killed him?

Her bear began to shift uneasily beneath her skin. Her mate might be in danger.

She was just about to call the detectives for help. Three could search the neighborhood faster than one. But then the lackluster breeze brought her the nauseating scent of Alan in full shifter battle.

Danger!

Her grizzly nearly burst out of her skin, but Tonya was experienced in keeping her reined in. But what to do? Alan was fully shifted. She couldn't call in the locals. They'd shoot him on sight. Which meant it was up to her and her nose.

Good thing that was exactly what her grizzly wanted. Letting her senses expand, Tonya tracked Alan's scent. Fortunately, that was an easy thing to do.

Over there. A few doors down. Backyard.

She started at a jog then quickly went full tilt. She burst through the gate quick enough to see the flash of a cougar tail as it disappeared through a door into the back of the garage. The yard was thick with Alan's stench, someone's blood, and damn, someone had ripped the shit out of the air conditioner.

She didn't pause, though she did take a breath hard enough to bellow, "Police!"

And then she heard the roars. Two of them. Cougar and…

Alan.

No time to choke on her fear. No time to even process the possibilities. She pulled her gun and ran through the door, ducking in case the cougar was waiting.

Good choice. The fucking cat leapt right at her the moment she crossed the threshold. Her nose told her it was the male cousin, not the bitch. His claws were razor sharp but his aim was off. He clipped her shoulder and a hot flash of pain burned through her body. Didn't matter. She was more than capable of rolling with the blow and turning it to her advantage. She came back up into a crouch with her gun aimed dead center at one pissed-off shifter cat.

Then she pulled the trigger. Twice.

Two shots dead-center mass. The cat went splat against a rusty sedan. Protocol said she needed to check him to be sure he was dead. Shifters could survive an awful lot, but more sounds banged through her brain. A fight. Right above her in the attic space. Damn it, how the hell did she get up there?

Into the house, through the kitchen, and then a door to a

stairway. She tore through them, her gun ready, only to fall back a step. Something heavy landed against the door, slamming it shut right in Tonya's face. Hell. She could hear the battle, but it would be suicide to try and push into the middle of a shifter fight.

Her other senses fed her data. Scent came with the most information. Alan's blood. Cougar shifters. Illness. But how many attackers? The scents were too varied for her to process, and the sounds completely chaotic. Hiss from a cat. Grunts from Alan. Thank God he was still alive, but the battle was crashing into walls and someone was screaming. A boy? It was too hard to tell.

But she couldn't just sit here and wait. Not with Alan fighting for his life. She'd bet on him to win out in the open, but in so tiny a space, the cat would have the advantage. She had to do it.

"Police!" she bellowed, then she shoved open the door.

Her mind cataloged the scene with clinical precision. Alan and a cougar were grappling. They were rolling about the floor in furious battle. Two small beds, one smashed to splinters, the other filled with a small unconscious girl, flushed with fever. But it was the boy who grabbed her attention. He was standing protectively over the girl, a pistol in his hand as he aimed at the combatants.

"Police!" Tonya barked. "Put it down!" She hated to aim at the boy but she couldn't let him shoot Alan.

The kid didn't even flinch. His eyes were trained on the fighters just as Alan heaved the cat away from him. He didn't shove her far. The cougar had her jaw locked on his shoulder, but it was enough to get some distance. And to tear her free from his body.

God, he was covered in blood and he stumbled as he got free. His face was thick with fur and large jaws, but he was still fighting.

"Elisabeth!" Tonya bellowed as she resighted on the cat. "Stay down! Elisabeth!"

She was about to yell something at Alan. Something about stepping away or *Don't fucking bleed out*. But she didn't have the breath. Then, to her relief, Alan straightened up. Jesus, he was bleeding from a dozen different wounds, but he was standing tall as he faced Elisabeth.

Tonya's gaze cut to the bitch. She was struggling on a damaged leg, fighting to right herself. Right there was the opening. Alan was fast enough to close the distance and snap the animal's neck, but he didn't. Instead, he started to shift back to human.

Tonya couldn't believe it, but there it was. His jaw shrank, his bared teeth slid away from view, and his claws became hands.

"Fuck you, bitch. My mother was a bear."

Then he turned away from her, his gaze landing hard on Tonya's. Then he nodded and it was enough for him to communicate everything she wanted to hear. He was telling her to take care of Elisabeth. She had the gun, now pointed straight at the cougar. He was going to save the kids. So he started crossing to the cot.

Bang! Bangbangbang!

Elisabeth fell back in a spray of blood and torn flesh.

Alan jerked his gaze back to Tonya, but it hadn't been her. It was the boy. Pulling the trigger as fast as his shaking fingers could manage. Shit, he was emptying his clip into Elisabeth.

Alan was the one who ended it. Long before Tonya could order the kid to stop, he slapped out, not with his claws, but with his hand. He chopped at the boy's wrist, knocking the pistol wide. The boy rounded on him, his eyes turning to slits. *Hell.* The boy was another forced shifter like Alan. Had to be as another stink permeated the room.

Time for shifter battle number three.

But before it could happen, Alan leapt. He tackled the kid and covered him with his own body. Not pinning him, but full-body protection even though the boy was the one who creating the problem.

The child screamed and the stench grew thicker. Tonya saw fur and teeth. *Hell.* A writhing mass of animal fury trapped between Alan and the floor.

"It's over. Get control." Alan's low voice continued as a steady murmur against the roaring fury of the boy. "I know you're pissed. I hear you."

Tonya stayed tense. She didn't want to shoot the kid, but she sure as hell didn't want Alan getting ripped to shreds. Best she could do to help was find the gun and secure it. She took care of that then glanced at Elisabeth.

Score: one dead villainess. Even a shifter couldn't come back from having her brains splattered against the wall. Next stop was the little girl. Damn, the child was burning up.

And all the while, Alan kept murmuring to the boy. "I know you're angry. I hear you."

In time, it worked. The boy stopped squirming, either because he'd found a way to pull it together or because Alan was squashing the breath out of him. And in the silence, he gasped out one furious sentence.

"Take. Sister. Doctor!"

Which is when the two local cops came thudding up the stairs. Heavy feet. Rapid pulse. Tight stench of adrenaline.

"Don't shoot!" Tonya called. "We're contained." And she prayed that they were. The last thing she needed was two local cops seeing a half-shifted boy.

"Are you all right?" one of the detectives called as he cleared the top step.

Alan was the one who answered. "Call an ambulance."

And when Tonya looked over, she saw that the boy was completely human again. As was Alan, though his shoulder looked a bloody mess as he wrapped up the girl in a blanket and lifted her up in his arms.

"She needs my doctor," Alan said as he looked at Tonya. She didn't need to guess at his meaning. The girl was going through the same process as Alan had. As the boy obviously had. The girl's shifter DNA was activated and it wasn't taking well.

"I'll take care of it," she said.

Alan nodded and the cops stepped out of the way as he started down the stairs. One had already called for an ambulance. The other was taking in the scene, his eyes wide and horrified.

"Is the animal downstairs—" she began.

"Dead," he answered. "Jesus, who would leave kids with two wild cougars?"

Tonya didn't answer. There was no explaining the logic of this to anyone. Besides, her attention was on Alan. God, he looked awful covered in blood, and yet she'd never seen him more powerful. More in control. He seemed magnificent to her, and she started to follow him. Just like she'd always follow him. But the detective grabbed her arm, holding her back.

"What the hell happened here? And what is that smell?"

"I'll explain later. I need to—"

"You need to do it now, Deputy," the man said, his words hard. There were more words. Questions. Procedures. All the annoying law-and-order shit she'd sworn to obey the moment she first got her badge. She knew it was important, but she wanted to be with Alan. She needed to be with the man she loved.

"Let me make sure he gets to the hospital first," she said.

The detective gave her a quick nod, but kept a hand on her. She could have broken free, but what was the point? The scream of a siren cut through the air and an ambulance tore up the street. She'd barely made it to the driveway when the paramedics hopped out and took charge of the girl. Alan tried to step aside, but with all the blood still seeping from his shoulder, no one was letting him go anywhere.

She tried to get to him. All she needed was a single private moment to tell him how proud she was of him. He'd done it all perfectly. He was still alive. The kids were safe. And she loved him. She so completely and totally loved him.

But there was no privacy and no time. She caught his gaze once and held it. And in that moment, she read absolutely nothing. No resignation. No reassurance. Just an enigmatic stare before the doors shut and he was driven off to the hospital.

Gone.

Chapter Twenty-Three

*T*onya.

Alan felt his body respond to her presence. He hadn't even realized she'd made it to the hospital, but his skin prickled with awareness and his blood heated to a warm glow. She was behind him, probably coming into the ER from the nurses' station, and he felt his breath ease.

He turned and spotted her immediately, scanning her for injuries. No reason for her to have them, but he looked anyway. He saw her familiar lush curves but also the rest of her body, the tight shoulders that meant fear and the slight jerkiness that signaled exhaustion. His gaze went to her face, and their eyes locked. He watched as tension flowed out of her. He knew it when she scanned his body for injuries and when she reassured herself he was alive and well. Then she moved with renewed smoothness past a group of orderlies to come straight to his side.

"You look weird in scrubs," she said.

"Better than soaked in blood."

"How are—"

"I'm fine. My shoulder aches, but it'll heal quick. You?"

"Better now. Jesus, paperwork sucks. And I haven't even started it. Been answering the same questions until I thought I was going to explode."

They were talking in stupidities because neither of them knew exactly what to say. So he dispensed with all that shit and wrapped her in his arms. She flowed into him like water into the sea. He absorbed her strength, her relief, and everything he adored about her, then tried to give it back in the squeeze of his arms, the press of his lips, and the words he murmured into her ear.

"You were right," he said.

He felt her still and then slowly pull back, her expression bordering on smug. "Of course I was. About what?"

Everything.

He was still trying to phrase it, crafting words that would determine his future. But in the pause between thought and voice, her phone rang. She grabbed it with a curse, holding it up between them as if she were tempted to throw it across the room.

"Your brother," she said. "He's on his way up here but can't stop calling."

Alan smiled and lifted the phone from her hand. She gave it easily and added a gesture that he should deal with his family. Alan thumbed it on.

"Hello, Carl," he said without even waiting. "I'm fine. Tonya's fine. Go back home."

"Jesus, Alan!" The relief in his brother's voice was almost comical. "You're okay? There was a shooting. You—"

"I know. I was there." He looked at Tonya, his words more for her than for his brother. "I didn't even know there was a gun. All I saw was her."

"Kid grabbed it from Elisabeth's clothes when she shifted," Tonya said.

Alan nodded while his brother started to rant. "You didn't *see* it? Damn it, Alan, you're not a cop. Why were you—"

"Guess what, Carl," Alan interrupted. He waited a second for his brother to sputter to a halt.

"Yeah?"

"I'm fine. Tonya's fine. And ding-dong the bitch is dead."

Another long exhale. "So that's over."

"Yes. So go home. I'll need you to help from there. Grease some bureaucratic wheels and shit."

He could almost hear his brother's brain churning, piecing together possibilities. It took a moment, but the man finally asked the question. "You coming home, too?"

"Not to your place," Alan said, his gaze following Tonya as she looked around his shoulder to the curtained alcove behind him. To the two kids they'd rescued from Elisabeth's clutches. "You and Julie don't need a third wheel."

"Damn it, it's your home, too."

"Shut up, Carl, and listen. I'm bringing a couple of kids back with me. They need *special* medical attention. And a place to stay that isn't shifter central."

Tonya's head jerked around at his words, her eyes widening as she, too, began to piece his plans together. And then her face softened. The tightness around her eyes shifted into a smile that seemed to come from deep within her. And at that moment, he wanted nothing else than to kiss her. Because she was beautiful. Because she was already halfway to what he wanted.

So he thumbed off the phone and did it. He cupped her face and drew her to his mouth. God, she tasted so perfect. Like coffee and sugar and *her*. The way she opened for him was just what he needed. The way her tongue dueled with his was so challenging that his hands tightened in possession. And the way she purred so deep in her throat made his groin surge with hunger.

He had to talk to her. He had to *ask* her all the things that were bursting through his thoughts. But most of all, he just had to hold her.

"Alan—" she began as she pulled back.

"Don't run away yet," he said, rushing his words. "Not before I can talk to you. I need to find the right thing to say—"

She arched her brows. "I've just chased you all across the state. I chained you up to keep you from escaping. And I still have handcuffs. Just where do you think I'm going?"

"Nowhere," he rasped. "Not yet."

She touched his cheek, her caress tender. "Not ever."

He grabbed her fingers and pressed his lips to them. The words spilled out of him. Not the ones he intended. Not even ones he'd realized were coming out, but once spoken they locked inside his heart as absolute fact.

"I'm going to adopt them."

She jolted, her gaze hopping to the kids. The girl Lexi was

sleeping now. The ER had managed to get her fever down so she was considered stable for the moment while they waited for test results. It wouldn't tell them squat because no one here knew about shifters, but he knew from his own experience that she was past the worst of it. Once the fever came down, the body found a way to adapt to the new shifter abilities. They just had to watch her and make sure she continued to regulate herself.

The boy Jordy was sitting by his sister's bed, holding her hand. He'd been pronounced healthy, but Alan knew that was an illusion. The boy had killed Elisabeth. And though the bitch had certainly deserved it, that wasn't going to stop the nightmares to come. He needed someone to help him through the anger and the guilt.

And then both kids needed to figure out how to handle being an entirely new and unique type of shifter. Counting Alan, there were only three created shifters in the whole world. They probably ought to stick together.

Meanwhile Tonya pursed her lips in thought. "That'll take some speedy legal maneuvering."

"Good thing I'm a lawyer."

She turned to look at him. "And it'll take time. And patience."

He nodded, feeling tongue-tied the moment he met her eyes. "I know. I didn't think I could do it, but…" He shrugged. "When I was out by Rand Lake, there was a man who showed me how. Simple words and patience. Turns out it works with toddlers and shifters both."

She chuckled, as she leaned into his arm. "Tell me something I don't know."

"I want to marry you."

They both started, surprised by his words. He recovered first.

"You were right about everything. That I needed time. That I'll find my balance."

"And you have."

Yes. No. Maybe. "It's all happening so fast. I'm still screwed up. So are the kids."

"So we'll take our time. Just don't run away again."

He lifted his shoulder in a halfhearted shrug. "I can't abandon them. I know where they're at, and it's not a good place."

She nodded, her gaze drifting to the kids. "Then all I need to do is stay close to them."

"No," he said as he pulled her tight. "Just stay close to me. Just…wait for me to be ready. I think I can get through this, but only if you're with me." She smiled, her face so soft that he couldn't resist stroking her cheek. From letting his thumb explore the texture of her lips even as she spoke.

"You picked life instead of death."

"I picked you," he countered. "I picked the kids." He took a breath, trying to explain everything that had happened in those few short minutes when he'd been fighting for his life. "Do you know what's good about being a shifter?"

Her lips curved. "Tell me."

"It's the instincts. The minute I stopped fighting it, all those instincts made everything thing clear. It wasn't just that I could fight better."

"You already had martial arts training, Alan. That helps enormously. Shifter and man—they become one."

"They are one," he said, feeling the truth of it inside himself. "And my instincts chose saving the kids rather than killing Elisabeth." Did she remember? "I left her to you, Tonya. I was going to let you arrest her."

"I know. I saw."

She had? Good. "But now I need to help them," he said looking at the kids. "There's a thousand little adjustments, and I'm the only one who can teach them. Plus, I'm pretty sure I can get group rates on therapy."

Her chuckle warmed him inside and out.

"But it'll only work if I stay in balance. If I have a smart woman by my side willing to do anything to keep my head on straight. Even chaining me up in a basement. And then risking everything by taking them off."

Her expression flashed through guilt and regret. "I shouldn't have—"

"Yes, you should have." He took a deep breath. "You did everything perfect. You are perfect—"

She snorted at that.

"And even if you aren't, I love every single flaw and mistake. I love that you've never lied to me. I love that you're not afraid to do what's necessary. And I love that your bear wants me even when I'm fucked up."

"It's not just my bear."

"It's you, Tonya. I love all of you, and I want to spend the rest of my life proving that to you."

She smiled, the expression like the sun breaking through on a cloudy day. "Don't prove it to me. Just stick around. Love me."

He dropped his forehead to hers and said the words he wanted desperately to say in front of a minister. "I do."

"I do, too."

Their kiss was sweet this time. Gentle, tender, and it burned through his blood in a wildfire of passion. Civilized and wild, all at once.

He could do this. With her at his side, he could do anything.

Chapter Twenty-Four

One Year Later

I do." Tonya's voice echoed strongly in the judge's chamber. A big sound given how many people were stuffed into this tiny space. Her brothers. Alan's family. And of course the most important ones were crowded right next to her.

Alan grinned and, at the appropriate moment, he said his words, too, adding an extra one for flair. "I absolutely do."

Cocky man. She absolutely adored him and the life they'd created. After catching Elisabeth, she'd been promoted to under sheriff and would soon take the full role when the current one retired. Her position as beta was solid, if not always thrilling, given the paperwork required. And Alan surprised them all by running a successful law practice for shifters. Turned out that once he stopped working just for the Gladwins, shifters throughout the state came to him for legal help.

He hired Julie as his assistant and they were so busy that he was expanding his office.

But that was nothing compared to watching Jordy and Lexi settle in with the Gladwins. Shifter kids were normal around here. Cat-shifters? Not so much. But it didn't seem to matter as the problems of balancing instinct against civilized behavior was common between the species. After the medical issues were stabilized, the kids had started attending school as if they'd been there all their lives. And though certain adjustments took longer than others, a single school year had seen all of that even out.

Which made this moment even more special. Finally. After everything, she was finally becoming a mother. Not just a wife, which had happened a half hour earlier, but now a mother of two wonderful kids.

"So now," the judge said, "if each of you would please sign."

They passed the adoption paperwork around from Alan to Tonya, then to Jordy and Lexi. One by one, they created their lives in solid black ink.

"Then it is my absolute pleasure," the judge continued, "to pronounce you all a family."

Then Carl stepped forward, dropping a kiss to each child's forehead. "And officially a member of the Gladwin Bear Clan. We'll be here for you always, no matter what."

Tonya watched the kids' faces closely. They were both beaming even if Jordy wasn't a big one for kisses. He was an eleven-year-old boy, after all.

"And now," Carl continued. "For the fun part."

Alan chuckled and looked at his watch. "Dessert isn't for another three hours. Whatever could you have in mind?" He was teasing. All the adults knew exactly what was coming. And if the kids had a guess, they didn't know for sure.

"Well," said the judge, as he shrugged off his robe. "I guess I don't need this." All he wore beneath were a pair of extra, extra large basketball shorts.

Jordy and Lexi's eyes danced with excitement.

"For real?" Lexi breathed.

Tonya nodded. "If you want to."

Jordy looked out the window. They were a short mile from a private woods that attached to the Gladwin State Park. "Right now? With *everybody*?"

Alan chuckled. "If you want to."

The two kids looked at each other, checking in. It was a habit they had of sticking together no matter what they faced, and it warmed Tonya to see it happening now.

"We do," they said together, and right there were the last two wonderful "I dos" of the day.

It was quick, joyous work to pile everyone into their cars, trucks, or SUVs as they headed to the private picnic area for the Gladwins. The tables already groaned under the weight of the food. The whole clan had turned out to welcome their newest members. But before they could get to the serious business of eating, there was something more fun to do first.

The run. A pell-mell tumbling, frolicking as animals in the woods. The monthly party had been reinstated by Becca, Carl's new wife, who had changed things around so that the run came first and the food second. Everyone looked forward to the party, and everyone, at the moment, was waiting on Carl to start it. Except he wasn't doing it yet. Instead, he looked at the kids.

"Want to start us?" Carl asked, as he pulled off his shirt.

"Really?" Jordy asked, his gaze going to the hundred-plus people gathered there. Not all of them would turn into bears. In fact, only thirty or so were strong enough to shift on a regular basis. The others would hang back, talk, work, or watch the children, as they started in early on the food. "But…" He swallowed as he looked at his sister. "We don't exactly look like the rest of you."

"Nah," quipped Alan as he unbuttoned his dress shirt. "We look better."

"Even if you don't *smell* better," teased Mark who was already standing naked at the edge of the picnic area.

"They smell pretty good to me," Tonya called as she shrugged out of her dress. She was going to relish this run because it was probably the last time she could participate in one of these parties as a bear. At least for another seven months or so. Shifting in the later stages of pregnancy was not a good idea.

Then it was all eyes on the kids as they took each other's hands. This would be the first time they did this in public. It had taken months to get them to control it, and even longer to manage the individual aspects. Now they could pick what parts of their bodies became covered in fur, what bones shifted how, and best of all, whether they wanted that defensive odor or not. Usually the answer was *not*.

Then the wait was over. With a nod to each other, her children shifted into their half-cat form. Beautiful golden fur, pert ears, and sharp teeth appeared. Lexi even sprouted a tail. She looked like a young, beautiful cat woman. Jordy went with large, sharp claws and bright green slit eyes.

"Catch me if you can," he hollered.

"Cats rule, bears drool!" Lexi cried with a challenge.

Then they were off, first the kids and then Carl, shifting from human to bear in a single leap. Roars echoed around them as the rest of the clan sprang forward in shades of brown and black. Alan was just about to go, too, when she caught his hand.

"Hey, Papa," she said, as she tugged him back.

"Yeah, Mama?"

"You going to stay behind with the baby when we do this next year?"

"The ba—" His eyes abruptly widened and his gaze dropped to her belly. "Seriously?"

She nodded, grinning.

"Best. Day. Ever!" he cried as he swung her into his arms.

Then she kissed him, her heart overflowing with love. Definitely the best day ever. Except for every single day to come.

The first version of this story started with Alan in the hospital, but my editor thought we needed a little more of Alan and Tonya as they were before his kidnapping. I wrote two new chapters, but that ended up slowing the pace too much. Writing is all about refinement, so in the end, we picked the car scene as the one to keep. That left this scene out in the cold. Unable to let it disappear completely, I opted to include it as a deleted scene.

So here you go! A scene from seven years before our story starts!

—Kathy Lyons

Chapter One—Deleted

Seven years ago

W ho the hell are you? And where is my sister?"

Tonya Kappes arched her brow at the most annoying of her three older brothers. And then, just to piss him off, she adjusted her ample cleavage until it strained the bodice of her Christmas elf outfit. The neckline was low, the skirt short, and her red stiletto boots were the perfect finishing touch. She looked hot, and as she was now of legal drinking age, she was going to thoroughly enjoy herself at the Gladwin bear clan's Christmas party.

"I just have to put on some lipstick, and then you can drive me to the lodge." She had her driver's license, of course, but with herself and her three older brothers all home for Christmas, there wasn't an extra vehicle to be had.

Simon folded his arms across his chest. As a bear-shifter, he was a big man. But since getting into the Army Rangers, every part of him was cut like granite. His biceps bulged like cannons as he glared at her. "I am not taking a slut to a kids' party."

"Watch your mouth," she snapped, fighting to keep her temper—and her bear—under control. Certainly she'd explored in college, but nothing approaching slutdom. And she wasn't a child who rose to the bait anymore. So she turned and faced Simon with her chin lifted and her shoulders thrown back. "I was a tomboy child, thanks to you three." She gestured vaguely downstairs to where her other brothers were making inroads on her mother's Christmas apple pie. "But I'm a woman now, and I'll dress how I like, when I like."

Simon's brow arched, but beyond that, his attitude didn't soften one iota. "Who is this new 'womanliness' for?" He cupped his hands around imaginary boobs and she rolled her eyes at him.

"It's for me. After all, I've got 'em, right? Might as well—"

"Don't finish that statement. I don't need any more nightmares, thank you very much."

He didn't have nightmares…yet. As far as they knew, he was still training, though there was a new secretiveness to her brother. It was only normal, she supposed, as was her stepping fully into her sexuality. All perfectly normal. So she lifted up a tube of bright red lipstick and applied it expertly to her full lips. Her brother mock shuddered, but then his expression turned serious.

"Come on, Tonya. You're better than this. Do you mean to tell me that this"—he gestured to her outfit—" is who you are?"

She folded her arms, plumping her cleavage just to watch him flinch. "There's nothing wrong with wanting to look sexy."

"It's not about sex." He looked like he wanted to vomit just from saying the word. "You're a senior in college now. It's about time to think about who you're going to be as an adult."

"I am thinking about that." Or more specifically, *who* she wanted to be *with* as an adult.

"And slutty elf is what you came up with? You're getting a degree in criminal justice. You loved your anthropology classes. And you're no slouch in the science department."

"And I'm going to a party, not applying to graduate school. Guys don't care about brains."

"The smart ones do."

She paused, wondering if that were true. But Alan Carman already knew she was smart. Now she had to prove that she was sexy. "I've got to get him to notice me first."

"Dress like that and that's all he'll notice. This isn't you, Tonya. Be yourself and the rest will fall in line."

She dropped her arms and lifted her chest. "These are part of me. I'm just not hiding them anymore." In fact, she'd spent most of college trying to figure out her feminine side. She was looking forward to finally unveiling it.

Simon sighed, shaking his head as he turned away. "He better be worth it," he said over his shoulder. "Because if he isn't I'm going to kick his ass. And then I'll start on yours."

He was, she thought with a grin. Alan Carman, the second son of their alpha, was certainly worth all the makeup and sexy clothing she owned.

Sometime in the last year he'd grown from the lanky, nerdy kid in high school to a tall, well-dressed man with shoulders that might not be bear-shifter broad, but filled out a suit like no one her own age. She'd watched him all summer as he worked going door to door selling magazine subscriptions. Even in ninety-degree heat, he'd worn the required suit and spoke gently to every person. She'd bought subscriptions for each member of her family. Nothing had happened between them then because she'd been dating an artist back at college. But she hadn't been able to forget how he'd looked or that he took the time to learn every family in Gladwin by name. Not just the shifters, whom he'd known all his life, but the others. The normals who weren't in on the shifter secret. Even the ones who were ignorant rednecks who wouldn't read a magazine if their lives depended on it.

Now it was Christmas and she'd broken up with her artist, mostly because she couldn't stop thinking about Alan. And because Mr. Artiste had turned into a needy jerk. She was free and clear, amorously speaking, and it was time for her to see if Alan had grown in other ways. They'd kissed once on his fourteenth birthday, and it had been the hottest kiss she'd ever had. Of course, she'd had next to no experience then, so who knew if it had really been as good as she remembered. Tonight, she planned to find out.

It took another half hour to leave her house because her brothers couldn't resist mocking her attempts at being a girl. She counted it a measure of her maturity that she didn't punch them out. And frankly, they seemed to be surprised by her new restraint as well. But that was college for you. It expanded a girl's mind, body, and ability to put her brothers in their place.

She put a little extra swagger into her step as she walked into the Christmas gathering. The lodge was really the cafeteria of the Gladwin shifter kids' camp, but it functioned as the meeting place for all clan events including the annual Christmas party. Everyone was there before them. That suited Tonya just fine as she wanted to make an entrance in her outfit. And sure enough, the moment she sauntered in, more than one head turned her way.

Awesome. Except not a one of them was the man she wanted to see.

"Jesus, Tonya," a voice drawled to her right. "When did you become a girl?"

Carl. Her high school sweetheart and the man who'd nearly gotten her pregnant when they'd gone at it as hormonal bears. He also happened to be Alan's older brother.

She turned, her chin lifted. "I've always been a girl. Nice of you to finally notice."

"I believe I noticed plenty in high school," he said, his light blue eyes lighting with appreciation as he took in her cleavage. "But there's no harm in continuing to look, right? If you'd dressed like that way back when, I don't think we would have ever broken up."

Yeah, they would have because they'd gone to different colleges. And because high school desires were different than adult needs. Everything about them had been hormones, though it had been really fun while it lasted.

"So where's your brother?"

Carl rolled his eyes. "Mr. Snobby is back at the house with the nonshifters."

"What?"

"He's all about having nonshifter friends now. Like we're smelly apes or something." Carl huffed out an annoyed breath as only an older brother could. "So he's hosting a party up at the house. For those not in the know."

"But this is a Gladwin *clan* gathering. And he's part of the *clan*."

"Talk to him." Carl spoke in an offhand way, his gaze traveling over the crowd to zero in on Missy Clarke. Their former classmate stood near the Christmas tree and was showing off long legs that had been colored by the best tanning beds in Michigan. "He says he'd rather be with his own kind."

"That's bullshit, and you know it!"

Carl raised his hands in surrender. "You're preaching to the choir." Then he moved away, his own swagger pronounced as he headed in Missy's direction. Tonya dismissed him as she headed for the exit. The Carman home sat across the street from the camp, as they were the ones running it. It was hard to stomp across the street in stiletto heels, especially since this was December in Michigan. Ice and drifts of snow made everything slick. Thank God her shifter metabolism kept her warm in her outfit. Without it, she would be one frozen elf.

The house was ablaze with lights and the door to the two-story cabin was unlocked. She heard Christmas music set too loud and a zillion scented candles stunk up the place. It probably wouldn't be bad for a normal human, but this was hell for someone with enhanced senses. WTF? Alan was usually way more considerate than that.

She stepped inside, wrinkling her nose against the mixed scent assault. She noticed around a dozen people milling through the house, all of them normal as far as she could tell. Then two seconds later, skinny arms twisted her around. If she hadn't been in stilettos, she could have stopped it, but she was unsteady on these things, especially on the polished wood floor. So she spun around and felt wet lips slam into hers. *Ugh!*

Jeremy Turpin. She could tell by the mixed scents of chewing tobacco and electrical tape. He'd been a slimeball in high school and remained a waste of space as an electrician. She shoved him backward with as much as leverage as she could handle in these boots. Which put him against the wall with a satisfying thump.

"Ugh, Jeremy, what the—"

"Mistletoe!" he gasped as he pointed up. Sure enough someone had dangled plastic mistletoe such that it hung badly over the doorway.

"That isn't even real, and if you try that again—" Her words cut off as she heard a chuckle. Melodic and sweet, it warmed her belly in wholly new and exciting ways.

Alan. She turned toward the sound. He was in the kitchen, and as she listened, she heard him murmur, "Merry Christmas," to someone.

"Merry Not-Jesus'-Birthday," came a giggling response. "Because, did you know, Jesus wasn't actually born in December, right? Early Christians needed a holiday to compete with the pagan winter solstice. People were coming to both, you know, and that was just, you know, holiday shopping, instead of real religion."

Tonya rolled her eyes. Someone was both drunk and a know-it-all. She rounded the corner, ready to share a look of disgust with Alan only to hear him chuckling, deep and low in his throat.

"Religious history is so fascinating."

Religious history? Or cleavage the size of…well, sized a couple cups bigger than Tonya's. And on a blonde with a heart-shaped face and soft waves of hair draping tantalizingly across her low cut blouse. She was leaning against the stove and trailing her hand across Alan's chest while he gazed adoringly down at a spot inches below her chin.

Jesus.

Tonya must have made a sound. She didn't mean to, but Alan looked up and his eyes widened at the sight of her. *Yeah, take that religious history Barbie.* And then the bastard spoke.

"Tonya? What the hell are you wearing?"

She looked down, abruptly self-conscious. Which pissed her off because even in front of her brothers she hadn't felt stupid. "Last year you were an elf, remember? I, er, thought it was a great idea and so, um…"

"You teased me mercilessly."

Yeah, well, that was because she was still with the artist and hadn't wanted to notice how hot his butt looked or that he had great legs in elf tights. "So, um, now you can tease me back."

"Isn't it interesting," piped in the blonde, "how people on the cusp of adulthood often revert back to childish behaviors? I absolutely understand that push-pull, having gone through it myself a few years ago. But eventually, a woman has to embrace her maturity more than her—"

"Cleavage?" The word just spilled out of her lips, and Tonya silently cursed herself for resorting to boob comments. And just as she knew would happen, the blonde took full advantage of the slip.

"Oh? Well, yes, I'm afraid I've been generously endowed. But I'm thinking of getting a reduction because it makes it so hard for people to appreciate my intelligence. I'm so glad I have more to offer than just a pair of tits." Then she stroked Alan's face, drawing his attention back to her. "And that Alan is smart enough to see my full measure."

From the look in Alan's eyes, he'd been "measuring" her from every angle in his imagination. Or maybe in real life, too, because the bastard's expression softened into fondness. "I love talking religion with you."

"Saying, 'oh God,' doesn't count as religion, Alan." WTF? Why did spiteful-bitch comments fly from her mouth?

The blonde chuckled, a sound worse than nails on a chalkboard. "That's why we spice it up with Yahweh, Jehovah, and El Shaddai."

Tonya wanted to go El Shaddai on the woman's ass, but she bit it back. She was done with immature displays of temper. So she forced herself to smile. "Alan, what are you doing here? You should be at the party at the lodge."

Alan's expression flattened. "I'm fine right here. With my friends."

"Jeremy Turpin?" she mocked. Then she held up her hand. "Whatever. Bring them over there. It's where everyone—"

"I'm not...*everyone*," Alan said, his voice hard. "I've never been *everyone*."

Shifter. He was saying he'd never been a shifter, but no one cared, least of all her. In fact, strong shifters needed to mate with a normal human or risk their children going feral. Which is why parties always included both kind. "But you belong with *everyone*. Over there."

"Why?" the blonde asked. "Why can't he stay here where he's happy? This is a lovely party," she said, gesturing to the main room where more normals from high school were clustered. Though it was hard to make out over the blaring music, Tonya cued into conversations about sports teams, weather, and politics. They were the usual conversations, and they were identical to the ones going on across the street. At the lodge.

"Why do you insist on segregating?" Tonya pressed. "What's wrong—"

"I'm not the one insisting," Alan said, his jaw firming. "There are conversations over there—attitudes—that make us unwelcome."

"Bullshit!" Tonya snapped. "You're the one holing yourself up over here."

Whatever Alan might have said to that was forestalled by the blonde. Her expression flattened into anger as she straightened up off the counter. "Look, elf girl, I'm sure the costume party is all kinds of fun and all."

"Tonya. My name's Tonya."

"Of course it is," the girl sneered.

When Tonya just stared, Alan explained. "Eleanor has a theory about why people use girl names that end in a vowel. It's part of her doctoral thesis."

The girl was working on her doctorate? Shit, just how old was she? "Your family is over there."

Eleanor sniffed. "His family is celebrating on Christmas Day. This is a community party done for political reasons like the appearance of unity and a biological need to reinforce stability through contiguous leadership."

Was there room for her teeth among that mouthful of words? "It's a Christmas party, not a political statement."

"Oh dear. Are you in school? Community college, perhaps?"

"I'm at the University of Michigan, thank you very much. And—"

"Tonya," Alan interrupted. "Maybe you should go back. You look really good in that outfit. I'm sure there are lots of guys—"

"And you prefer it here?" Tonya pressed. "With—"

"My girlfriend? Yes."

Oh. Right. So he was dating the walking encyclopedia with boobs. Tonya rocked back on her heels. "You know, Alan, I get it. You wanted someone as smart and normal as you." By which she meant freaky weird and book smart, not people smart. He'd grown up in the family of the clan alpha. He was one of the rare humans in on the shifter secret. He was well versed in animal behavior and had seen leadership up close and personal. That was as a far from normal as it got, and yet he'd picked the most ignorant woman she'd ever met as his girlfriend. One who spouted academic bullshit and thought it was truth.

Guess that proved all men fell for a big set of tits no matter who was wearing them. And in this, Tonya had to admit, her set were smaller than the triple Ds on Eleanor.

"Tonya—"

She held up her hand. "A doctorate and ample cleavage. She's a great choice, Alan. I'm sure you'll be very happy together." Then she spun on her stiletto heels and marched out.

When an alpha meets his match…

Don't miss the first book *The Bear Who Loved Me* in the Grizzlies Gone Wild trilogy by *USA Today* bestselling author Kathy Lyons, available now.

An excerpt follows

Chapter One

*M*ore. *Power.*

Thoughts came slowly to Carl Carman, but each word reverberated with power. That was the best part of being a grizzly bear. Simple words meant simple, strong deeds. Human complexities were nonexistent in this state, though they echoed in the back of his mind. He was on a mission, had come to this Christmas tree field on a clan purpose. That he took joy in what he did was a trivial detail.

Now.

He braced his legs, shoved his claws deep, and then he thought it. One word, and the power crashed through every cell in his body.

Destroy.

He did.

What he held, he uprooted.

What he gripped, he crushed.

Whatever he touched, he tore apart.

Joy.

He grinned though he grunted with effort. He tasted blood—his own—and the coppery tang was sweet. Human language tried to intrude in this moment, but the grizzly had no interest in it. His language was action, power delivered with thrilling ease. And it liked to rip things apart. So he continued and was content.

Until something else disturbed him. Red and blue flashes across his retinas. At first he flinched away from the lights, but they roused the rational part of him. Red. Blue.

Police.

With a roar of fury, he began to tuck the animal away. His bear fought the shift, holding onto his shape with every ounce of his determination. But in this, the man was stronger, the mind crueler. With steadfast will, he folded the grizzly into an envelope in his mind. It had taken him years to master it. Things that large don't origami into a tiny flat rectangle easily.

His bones shifted, most of the fur thinned and disappeared, though some fell to the ground. His face tightened, and the strength in his arms and claws pulled inside, shrinking as it was tucked away. He straightened, the grizzly hump now gone as the energy coiled tight inside. His eyes burned. Damn, how they burned. But in time that last vestige of dark power would fade and his normal cool green color would return. Quiet control and long, complex sentences would be his norm. Though his first words as human were always the last snarl of his bear.

"Shit."

"And Merry Christmas to you, too," said a familiar female voice, though that particular holiday had passed months ago. His vision settled, and he saw Tonya dressed in her patrol uniform as she leaned against her squad car. The lights were still flashing, and in the early morning dawn, those colors would be seen far and wide.

"Flip off those lights," he growled as he started searching for his pants. He was out here swinging in the breeze for all to see, and though that rarely bothered him, naked and vulnerable was not a good idea around her.

She opened the squad car and used one hand to flip off the lights while the other aimed her phone at him. Jesus, she was taking pictures.

"I'll tear that thing out of your hand," he snarled, "and I won't be gentle."

"Promises, promises," she said with a sigh. But she did drop the phone. "Doesn't matter. I already got my holiday screensaver." She pushed off the car and sauntered over, her hips swinging in a tantalizing rhythm. Tonya Kappes had short honey-blond hair, modest curves on her tall, muscular frame, and a dangerous look in her eye that had once tantalized his grizzly like honey. Now it just made him tired. "See?"

She was hard to miss. He might not want to marry her, but that didn't stop him from appreciating her feminine charms. But then a moment later, he realized she was talking about the image on her phone, flipped around for him to see.

Hell. "Give me that."

She tried to pull away, but he was faster and stronger. He

caught her wrist and squeezed until the cell dropped into his other hand. She might have fought him more, but a glare from him had her quieting, her head tilted to the side in submission. Then he looked down. There, full screen on the phone, was a video of him as a grizzly bear methodically destroying a field of Christmas trees. The telltale silver streak down his back flashed clear in the dawn light.

"Why would you record this?" he asked.

She flashed him a coy look that only pissed him off. "I like watching you work."

Bullshit. She liked collecting blackmail material on people. She'd never used it as far as he knew, but that didn't stop her from gathering intel on everyone. It was just part of her character and probably helped her be a good cop. But that didn't mean he had to like it. With a quick flick of his thumb, he initiated a factory reset of her phone.

"Hey!" she cried when she saw what he'd done. "That's evidence!"

"You here to arrest me?"

"You did just destroy Nick Merkel's best tree field."

"It had to be done, and you know it."

Her lips compressed into a flat line. "The Merkels' farm brings a boatload to the local economy. Hurting this field damages everyone."

"He refused a direct order to fix his pesticide platform." Pesticides were a fact of modern agriculture, and most farmers were extra careful about the area where the chemicals were mixed and stored. Not Nick Merkel. Spills were common and his platform leaked like a sieve. But he didn't seem to care because the runoff went away from his property. Too bad for him that Carl cared. A lot. "He's leaking poison into the groundwater."

She nodded, grim anger on her features. "So kill him and be done with it."

"You'd rather I murder him than destroy his prize field." It wasn't a question. He knew that shifter law gave him the right to kill anyone in his clan who openly disobeyed him. But the man in him keep looking for a more civilized punishment. Not so for Tonya.

"He's got a wife and two sons to carry on the farm. They'll fix the platform and still bring in money to the area."

Carl didn't answer. Tonya was a cop through and through. That meant black-and-white law and swift justice. If kids vandalized a building, they went to jail. If a man poisoned the land, he got killed. For the most part, shifter law bowed to human law, but there were two unbreakables. Don't hurt the land. Don't disobey the alpha. Nick Merkel had done both.

Something in the Merkel bloodline was just ornery. The man had been a thorn in Carl's side since Carl had stepped into his position as the alpha of the Gladwin grizzly-shifters, eight years ago. But Carl had seen firsthand what happened when a leader took the law into his own hands. He had sworn his tenure as Maximus of their mid-Michigan clan would not be one of terror and vigilante justice. So he'd done one step short of murder. He'd destroyed a field of Merkel's Christmas trees, cutting the bastard's pocketbook instead of his jugular.

"It won't work," Tonya said. "You'll have to kill him eventually."

"And then they'll crucify me for killing one of our own." He knew because that's what had happened when he'd taken control of the clan. Another idiot had challenged him, and he'd let his grizzly out. One bloody death later, and Carl was the acknowledged alpha. But then the widow had started grumbling. And before long, others had agreed that an alpha should never kill one of his own.

"It's an endless cycle," Tonya agreed. "You can't stop it. So get on with the next step and kill him. Deal with the next step when it happens."

"Just help me find my damn pants," he grumbled, unwilling to admit that there wasn't a way out.

Her lips curled into a slow smile. "They're locked in my trunk."

Carl's head whipped back to her. "Why?"

She shrugged, a roll of her shoulders that set her breasts to bouncing. "Evidence."

"Blackmail, you mean."

She chuckled, a low throaty sound. "Or just a way to keep you naked for a little bit longer."

She took a step back, her gaze rolling slowly down his torso. Jesus, she was bold. She had a way of making even the most exhibitionist of his set feel dirty in a completely teenage horny, fuck-'em-fast-and-furious kind of way. But he'd left those hormones behind years ago.

Then he caught her scent. "You're in heat."

Damn it, if he hadn't been so absorbed in dealing with Nick Merkel, he would have noticed it right off the bat. No wonder he was keyed up around her.

She arched a brow. "Ticktock goes the biological clock."

"Give me my clothes. I am not fucking you. And especially not in the middle of a destroyed Christmas tree field."

She chuckled. "I don't care where we do it, Carl, but we gotta do it."

"No, we really don't."

He watched hurt flicker in her eyes. It didn't even touch her face, but her eyes flinched, and it was more telling on her than a scream on anyone else.

He didn't want to insult her. He had some warm feelings for her. They'd known each other all their lives, but cuddling up to her was like snuggling with a live hand grenade. He could control her. She always submitted to him eventually, but who wanted to spend their off-hours in a constant game of dominance and submission? He wanted someone he could relax and have a beer with. Around Tonya, he'd be on duty as the Gladwin Max 24/7.

"All right," she said as she folded her arms across her chest. Her breasts plumped nicely, and his bear took notice. The rest of him was seeing that despite her words, Tonya had not given in. "Let's look at this logically." She almost sneered the last word. Grizzly clans were not known to be deep thinkers. Something he daily tried to change.

"Not until I'm dressed."

She didn't move. "Our bears are compatible. We established that as teenagers."

"Everyone's compatible at sixteen." And back then, they had "compatted" as much as possible for a hot, horny month. But even at sixteen, he had grown tired of the constant power play.

"You're Maximus now, but you need a strong wife at your side to hold the position. Merkel openly defied you. Unless you do a massive show of strength, more will follow. The last thing we need is a civil war inside the clan."

He knew this. It had been burning through his brain ever since Merkel had refused to fix his platform. Carl had tried to sic the EPA on the man, hoping that human justice would help him out, but the organization was overloaded and undermanned. The earliest they could get someone out to check on violations was three weeks away. Hence his morning rampage.

"We're short on numbers as it is," he growled. "I'm not going to murder my own people."

"You don't have to," she said. "I will."

"Tonya!"

"I'm a cop and the strongest she-bear in a hundred miles. Get me pregnant and my brothers will line up to support you."

"They could line up without me getting you knocked up."

She shook her head. "That's not how it works and you know it."

True. Family loyalty trumped clan groupings all the time. It was the reason Merkel's wife and sons hadn't taken care of their father themselves. That kind of betrayal was nonexistent within shifter communities. Tonya's family was large and powerful, and there were rumblings of them splitting off to establish their own clan. Or of them taking over his. That would all end the moment he impregnated Tonya. If she became his Maxima, then that would fold her family into his, locking up the leadership for generations to come.

But he just couldn't do it. They'd drive each other insane inside a year. Besides, he had a better idea, but first he had to end any romantic ideas between the two of them.

"I think of you like a sister," he began, and it was the God's honest truth.

She didn't argue. Instead, her gaze drifted down. The shift was slow and deliberate, and he forced himself to let his hands go lax, opening up his entire body for her perusal.

Flat. Flaccid. And absolutely uninterested despite the fuck-me pheromones she gave off.

She didn't speak. There was no need to. She simply lifted up the car key fob and pressed a button. The trunk popped open, and he finally got his hands on his clothes.

They didn't speak as he dressed. He didn't even want to look at her. He'd hurt her, and the guilt weighed heavy on him. Maybe the others were right. Maybe there just wasn't enough bear in him to effectively lead the clan. His uncle had been so much bear he was almost feral. When he'd been Max, he'd killed with impunity, destroyed at random, and taken the most powerful she-bear by force. It had been human cops who had killed him—with his own father's help—opening up their clan to another way to rule. Logic and law—human concepts that the Gladwin shifters desperately needed.

Ten years later, Carl had stepped into power, but everyone seemed to think he was more man than bear. He couldn't kill without exhausting all other possibilities. And he couldn't fuck the most powerful she-bear around just because she was in heat. Which left him with a fracturing clan and his best ally hurting as she answered a call on her radio. Some drunk teens were cow tipping a few miles to the east.

"I have to go," she said as she climbed into her cruiser and shut the door. But the window was still open, so he leaned in.

"Tonya, you're still a valuable member of the clan. Maybe my most—"

"Save it. I've heard it all." They'd had this argument in one form or another since they were old enough to marry. The only sop to his guilt was that she wanted the power of Maxima way more than she wanted him.

"I have a better idea," he said. "Be my beta."

She froze, her eyes widening in shock. "Alan's your beta."

His brother, Alan, had served as his second from the very beginning. It kept the power in the family, but Alan had never shifted. The grizzly DNA had missed him, and the man couldn't hold the position for much longer. Privately, Carl believed that's what had sparked Merkel's latest round of disobedience. The idiot hoped to force Carl's hand into making a compromise and giving him the beta honor.

Never going to happen. He needed someone he could trust as his second.

"I know it's unorthodox," he continued, "but I can't think of anyone better."

"Unorthodox? A female beta is unheard of! You think you have problems with Merkel now? Every shifter in the state will be calling you a pansy-assed *human*."

A big insult in the shifter community. Everyone seemed to believe that the animal side was the power center. The *male* animal. But if any female could change their minds, it was Tonya.

"A female beta makes the clan look weak. Those Detroit bastards will be on us in a split second."

"The Detroit clan has their own problems. They're not looking to start a war with us." He hoped.

"You should ask one of my brothers."

He'd thought of that, but he didn't trust them like he trusted Tonya. He'd known her since they were children. Everyone expected them to marry, so they'd been shoved together from their earliest moments. He knew the way she thought and which way she would jump. In most things their opinions aligned, though she tended to more to a black-white rule of the jungle, while he tried to think a problem through. All of that added up to her being an excellent beta.

"I chose you. Swear unwavering loyalty to me, and we can hold the clan together without marriage. That's what you really want, anyway."

She arched a brow. "You underestimate your attraction as a mate."

"Bullshit. You want the power."

"And the hot sex."

Carl rolled his eyes. "So get a gigolo and be my beta."

She shook her head slowly, not in denial but in stunned amazement. "You're trying to drag the shifter community into a modern mind-set. It's going to backfire on you. We're just not as logical as you." To her credit, she didn't sneer the word "logical" like most shifters would.

"Will you do it? I can announce it at the next clan meeting."

He needed time to tell Alan, and that was not going to be a comfortable discussion.

"Yes," Tonya said, being typically decisive. Then she pushed the car into drive, but she didn't move. "One more thing: You had a message. That's why I came out here to find you."

He frowned. Damn it, she should have told him that first thing instead of trying to trap him into mating. "What?"

"There's trouble in Kalamazoo."

"What?" The word exploded out of him, but Tonya didn't hear it. She'd already hit the gas and was roaring away.

Just as well, he thought as he sprinted for his truck. Even clothed, there was no way to hide his reaction at the mention of that place where *she* lived. He hit the freeway with his erection lying hard and heavy against his thigh.

Bear meets girl…

Read *LICENSE TO SHIFT*, the second book in the Grizzlies Gone Wild trilogy, by *USA Today* bestselling author Kathy Lyons, available now.

An excerpt follows.

Chapter One

*F*emale.

Mark Robertson's nose twitched, and he moved to explore the scent.

Fertile.

He pursued, the spice of her as sharp as a hook.

A sound grated on his nerves and his hackles rose in irritation. The female was here and he was already thick with the drive to mount her.

Close.

He would hunt her, and she would succumb.

Part of him was uncomfortable with that predatory thought. It disliked the absolute ruthlessness with which he would claim his mate. But that voice was tiny and uninteresting. When it came to mating, there were no limits. Offspring were imperative. Taking a female urgent. He would hunt this female unto the ends of the earth.

If only the damned noise would stop.

He blocked out the sound, refocusing on the female, but she proved elusive. The scent was there, the draw undeniable, but he had to wake to find her.

Wake.

He did, though the struggle to consciousness was hard. He'd been dreaming, he realized. And someone was making a noise that pounded in his temples. The grizzly part of him wanted to obliterate the sound with his claws. The man in him barely had the wherewithal to comprehend it was the door buzzer.

He shoved to his feet, his movements lumbering and awkward. He banged into a desk and howled in rage, the sound waking him enough to open his eyes.

Home.

He was in the place bear and man coexisted in relative peace, but the sound was forcing him to leave it. That didn't bode well for whatever idiot was leaning on the buzzer. He inhaled, pulling in the scent of humming electronics, stale coffee, and fertile female.

Well, at least that part had been real. A woman stood on his doorstep, which made her easy prey.

He stumbled to the stairs, climbing angrily out of his basement den. The raw buzzer sound ate at his control, and each moment it continued made his teeth bare with fury. The man in him prayed it was the female, otherwise the grizzly would kill it. This was his most dangerous time—when bear and man fought against each other for control. It made the animal unpredictable and the man insane.

The clamor paused, giving him a split second of relief. And

then it began again, the renewed racket even worse because of the brief respite.

He had no dexterity to manage the locks. The bear tried to rip the door open, but it was steel reinforced and would not budge, though God knew he tried. The frustration nearly undid the bear, but the man took control. He slammed his hand down twice trying to break the lock before he thought to twist the deadbolt. The chain was harder, requiring more focus, and his higher cortex was recruited to handle the fine manipulation. Higher cortex was controlled by the man, which forced the beast back into sullen bitterness.

This was why I layered a dozen different locks on his door, the man gloated. So it would require higher brain function to open and thereby save whatever idiot thought they could wake him. The bear remained silent, biding its time until the man managed the locks. And when the task was done, the bear attacked.

It surged to the fore, hauling on the doorknob with all its strength. It still required the man to grip the knob, but beyond that, the grizzly was in control. Worse, it was whipped into a frenzy by the buzzer and the female.

Still, the door would not open.

He roared in frustration. The grizzly wanted to rear up in fury, but since the man was already standing, this merely reinforced his upright position. And with that, a large yellow sign came into view. It was a black arrow on a yellow placard, the color so bright it hurt his eyes even in the semi-light of the front alcove.

It took the man to understand it. And it took another eon of that relentless sound for the man to establish control. That, of course, was why the newest lock and sign were there. It could only be managed by a man. The bear would destroy it, thereby trapping him indoors forever.

But he was a man still. At least enough so that he could control himself. So he beat the grizzly back, forcing it into a tight compartment of his mind where it clawed at its cage. The arrow pointed to a keyboard hung on the wall. To open the door, he had to type in six numbers and four letters. The animal had no prayer of remembering the sequence, but the man could do it, though he fumbled it twice before managing it on the third attempt.

The door unlocked with a loud *thunk* of electric magnets shutting off. Then he twisted the knob and hauled the heavy thing open.

First thing he did was slap her arm away from the buzzer. He tried to modify his strength so as to not break her arm, but the grizzly demanded violence for the assault on his ears. She gave a squeak of alarm, but it wasn't a cry of pain, so the man in him was reassured. And while she stood there, her mouth open in shock, he took the time to use all his senses, orienting himself to the world outside his den.

It was afternoon on a Michigan summer day. The sky was overcast, which was a blessing on his eyes. It also kept the air from being too hot. His home edged the Gladwin State Park, a rustic cabin that belied the expensive electronics that kept his basement a hum of activity.

But that was behind him. In front was a woman, lush and fertile.

He cared little for her coverings—crisp linen pants beneath a polyester blouse. What he focused on was the scent of her body and the flush on her cheeks. The animal in him smelled for disease and found none. He also evaluated the power in her body, the width of her hips, and the full, lush roundness of her breasts. The grizzly pronounced her exceedingly healthy to carry young. The man liked the sight of her cleavage and the length of her legs. Neither cared that her mouth hung open in shock, though they noted the quick tempo of her breaths.

"Uh, hello," she said. There might have been more words, but he didn't have the brain function to process sentences yet, and even if he did, her voice drowned out the sounds of the forest. He had been asleep for a while, and he needed to be alert for danger. He would brook no interference now that the fertile woman had presented herself at his door.

So when she kept speaking, he growled at her. Low and guttural. She snapped her mouth shut on another squeak, which he found strangely funny. He sniffed the wind, finding the usual mix of civilization and woods. Nothing of note except for this woman, whose scent mixed feminine musk with citrus. Oddly appealing.

So he turned his full attention back to her, mentally dissecting the smell—what was shampoo, deodorant, and her. He liked *her*, and he felt his organ thicken in desire.

A memory teased at his mind. Did he know this woman? He studied her sturdy body, seeing the lush curves and wide hips, good for carrying young. If he took this woman now, she would conceive his young. He could overpower her here, rip off her coverings, and release his seed inside her within moments. It wanted it with a fierceness that alarmed the man.

So he forced himself to turn away, heading for the one thing that helped most when his control balanced on a knife's edge. It required him to turn his back on her, but he did it while he lumbered to the kitchen and the acrid scent of cold coffee.

He found it on the counter. A banged-up metal mug that waited for situations just like this. He grabbed it and swallowed the cold brew, praying it would work one more time. It would push the brain cells into life and thereby suppress the animal a little more. Then he could live for another day as a man instead of a beast.

He heard her follow him. She wasn't in the least bit quiet as her sandals slapped on the hard tile of his front hall. He heard her draw breath, probably to speak, and he whipped around to glare at her. He was not human yet. She would wait until he was. Anything else was too dangerous for her.

But when he spun around to growl at her, he was struck again by how pretty she was. Not her scent, but her features. Round face with a pert nose. Large brown eyes and curly hair pulled into a messy bun. She wore makeup, though lightly, and she'd chewed off any hint of lipstick. She had a light brown mole near her right ear just above her jaw, and he wanted to lick it to see if he could detect the change in texture with his tongue. And then there was her mouth, soft and red. She was biting her lower lip on one side. It was an endearing, human sight that made the man happy. The bear didn't care about such details. Minute shifts in expression on a human face meant nothing to it. But as long as he could see the flash of a white tooth as it tugged at her lower lip and know she was uncertain, he knew he was still a man even if he couldn't form actual words just yet.

Again that hint of knowing her teased at him, through both bear and man. She was familiar, but he hadn't the focus to isolate the memory. He needed more caffeine, but the metal mug was empty. Fortunately, he knew the next steps by heart. It was a complicated process, but that was part of the plan. The more he used his brain—even to fire up an expensive espresso machine—the better for everyone.

So he did. He turned on the machine, pulled milk from the refrigerator and honey from the cabinet. He did everything by rote, while each motion reinforced the human side of his personality. He ground the beans, measured out the espresso shots, and filled a large mug. Without conscious decision, he added chocolate and whipped cream, then drizzled the honey across the top before offering it to her.

A gift for the woman who would be his mate.

No.

The man cut off the thought, knowing that it came from the animal. This was a gift for the woman who'd risked her life by waking him. That made her stupid, not a life mate. And why the hell would she come here when she was fertile? Good God, who would be that stupid?

Every *normal* human woman would be that stupid, he answered himself. It was only the shifters who scented fertility and thought about what that broadcast to the world. Which meant this woman was fully human and completely ignorant of his kind.

He ought to throw her out of the county. Until her cycle ended, she was a temptation to every young boy in the flush of his first season. Though, if he were honest, she was in the most danger from him.

She looked perplexed as he held out the drink. He ought to be drinking it instead of giving it to her. He needed all the caffeine he could get right then. But she was his female—*a woman*, the man corrected, and not his at all. She was a woman in his home and this was as polite as he could manage. If she took it, though, that would seal her fate. The grizzly would take it as a sign of agreement to mate.

There was nothing Mark could do to stop that. Her only hope was if she left while he remained in control of himself. Which made it the man's job to get rid of her as soon as possible. For her own sake.

And all the while, he just stood there, his hand beginning to burn from the heat of the mug.

Take it, the bear urged.

Run, the man screamed. *While you still can.*

But no words formed on his mouth. And after a long, slow moment, she reached out and lifted the mug from his fingers.

Her touch was light, the brush against his skin sending bolts of desire into his hard dick. It jerked toward her, but he didn't move beyond that. And then she smiled, her expression clear enough for even the bear to understand. A wary greeting. Her face said, *Hello.* And maybe added a *thank you* as she pulled the drink to her mouth.

He watched, mesmerized, as her lips pursed against the white cream. Her eyes drifted closed, and her throat shifted as she swallowed. Then he heard it. A soft release of sound, too quick to be a purr and yet was undeniably delight.

Oh, hell. She was appreciating his gift. His cock stood up ramrod straight, and if his muscles hadn't been locked tight, he would have reached for her. She'd accepted his gift of food, even murmured her appreciation of it. She was his now, according to the grizzly. The man wondered if she'd just signed her death warrant.

She lowered the mug and licked the cream from her lips. His breath caught, and he had to tighten his hands into fists so that he wouldn't reach for her. He had to leave before the grizzly caught him unaware. Willing or not, the bear would impregnate her because that was its number-one, absolute drive right now. *Get her with child.*

With a strangled sound, he jerked himself back to the machine. He could make his own drink and pray that the caffeine helped him keep the grizzly caged.

So long as she didn't speak. And if she touched him, she was doomed.

He began to order himself about, his mind becoming a drill sergeant to the body. Put in the coffee, slam on the machine, watch the dark liquid of sanity pour from the spout. He focused on those simple details while beside him he heard her breath catch. There'd been fear in her scent from the beginning. An acrid tang that helped keep him away from her. The man detested that scent and would do nothing to make it continue. But now he wished it would overwhelm him. Now he wanted her to be bathed in the scent because while he tried to focus on making coffee, he scented her arousal. The musk deepened, the scent akin to roasted nuts. He knew that scent. It was imprinted on his brain as clearly as a brand.

Who is she? He wanted to remember.

He finished making his latte, sweetening it only with honey before gulping it down. It seared his tongue and burned his throat, but it was better to feel pain than smell her. It was a skill he'd perfected in these last years while slowly going feral. He focused on one sensation and blocked out the rest. His throat burned, therefore he couldn't know that she was attracted to him. He couldn't be drawn in by her body's interest because all he felt was his own scorched tongue. Or so he told himself.

And then—thank God—she did something smart enough to preserve her virtue. She began to speak, her words high with nervousness and too rushed for him to process without recruiting his higher cortex.

Yes. Yes. Make me think. Make me hear. But for God's sake, don't touch me.

More words. What did they mean?

"...my father...computer...notes...have them?"

It took three tries before he could form a word. Even so it came out more like a grunt. "No," he said. Then the most important thing for her own safety. "Leave."

"...can't."

Hell.

About the Author

Kathy Lyons is the wild, adventurous half of *USA Today* bestselling author Jade Lee. A lover of all things fantastical, Kathy spent much of her childhood in Narnia, Middle Earth, Amber, and Earthsea, just to name a few. There is nothing she adores more than turning an ordinary day into something magical, which is what happens all the time in her books. Winner of several industry awards, including the Prism Best of the Best Award, a *Romantic Times* Reviewers' Choice Award, and Fresh Fiction's Steamiest Read, Kathy has published more than fifty romance novels, and she's just getting started.

Check out her latest news at:

KathyLyons.com

Facebook.com/KathyLyonsBooks

Twitter: @KathyLyonsAuth

CPSIA information can be obtained
at www.ICGtesting.com
Printed in the USA
LVOW11s0114231216
518335LV00001B/23/P